LARAMIE NELSON RIDES AGAIN!

In Zane Grey's *Raiders of Spanish Peaks,* Laramie Nelson, foreman of the Spanish Peaks Ranch, saved the Lindsay family from ruin, and appeared to have stilled his restless spirit with his love for Hallie Lindsay, and a respected position in the community.

But Laramie Nelson was not a man to be tied down. Soon he was back on the trail—and ready to face the frontier once more.

Other volumes in
the Romer Zane Grey series:

Zane Grey's Laramie Nelson:
The Lawless Land

Zane Grey's Buck Duane:
King of the Range

Zane Grey's Arizona Ames:
King of the Outlaw Horde

Zane Grey's Yacqui:
Siege at Forlorn River

Zane Grey's Nevada Jim Lacy:
Beyond the Mogollon Rim

Zane Grey's Buck Duane:
Rider of Distant Trails

Zane Grey's Arizona Ames:
Gun Trouble in Tonto Basin

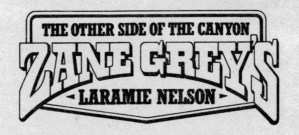

ROMER ZANE GREY

Based on characters created by Zane Grey

LEISURE BOOKS　　　NEW YORK CITY

A LEISURE BOOK®

July, 1999

Published by
Dorchester Publishing Co., Inc.
276 Fifth Avenue
New York, NY 10001

ISBN 0-8439-4610-5

Printed in the United States of America.

CONTENTS

The Other Side of the Canyon   7

Showdown at Lone Tree   77

Last Stand at Indigo Flats   147

The Other Side
of the Canyon

1

Laramie Nelson topped a small rise in the road and drew his horse up, letting him blow. He eased one foot out of the stirrup and hooked a leg over the saddle-horn while he rolled a cigarette.

It was mid-afternoon of a July Kansas day, hot and dusty, and he'd ridden west out of Dodge at dawn, his destination a small town a few miles up ahead. He was saddle-sore and had strong misgivings about what he would find waiting for him ahead.

Laramie was tall, slim, sandy-haired. He lean face was lightly dusted with freckles, and in repose had a melancholy cast, his smile a rare and sudden thing. His eyes, slightly squinted from years under the glare of the sun, were gray. His clothes showed much wear. Even his gun belt, slung low on his right thigh, was worn, the holster shiny with use. Only the long spurs on his dusty boots glinted, winking like silver in the sun.

Now he cocked his head as a train hooted mournfully almost two miles distant. He knew the tracks ran parallel to the road a mile to the north. Wingfoot snorted and pawed the ground, dust puffing up like smoke signals.

"All right, hoss, all right." Laramie swatted the horse affectionately. "Since you're so anxious, let's ramble on."

Wingfoot moved out at an easy lope. Although the area was in the grip of a long drought, it was pretty country, cattle country, flat plains with a few gentle hills folding back into the blue distance. The open grassland was dotted with clumps of trees. Cattle stood in clusters under the trees, heads drooping listlessly in the still heat.

Suddenly the silence was broken by rapid gunfire off to the right. Then the train whistled again, an angry blast, followed by the screeching sound of tortured metal as the train ground to a halt.

Laramie heard more shots, scattered now. Without hesitation he turned Wingfoot with his knee and touched spurs gently to his flanks. Within seconds Wingfoot was running flat out, Laramie leaning forward, urging him on. He unslung his Winchester and held it ready.

Wingfoot burst out of a grove of trees about two hundred yards from the stalled train. About a dozen horses were gathered at the mail car, which was open. Several of the horses were riderless. But even as Laramie rode pell-mell toward the train, five men boiled out of the mail car, forked their horses, and the bandit crew rode off at a fast gallop, traveling away from Laramie. One rider trailed several yards behind the others. All wore masks.

Aside from the fact that Wingfoot was already winded and hadn't a prayer of catching fresh horses, what chance did one man have against a dozen armed and ruthless train robbers?

Laramie reined Wingfoot in. As his mount came to a ploughing, stiff-legged halt, Laramie stood up in the stirrups and aimed his Winchester at the lagging rider. He followed the man in his sights for a moment, then squeezed the trigger. For a moment he thought he had missed.

Then the rider threw up his hands and tumbled into the dust, his horse racing on. Now one of the bandits turned and rode back. He rode in a strange way, back bent, neck crooked up like a hovering buzzard. Laramie figured he intended carrying the wounded man off on his horse. Instead he reined in above the fallen man, drew his gun and took deliberate aim. He fired twice, then sent his horse scampering after the others.

Laramie kneed Wingfoot into life and pounded toward the train. Out of the corner of his eye he saw a small man in Eastern clothes hop down out of the mail car and began firing after the fleeing bandits. But they were already out of pistol range.

At the fallen train robber, Laramie pulled Wingfoot in and left the saddle, landing on his feet like a cat, rifle muzzle centered on the prone man's chest. The bandit's bandana mask had fallen off.

The uncovered face was lean, gaunt. A weak mouth spoiled darkly handsome features.

Laramie grunted and dropped to one knee. "Ned! Ned Cooper!"

The man's eyes fluttered open. A startled look swept his face. "Laramie!" A faint smile moved like a shadow across his mouth. "It's been a long time, pard."

"Yeah, a long time," Laramie echoed. "But I don't understand how you..."

"Laramie..." Ned Cooper heaved himself up on his hands, the tendons in his suburned neck standing out like ropes. He stank of sour sweat and the blood that bubbled up out of his chest. "Elizabeth... Tell Elizabeth that I..." A spasm of agony contorted his face, blood poured from his mouth in a bright flood, and he fell back his eyes staring and lifeless.

Laramie heard the hard pound of footsteps and glanced up. The man in Eastern clothes skidded to a stop and said in an Eastern voice, "Give me that damn rifle!"

There was a bloody gash across the side of his head. Without waiting for permission, he snatched the Winchester from Laramie, dropped to one knee and began firing at the bandits. They were far out of range, of course, the last few just disappearing over a distant rise.

The Easterner realized this. He scrambled to his feet with a curse and lunged for Wingfoot. Laramie barred his way.

"Whoa now, stranger," Laramie drawled. "My horse is tuckered out. And even if he wasn't, what could an Eastern dude like you do against a dozen armed bank robbers?"

The Easterner glared at him. "Dude, is it? Damn you, cowboy!"

The man was at least six inches shorter than Laramie. His face was round, plump, innocuous as a babe's. Even bristling with outrage, black button eyes snapping, he

10

looked about as dangerous as an aroused rooster. Laramie suppressed a smile.

Abruptly the sand seemed to run out of the smaller man, and he muttered, "You're right, blast it! I'd be plucked bare as a prairie chicken caught in a tornado!"

Laramie glanced down at the man on the ground. He stooped and closed Ned's eyes.

"You know him?"

"Yeah, I know him," Laramie said absently. His thoughts were elsewhere. Was Ned the reason Elizabeth had left an urgent message for him in Dodge, a message pleading for him to come to her? The last time he'd seen Elizabeth she'd been Mrs. Ned Cooper.

The Easterner was speaking, "It's their trademark, you know."

Laramie focused his gaze on him. "Whose trademark?"

"The Taggert brothers and their gang. They never leave one of their members alive behind to identify them or tell where they hide out between holdups."

Laramie had heard of the Taggert bunch. They made a specialty of robbing trains and had terrorized the railroads for close to two years. He said, "You seem to know quite a bit about the Taggert brothers."

"I should. I'm out here to round them up. I'm Brock Peters—with the Pinkerton Agency. The railroads hired us to break up that bunch."

Laramie took the man's proffered hand, muttered his own name. He was struck with astonishment. One man, and an Eastern dude at that, sent to round up a dozen desperados like the Taggerts? He swallowed a laugh and tried to keep a straight face.

But Peters must have read something in his face, for he said ruefully, "I know, I'm not doing so good. They laid a gun barrel alongside my head and I was out for a spell." He touched his fingers to the head wound and winced.

At that moment a portly man in a conductor's uniform bustled up. He looked pale around the mouth, but he was

11

swollen with an air of self-importance. "Mr. Peters, we have to get this train moving again. This has thrown us off schedule as it is."

"When did you ever keep on schedule?" Then Peters waved a short-fingered hand. "But you're right. Have somebody unload my horse and you can proceed." The conductor started off, and Peters called after him. "Wait! You'd better load this onto the train." He indicated Ned Cooper's body.

"No," Laramie said curtly. "I'll take his body into Cottonwood Springs, to his wife. It's only a short ride."

Peters looked at him, eyes narrowed in speculation. "Is that so? His wife, huh? All right." He motioned the conductor on. "I'll ride in with you, Nelson."

2

Peters could ride a horse. Laramie Nelson had to grant him that much, even if he did look slightly ridiculous in the Eastern clothes, button shoes on his small feet, round hat perched atop his head like an upturned bowl. Laramie would have laughed, but he didn't feel much like laughing with Ned Cooper's body draped across Wingfoot in front of his saddle.

As they reached the road and headed west, Peters took out a small, thin cigar and lit it. He said, "You want to tell me about him? What's his name? Ned Cooper?"

"There's not much to tell," Laramie said slowly. "I knew Ned...about five years ago, I guess. We punched cows together for the same spread, the Lazy H outfit out in Colorado. We were good friends then. Then he met this girl. I was kind of sweet on her, but she married Ned. I stayed around for the wedding, then rode out. That was the last time I saw Ned."

Laramie was silent for a minute, reflecting on what had happened during those five years: range drifting with his inseparable pals, Lonesome and Tracks; the rewarding,

12

challenging months as foreman of the Spanish Peaks spread over in Colorado, and the day of sudden death and passion that climaxed them.

For awhile, Laramie had thought he'd found a final home there, heading the cattlemen's protective association, headily in love—a love that was strongly returned— with Hallie Lindsay, his boss's turbulent daughter.

But perhaps their love had been too passionate, the settled life too restricting. Something had burned out between them, and Laramie had known it was time to be riding on. It was the hardest choice he had ever made, and making it had changed him—at least temporarily. The hell-raising daredevil whose reputation had spread through the West was quieter now, thoughtful rather than carefree.

And he was looking for *something*—a new kind of life, maybe—something that would call on his skill, his wits, his nerve, a way of life that would be a real test for him. . . .

Peters' voice recalled him from his reverie.

"Five years since you saw this Cooper—and you just *happened* to be riding by today?"

"Oh, that. I found a letter waiting for me in Dodge from Elizabeth, that's Ned's wife. The letter said she wanted to see me. So I rode out of Dodge this morning."

"She say why she wanted to see you?"

"Nope. Just said she needed my help bad. If you mean did she mention Ned . . . no, she didn't."

The note had been brief, cryptic. *Dear Laramie, I need help badly. You're the only one to turn to. I've heard that you ride into Dodge City occasionally. If you get this, will you come to the aid of an old friend? Please?*

Peters was speaking. "Did it ever strike you that this Cooper had it in him to turn sour?"

Laramie took his time about answering, his thoughts circling back into the past. "Reckon I never thought much about it one way or another. Oh, he was always a little wild, always in a tearing hurry to get things done, but I

13

thought getting hitched had settled him down some."

"Apparently it didn't," Peters said grimly. "But he's settled down now. Permanently."

Laramie felt a pull of anger, but he held his peace. Peters was right, looking at it from where he stood. They rode awhile in silence, the only sound the creak of saddle leather, the dull plop-plop of hooves in the dust. Although it was now well past mid-afternoon, it had grown hotter. There wasn't a breath of air. Clouds boiled up low on the horizon to the north, like hills humped in the distance, but Laramie figured it was probably a false alarm. A real gully-washer of a rain right now would be welcome, but Laramie doubted it was in the cards.

"Nelson."

Laramie glanced over at him.

Peters jerked his head at Laramie's low-slung, well-worn Colt. "You good with that?"

"I know how to use it," Laramie said evenly.

They locked stares for a moment, neither giving an inch, then Peters let smoke drift out of his mouth and said dryly, "Yes, I'm sure you do."

The sun had dropped out of sight by the time they rode down the dusty main street of Cottonwood Springs. Cottonwood Springs was little more than a cluster of wooden, false-fronted buildings, all leaning south as though once struck by a particularly severe norther. As they rode along, butter-yellow light spilled out of some of the buildings.

People strolling along the boardwalks halted to stare at them, two strangers on horseback, one man draped across a horse like a sack of grain, then hurried on with faces averted.

Laramie reined Wingfoot in toward a hitching rail and called out to a man on the walk, "Where can I find Elizabeth Cooper?"

The man stopped as though jerked up short at the end of a halter, peered up at Laramie, then swept an arm west.

14

"She lives on the west edge of town. Last house on the right." The man ducked his head and hurried on.

Laramie glanced over at Peters. "Whole town seems spooked."

Peters shrugged. "The Taggert brothers probably rode through here, either coming or going. They're enough to tree any town."

The last house on the edge of town was old, weathered, badly in need of paint. A border of flowers had been planted across the front of the house. Most of them were dead, the others wilted and drooping. There was a light in the window.

Laramie sighed as they reined in before the house. He had no stomach for what he had to do. He caught Peters' glance. The man nodded understandingly, indicating he would stay outside.

Laramie Nelson dismounted stiffly and strode to the door. He rapped firmly with his knuckles. After a moment he heard the sound of footsteps, and the door opened. The years hadn't been kind to Elizabeth. Her face looked drawn, thinner than he remembered it. The brown eyes, staring at him without recognition, were dull, tired.

"Yes?" she said in a neutral voice. Her black hair, falling to her shoulders, was lusterless, stringy, and she brushed a strand of it out of her eyes. Her face was flushed and damp.

He said quietly, "Hello, Elizabeth."

Her face came alive. "Laramie! I didn't think . . ." Long dress sweeping the floor, she rushed at him and seized his hand. "You came! Thank God!"

"Elizabeth . . . I have bad news."

Her hands tightened convulsively on his, the nails biting into his flesh. "Ned?"

"I'm afraid so."

She dropped his hand and pushed past him. There was enough light to show the two horses and body draped across one. Laramie, thinking she was about to run to

15

Wingfoot, started forward to hold her back.

She didn't move. "Is he . . . ?"

"Yes, Elizabeth," he said gently. "He's dead."

She turned to him then, and said in a dead voice, "Will you bring him in, please? The back bedroom."

Laramie went back to Peters and together they carried Ned Cooper inside, Elizabeth showing them the way, carrying a lamp. The interior of the house was clean, the splintery floors still damp from a recent scrubbing, and starched curtains covered the windows, but the furnishings were pitifully few. There were four rooms in all. A large parlor with a fireplace, a kitchen with an iron cookstove, a short hall opening off onto the two bedrooms.

Elizabeth set the lamp on a chest of drawers in the back bedroom. They placed Ned Cooper on the narrow bed, and Laramie removed his boots. Elizabeth took a quilt from the chest and spread it over him.

Laramie and Brock Peters stood aside silently while she stood looking down at her dead husband, hands clasped before her. Her face revealed nothing. Then she bent and pulled the quilt up over his face and turned to them. She pushed the strand of hair out of her eyes.

"I expect you men are hungry. I have a pot of stew cooking. It's soon done. There's a pump out back where you can wash up."

As they washed, Peters said, "Seems to me she takes it calmly enough, her husband fresh killed and all."

"What'd you expect her to do? Beat her breast and scream?" Laramie demanded. "This is the west, Peters. We're used to violent death, even our women."

"That wasn't quite what I meant. She didn't seem at all surprised, as though she'd been expecting it."

Laramie, splashing water over his face and chest, only grunted in reply. His mind was busy with a larger question. Should he tell Elizabeth it was his bullet that had knocked Ned off his horse? Would she hate him for

16

that? He wasn't sure if his bullet or the bandit's had killed Ned, but it really didn't matter. If he hadn't shot Ned off his horse, he'd still be alive.

Elizabeth was putting supper on the table when they re-entered the house. Laramie unbuckled his gunbelt and hung it on a peg just inside the kitchen door, then bent a hard look on Peters. Peters looked obstinate for a moment, then shrugged and took a small gun from the waistband of his trousers and hung it alongside Laramie's.

Laramie said, "Elizabeth, this is Brock Peters. He's a Pinkerton man. He was with me when Ned..."

"How do you do, Mrs. Cooper," Peters said courteously.

"How do, Mr. Peters." Elizabeth's glance jumped to Laramie. "I want to hear about it, but eat first."

The two men sat, and Elizabeth served them before sitting across from them. She put food on her plate, but she did little more than pick at it. The stew and the fresh-baked bread were delicious. Laramie felt uncomfortable about eating with Ned Cooper laid out in the back bedroom, but he discovered he was ravenous. And Peters pitched in with a good appetite, so Laramie ate heartily.

When they were done, Elizabeth served them mugs of steaming coffee. Laramie rolled a cigarette, and Peters asked Elizabeth's permission to light one of his little cigars.

Elizabeth said, "Laramie?"

He sighed heavily and leaned back. "Ned was in on a train holdup, Elizabeth, with the Taggert gang. They took a payroll off the mail car and got away clean. All except Ned." He took a deep breath and said harshly, "I shot him, Elizabeth. Of course I didn't know it was Ned at the time, he was masked, but I shot him."

Elizabeth nodded slowly. Laramie Nelson could detect no animosity in her attitude.

Peters spoke up, "I think Nelson only winged him. It was one of the Taggerts who finished him off. That's their trademark."

Elizabeth nodded again. "Lyle Taggert, most likely. They're both mean but Lyle's the meanest." Bitterness burned in her voice like acid. "I told Ned they'd kill him without batting an eye if they ever had the slightest excuse."

"What happed to Ned?" Laramie asked. "The Ned I knew was a little wild, but I'd never have figured him for something like this."

"He wasn't the Ned you knew, Laramie, hadn't been for a long time. Ned was a weak man. I knew that before I'd been married to him a year."

The brown eyes gazed into Laramie's, and he remembered the girl she had been—and the half-formed desires he had felt—and he knew she was remembering, too.

Faint color touched her cheeks. She pushed the hair out of her eyes and hurried on. "But I'd made my bargain, so I stuck with it. Ned failed at everything he tried. He'd fail in one place and we'd drift on to another. He always blamed something or someone for his failures, never himself. The last thing he tried was farming and you know how much he hated farming, Laramie. But he even failed at that.

"The railroad wanted our farm. Ned thought he could hold out and force them to pay a steep price. He was wrong. They could afford to wait and freeze him out. In the end he was forced to let them have it for almost nothing. That was six months ago. Somehow that seemed the last straw. He blamed the railroad and could think of nothing but getting even. The only way he could see was to rob them and he couldn't do it alone."

"So he joined the Taggerts," Peters said.

"He joined the Taggerts. He practically had to beg them. I didn't even know he'd been taken in. He didn't tell me." Her voice dropped to a whisper, and she stared down at her plate. "And he even failed at that, too. Poor, doomed Ned." She got up to refill Peters' coffee mug.

"And that's why I sent for you, Laramie. I was desperate. I did everything I could to talk him out of it. Nothing worked. I thought maybe you could."

Laramie heard a noise at the kitchen door and glanced that way just as a tall man dressed in black stepped in. He held a sixgun at waist level, aimed at the table.

"All right, you two buckos! Keep your hands on the table or I'll blow your heads off!"

3

Elizabeth looked around at the intruder. "Oh, for Heaven's sake, Claude! What do you think you're doing?"

The man jerked his head without taking his gaze from Laramie Nelson and Brock Peters. "You stay out of this, Elizabeth. This is law business." He moved closer to the table.

It was then Laramie noticed the marshal's badge pinned to his fancy vest. He wore crossed gunbelts, his left hand hovering near the pearl handle of the holstered gun. He was a commanding presence in his black clothes, with broad shoulders, piercing black eyes, heavy moustache and hawk nose, yet Laramie sensed an uncertainty in him.

For some reason he never afterward understood, Laramie looked over at Peters, who was holding the nearly full mug of coffee cupped in his hands. Peters nodded almost imperceptibly. Laramie tensed himself, and Peters moved with blinding speed, tossing the scalding coffee into the marshal's face and throwing himself sideways off the chair.

At the same instant Laramie moved also, to one side and down, scuttling bent over under the protecting lee of the table toward the marshal.

A hoarse bellow of pain erupted from the marshal and

19

the gun roared. Laramie straightened, coming up almost in the marshal's face, ready to whack him with his fist. It wasn't necessary. The marshal was pawing at his streaming eyes with his free hand. Laramie snatched the gun from his unresisting hand and plucked the other from his holster.

Elizabeth came with a towel and guided the marshal to her chair and began swabbing gently at his eyes. "You're an idiot, Claude Rigney!" she scolded.

The marshal said plaintively, "There was no need to do that. I could have been blinded!"

"Oh, I don't think so," Peters said blithely. "Mrs. Cooper's coffee isn't *that* bad. And I don't like strange men pointing guns at me. It makes me nervous."

"But I'm the law here!"

"That cuts no dice with me," Peters retorted. "I've seen lawmen turn sour before."

"Just what is it the law wants with us, Marshal?" Laramie asked.

"It was told to me that you two rode in here with a dead man, that you came out here with him." Rigney's eyes were better now. He squinted at Laramie. "Is that right?"

"That's right."

"Then why didn't you come to me?"

"Because it's Ned, that's why!" Elizabeth cried.

Rigney twisted his head up to stare at her. "Ned?"

"He was killed trying to rob a mail car. Lyle Taggert killed him!"

Rigney scowled across the table. "What part did you two play in the robbery?"

"I'm Brock Peters, Pinkerton man. I'm out here after the Taggerts."

"And I'm Laramie Nelson."

Rigney's gaze sharpened. "Laramie Nelson? I've heard that name. You're a gunfighter, ain't you?"

"I can use one, if it comes to that."

"We don't care for gunslicks in Cottonwood Springs!"

20

Rigney said in a high voice. "You remember that!"

Laramie drawled, "I'll keep it in mind."

"Oh, stop it!" Elizabeth stomped her foot. "Laramie's an old friend, Claude. I wrote him to come!"

Peters had just lit a fresh cigar. He said through a cloud of smoke, "Suppose we could round up a posse and ride out after the Taggerts, Marshal?"

"The people in Cottonwood Springs stick pretty much to their own business," the marshal said stiffly. "They're not much interested in helping the railroad."

"Seems to me there wouldn't *be* any Cottonwood Springs, or not much anyway, except for the railroad."

"The truth is," Elizabeth said scathingly, "the people here are scared silly of the Taggerts. They dig a hole every time they hear the Taggerts are coming!"

Rigney said, "Now Elizabeth, you shouldn't be so hard on the folks hereabouts. They have families to think of."

"Huh!" Elizabeth was magnificently scornful.

Peters drew on his cigar. "I guess that leaves it up to me then. I'll have to ride after them myself."

Laramie stared. *"You?"*

"That's what I said," Peters said, unperturbed. "Of course, it would help considerable if I knew where they hide out between jobs."

"I know," Elizabeth said.

They all gazed at her in astonishment, including Marshal Rigney.

"Well, I do!" She faced them defiantly. "I rode out there once with Ned when he was trying to join them. The Taggerts didn't know I was with him. I stayed behind in camp and Ned rode in alone. They hide out in a blind canyon, only one way in and out. It's over in—" She stopped abruptly, her glance skipping from one to the other.

"Well, Mrs. Cooper? Where?"

"No." She swung her head from side to side. "A

bargain first. The only way I tell is to go along. I lead the way in!"

Laramie's breath exploded. "You can't mean that!"

"I mean every word of it!"

"Elizabeth . . . I'm the law here and I'll handle this," Rigney said somewhat pompously.

"No," she said stubbornly. "I go along or you get nothing from me. I aim to see the Taggerts pay for Ned's death. Maybe he was weak, maybe he deserved what happened, but they're to blame!"

"All right, Mrs. Cooper," Peters said. "I'll accept your terms. We'll start early tomorrow morning."

"No," Elizabeth said again. "First, I have to bury Ned."

Laramie was listening with mounting disbelief. His respect for Peters had grown. Whatever else he was, the little man had guts. Throwing the coffee in Rigney's face had proved that. But even so . . .

He said, "You must be out of your minds, both of you! An Eastern dude and a woman going after the Taggert bunch!"

"Nelson, I've had enough of 'Eastern dude.'" Peters' eyes were flinty and cold. "I'll have to ask you to put a stop to it."

Taken aback, Laramie Nelson said, "You're right and I'm sorry. But that still doesn't make it right you should risk Elizabeth's life on such a jackass stunt. If you wants to risk yours, that's your lookout."

"And I should think it's Mrs. Cooper's lookout what she want to do. I'm not dragging her along roped and tied. She goes, it's of her own free will."

"He's right, Laramie. It's my life to risk, so I'll thank you to stay out of it," Elizabeth said distantly.

"Oh, for—!" In disgust Laramie thrust the guns at Rigney. "Take these back, Marshal, before I shoot myself."

Rigney stood up, holstered the guns with a show of

dignity. He glanced at Elizabeth, started to say something, then settled for a nod, turned on his heel and strode out.

"Good riddance," Elizabeth muttered, staring after him. "He's a poor excuse for a marshal. All he could do for Ned before was threaten to arrest him for being drunk and disorderly."

A change had come over Elizabeth. She was no longer listless but seemed charged with energy. Her color was high, and she had shed her weariness like a cloak.

It would seem, Laramie thought as he watched her, that Ned's death had removed a heavy load from her shoulders. Either that or the prospect of revenging him had given her a new lease on life.

Now she faced around, her glance going immediately to him. "Laramie, forgive me. I didn't mean to sound so..."

"Forget it." He batted a hand at her, then shook his head, his face mournful. "I must be out of my mind, too, but I'll go along with you two idiots. Maybe I can keep you from getting killed. Although why I want to bother, I'm sure I don't know."

Elizabeth clapped her hands like a child. "Laramie, that's wonderful!"

"Yeah." Nelson turned to Peters. "We'd better go see if we can find a room for the night."

"Oh, no!" Elizabeth said in quick dismay. "There's no need for that. There's room here." Her gaze darted toward the back bedroom.

Laramie knew she was thinking of being left alone for the night with her husband's body. And something else occurred to him. She might be in some danger. He said, "All right, maybe that would be best. But I'll take the horses uptown and stable them. They'll need a rubdown and a good feed before heading out tomorrow."

Laramie strapped on his gunbelt and left the house with Peters. Outside he said, "You'd better stay with

23

Elizabeth. I want a look at this town. The chance of the Taggerts knowing that Elizabeth knows the location of their hideout is pretty slim, but it's possible. She'll never be safe again as long as the Taggerts are free."

"Glad you're going with us, Nelson. You'll lessen the odds considerable."

Laramie snorted. "Don't pat yourself on the back. It has nothing to do with you. The only reason I'm going is Elizabeth."

"The reason doesn't matter," Peters said cheerfully. "So long as you've decided to come with us."

Laramie led Wingfoot and Peters' horse away from behind the house where they'd been tethered by a tub of water and walked them toward the center of town and the livery stable he'd seen as they rode in. Once in the covering darkness, he allowed his face to relax in a faint grin. He still thought they were riding out on a foolhardy mission, but Peters had sand. He'd do to ride with.

Although it was only a little after nine, most of the town was already asleep, all the buildings dark except the two saloons directly across the street from each other. They were lit but even they seemed unusually quiet, with none of the usual loud voices and raucous laughter.

Laramie located the livery stable. There was no one around, but it was unlocked. He found a lantern hanging inside the door. He led the horses to two empty stalls, unsaddled them, gave them some grain and water, then rubbed them down with an old blanket. They were done eating and stood with heads drooping tiredly by the time he'd finished with the grooming.

He stood in the doorway of the stable for a moment, rolling a cigarette, his fingers performing the familiar task easily in the dark. He poked the cigarette into his mouth and struck a match on his bootheel.

He heard a faint sound off to his right, and a danger signal thrummed along his nerve-ends. Instinctively, he threw himself down and to one side before he saw a

24

firefly-flash of orange flame. He heard the sound of the shot as he hit the ground rolling. He rolled over twice and came up on one elbow, Colt in his hand.

He got off two quick shots at the place where he'd seen the wink of light, but he knew he couldn't pinpoint the spot well enough to hope for a hit. After the sounds of his shots died away, silence fell.

He listened intently but heard nothing. Something began to bother him. After a moment he realized what it was. It was much too quiet. The three gunshots should have aroused *some* attention. But there was no hue and cry. No lights came on. Nobody came running out. The saloons were only a few doors up the street, yet he saw no curious faces poking out to see what the noise was all about.

Either the whole town was too spooked to investigate or they had all been forewarned not to venture out.

But there was a more important consideration. Who had taken a shot at him and why? Had the Taggerts left someone behind who had learned they were riding out after them? Or had some young gunslick heard of Laramie Nelson's reputation and decided to add to his own rep? But that wasn't the way it was done. There was no glory in drygulching a well-known gunfighter. That was done with an open challenge and a shoot-out on Main Street with plenty of witnesses.

Without thinking, Laramie had rolled another cigarette. But this time he stepped inside the stable to strike the match. Then he strolled down the main street of Cottonwood Springs, taking his time, his gaze alertly probing every dark nook on the way. He didn't see a soul and reached the Cooper house without being challenged.

4

Laramie Nelson had been wrong about the rain. He awoke in the night to the sound of thunder, followed by the drumming of rain on the roof. It was still raining lightly the next morning, a gray and gloomy day.

"It's fitting, I guess," Elizabeth said. "Ned always liked wet, dreary and somber days just like this one."

There was only a scattering of the townspeople at the funeral. Marshal Rigney stood off to one side, resplendent in black, black slicker glistening in the drizzle.

A strip of canvas had been stretched across the grave in which rested a pine box holding Ned Cooper. The preacher droned the words. Elizabeth stood across the grave from him, Laramie and Peters flanking her. Water dripped from the canvas. The odor of fresh earth and raw pine mingled with the smell of rain.

Elizabeth endured without a tear until the preacher spoke the final word and gestured to two men with shovels. As the first shovel of dirt thudded onto the pine coffin, she sobbed once, wrenchingly, and turned blindly away.

"Laramie," she said in a taut voice, "I'll be ready to ride in a half hour."

Laramie nodded. "You go on back to the house with her, Peters. I'll get the horses."

Laramie had fallen into the habit of command, as he was accustomed to doing in any situation, but he was a little surprised at Peters taking his orders so readily.

As he headed toward the livery stable, he saw the sun break through in the east and he noticed that the rain had stopped. Was that a good omen? At least the heat had broken.

Wingfoot was rested and frisky, and Laramie had trouble getting a saddle on him. Finally he led the horses up the street and hitched them before the general store. Elizabeth had told him she would pack what food they would need. But Laramie bought a few items. Tobacco, a supply of shells both for the Winchester and his Colt. Then he paused for a moment, frowning.

Many days' riding across wild country lay ahead of

them—country where outlaws like the Taggerts, and bands of hostile or renegade Indians roved at will. And all they had was a couple of handguns and a rifle.

"We could use a troop of artillery," he reflected wryly.

Then one item of the storekeeper's stock struck his eye. He thought for an instant, then grinned broadly. "Now there's the next best thing. Some artillery," he told himself. "Could give some hostiles a mighty hot time."

Still grimly amused, he made a final purchase.

When he rode up before the Cooper house, there was a saddled horse waiting in front. It was a rangy, powerful-looking animal with a mean look.

Peters and Elizabeth emerged as Laramie reined in. Peters was carrying saddlebags stuffed with provisions. Elizabeth had a rifle under her arm. She was wearing boots, faded trousers and a man's shirt. She looked years younger, somehow a little rowdy. Even in a man's attire, she was clearly a woman, and a damned attractive one.

He said, "That's a pretty salty-looking animal, Elizabeth. Sure you can manage him?"

"I can manage him," she said spiritedly. "He's mine. I had to fight Ned like the dickens to keep him from selling Sam."

Laramie was amused. "Sam? That's a hell of a name for a horse."

She marched up to the horse and vaulted into the saddle without assistance. Sam reared, snorting. Elizabeth sawed on the reins, pulling his head back, talking to him in a low voice. The horse gradually subsided and stood pawing at the ground. Elizabeth glanced over at Laramie.

"I guess you've forgotten how well I can ride," she said.

"No, I haven't forgotten," he said soberly.

Laramie heard the clop of hoof-beats and looked around. Marshal Rigney was riding toward them on a big black horse, tall in the saddle, black clothes free of dust, pearl gun handles glinting in the sun.

Right out of a Ned Buntline dime novel, Laramie Nelson thought sourly.

The marshal pulled his horse up. "Since the robbery took place in my territory, I thought I'd ride with you."

"Afraid you'll get fired if you don't?" Elizabeth asked. "Isn't that it Claude?"

The marshal reddened, but he didn't rise to the bait.

Peters swung up on his horse. "Welcome, Marshal. One more man evens the odds that much more."

"You don't know Claude. Just wait," Elizabeth muttered. She chirped to Sam and started off at a trot.

Laramie swung Wingfoot in beside Brock Peters. "Any idea where we're headed?"

"Somewhere over in Colorado. That's all she'd tell me. About a week's ride."

"The Taggerts could be gone on another raid by the time we get there."

"Not the Taggerts. I've studied the way they work. They make a good haul, they hole up for a spell with good whiskey and lay around drunk until most of the money's gone. They won't move again for at least a month."

It was now mid-morning, and the sky was clear of clouds, the sun blazing down. It would be hot again before the day was over, but at least the dust had settled. Elizabeth set a good pace, always bearing west. Once Laramie rode up alongside her, but she didn't seem inclined to talk. Her face was shadowed with sadness, and he realized the funeral must still be on her mind. He respected her mood and dropped back to ride with Peters.

Rigney hung back, as though reluctant to be seen with them. Even when they stopped for a cold noon meal, he sat apart, not talking.

"Friendly cuss, ain't he?" Laramie drawled.

"He'll be no help," Elizabeth said.

Peters asked, "Can he use those fancy guns of his?"

"Oh, he can shoot, I'll give him that. He can shoot at something that doesn't shoot back!"

"You ever see him back down?"

Elizabeth shrugged. "Who's to back down from in Cottonwood Springs? Ther're no hardcases around, only Saturday night drunks to jail. Whenever the Taggerts rode through he always managed to be out of town!"

Laramie said, "You sure you don't just have a spite on for him because he tried to jail Ned for being drunk?"

He was sorry the instant the words were out, but it was too late Elizabeth glared at him, her mouth working, and he thought she was about to break into tears. Then she jumped up and walked stiffly to her horse and began cinching the saddle.

"A little hard on her, weren't you, Nelson?"

"Maybe." Laramie got to his feet. "Let's ride."

They pushed hard all afternoon and made camp at sundown in a grove of cottonwoods by a meandering creek. After the horses were unsaddled and turned loose to graze, Laramie said, "I'll see if I can get us a couple of rabbits for supper."

With the Winchester in the crook of his arm, Laramie trudged up a small, grassy knoll about a quarter mile from camp. There was still ample light by the time he topped the rise and paused to look around. He spotted a cottontail about forty yards away, ears up, sniffing the wind. As Laramie brought his rifle to his shoulder, a gun cracked behind him and the rabbit leaped convulsively and tumbled over dead.

Laramie wheeled about. A few yards behind him and to the right stood Marshal Rigney, smoke drifting from the snout of the pearl-handled sixgun in his hand.

The marshal's hawk face wore a meager grin. "Why waste a Winchester bullet on an easy shot like that?"

"You're pretty handy with that, Marshal," Laramie drawled. "But it ain't always such a good idea to sneak up behind a man like that and fire off a pistol."

Rigney stiffened. His eyes began to burn. "Who's sneaking?"

The sixgun was still in his hand, the barrel slanted toward the ground. Now it came up slowly until it was aimed dead center on Laramie's heart. Laramie stood easily, rifle held negligently in his left hand. He watched the marshal's eyes for the tightening that would mean he was about to fire. Laramie didn't so much as move an eyelash.

Then Rigney laughed harshly and holstered his gun. "You push a man pretty hard, Nelson."

Past him, Laramie caught a flicker of movement. Another cottontail bounded through the tall grass. The range was about forty years but this one was in motion, a much more difficult shot. Almost in one motion Laramie drew and fired. His bullet caught the rabbit in mid-air and flipped him over twice.

At Laramie's draw Rigney had sent one hand clawing for his gun, then had frozen in mid-motion.

"One apiece," Laramie drawled. "I reckon we're even so far."

Ignoring Rigney, he strode past and picked up his rabbit. It had been a grandstand play and could have backfired badly if he had missed. Laramie experienced a spurt of pride he recognized as being childish. Even so, he was glad he had carried it off. There was something about Rigney that rubbed him the wrong way.

He got a second cottontail before returning to camp. He heard another shot on his way back, and Rigney followed him in a few minutes later, also carrying two rabbits.

Peters and Elizabeth had fire going, a coffeepot bubbling and a spit built for the rabbits. Laramie and the marshal quickly skinned and gutted their animals and turned them over to Elizabeth. Not long after full dark they were all well-fed and sipping their coffee, Rigney again sitting off to one side, glowering and silent.

Although Elizabeth had cooked their supper quickly and efficiently, she was also unusually quiet. Now she gathered up the dishes and prepared to carry them down to the creek.

Laramie got to his feet. "Let me tote those for you, Elizabeth."

She surrendered them without a word and led the way down to the creek. There was a crescent moon, a silvery glow filtering down through the leafy cottonwoods. Elizabeth sat on a fallen log at the water's edge and washed each tin dish as Laramie handed it to her.

"Elizabeth," Laramie said tentatively. "I'm sorry for a couple of things I've said."

"That's all right, I didn't really mind."

"Then you're not sore? I mean...you've hardly said a word all day."

"It's not that, Laramie. It's not you. It's...*me!*" Her voice was fierce, angry. "I'm mad at myself. I can't *feel* anything! I know, at the grave I sobbed once, but I think that was because I'm so darned mad."

"Well...I understand the shock of something like this takes some time to get over. You'll be okay."

She shook her head. "No, no, you don't understand! I didn't love Ned. It's almost a relief to be rid of him." She brushed the hair out of her eyes. "And that makes me out to be a heartless, uncaring woman!"

"If that's the way you feel, why are you so dead set on getting the Taggerts?"

"Because they're responsible for his death, and he was my husband. They should be made to pay for that! The fact that I didn't love Ned makes it even worse!"

Laramie reflected on the female mind. What mere man could follow the reasoning of a woman?

"Laramie," she said in a softer voice. He saw that she was looking at him intently, eyes huge and shining in the moonlight. "All these years...did you ever think of me?"

"Why, yes, of course I did," he said warily.

"I did. I thought of you often, wondering what you were doing, how it would be married to you."

31

"Not good," he said lightly. "The kind of life I lead wouldn't be easy on a woman."

"But haven't you ever thought of getting married, settling down?"

Laramie's face turned hard. "I did, for sure," he said grimly, remembering Spanish Peaks...and Hallie. "But—it didn't take. I reckon I'm just a rolling stone, Elizabeth, never meant to settle down."

"Could that be because...?" She straightened abruptly. "You see? There I go again, talking about...I'm a hard woman, Ned not even cold yet."

"Not hard, Elizabeth. You could never be that."

"Thank you for saying that, Laramie." She got to her feet and placed a hand lightly on his arm. "Try to forget what I've been saying. Starting tomorrow, I'll be thinking only of what we're out here to do."

5

They ran into the band of renegade Indians the afternoon of the fourth day.

The country was more broken now, the plains left behind, and they had started to climb. Although they occasionally came across a herd of grazing cattle, they hadn't seen a farm all day. It was still hot, but the air was clearer, sharper, the nights cooler. And in mid-morning Laramie had seen a long blue smudge on the western horizon that he knew to be the shape of the Rocky Mountains. Two more days' ride and the Rockies would be looming up in all their awesome majesty.

True to her word, Elizabeth had been all business on the second day and since, setting a hard pace that covered many miles a day. It was quite clear that she knew where she was going, and she led the way unhesitatingly.

They were following a faint trail along the bottom of a deep draw, Elizabeth two lengths in front, when she pulled up sharply and pointed an arm up. "Look!"

Lined up on the north rim of the draw were more than a dozen Indians on small ponies and carrying rifles. They were still as statues.

Laramie and Peters reined in. Peters asked, "Hostiles?"

"It's hard to say. As far as I know, we're at peace with the redskins in this area. If they are hostiles, I'd guess a band of renegades. In any case we'd better take cover. We're sitting ducks like this."

Laramie raised his voice. "Take cover! Behind those rocks!"

In times past floodwaters had cut a small wash into the side of the draw, leaving huge boulders strewn about as though dropped by some playful giant.

Elizabeth had already swung her horse in that direction before Laramie shouted. Now, as Laramie and Peters sent their mounts racing after her, the frozen tableau on the rim shattered. Wild yells ricocheted across the draw, and bullets sang ground them. Then they were behind the boulders, miraculously unhurt. Rigney came pounding in behind them.

Elizabeth was already behind a boulder, levering her rifle. Laramie hit the around running, dropping to one knee beside her. The horses huddled back under the lee of the overhang.

The Indians on the far bank were riding back and forth, firing steadily. Laramie got off a couple of shots, then ceased firing. He shouted, "Hold your fire! They're too far out of range. We're just wasting bullets!"

Beside him, Peters asked, "What are they, Nelson? Apaches?"

"Apaches?" Laramie twisted his head around. Peters was cool, as unruffled as though sitting down to supper. "A hell of a lot you know about Indians! Apaches never range this far north. They're in the border states, desert country. Besides if these were Apaches, we'd've been dead before we knew they were within miles of us."

Peters shrugged "So I don't know about Indians. Back

east we're always reading about the warrior Apaches. What are these, then?"

"Hard to tell. Could be Comanches, Cheyenne. Could even be a mixture, renegades banded together to raid and plunder."

Marshal Rigney slid in beside them, crouching low, ignoring the dust around his boots. He was breathing heavily, his face pale and drawn. "Whose idea was this? We're pinned down here like flies on molasses!"

Laramie gave him a cold stare. "We had little choice as I saw it. If we'd tried to ride down that draw, either way, they'd have picked us off one by one. The only way they can get at us here is head-on. They can't get at us from above." He glanced up. "That overhang protects us."

"They can keep us pinned down here until we starve to death or die of thirst," Rigney said sullenly.

"They may get tired before then. This ain't a war party out for blood. They're looking for loot and I'd say we don't look like much. Except for you, in that fancy outfit." Laramie raked Rigney with his gaze. He was beginning to wish he had heeded Elizabeth's warning. "If you don't like it here, Marshal, ride out. Nobody's holding you back. Me, I like it just fine."

Peters broke in, "What do you think they'll do, Nelson?"

"Oh, they'll make a try at us. Maybe more than one, but we're located pretty good here—"

"Here they come!" Elizabeth shouted.

Laramie peered around his boulder. The Indians were plunging down the sloping side of the draw, the horses stiff-legged in front, hindquarters skidding in the shale. Now the first one reached the bottom and came at the boulders on a slant, the little pony running all out, belly skimming low over the ground. The others were strung out behind him. The Indians rode low, firing and yelling as they came. The noise was deafening.

"All right...now!" Laramie yelled at the top of his voice.

They began firing steadily, the shots echoing and re-echoing like whipcracks. The charge was broken less than thirty yards from the nest of boulders. The Indians turned their ponies in a tight circle and rode back the way they came, dust screening them now from view.

As the dust settled, Laramie counted four still bodies. "Not bad. Anybody hurt?"

He looked around. Elizabeth gave him a pale smile. Peters winked. He was beaming and excited, the bowler hat perched on his head at a cocky angle.

Rigney said, "They made it within twenty yards of us. The next time they may ride right in before we can turn them!"

"Will there be a next time, Nelson?" Peters asked.

Laramie squinted at the sun. There was less than an hour to go before sundown. "Yes, they'll make at least one more try. Between sundown and dusk, when they'll be harder to see."

"And if we turn them back, what then?"

"Then we wait and see." Laramie got to his feet. "We'd all better have a drink. I'll get the canteens."

He propped his rifle against the boulder and walked back to the horses. He didn't make any effort at concealment. The Indians were all grouped across the draw, powwowing. Some Indians he'd known were good shots, but he'd never known one *that* good at this distance.

The horses were a little spooky. Laramie spent a few minutes quieting them, then returned with the canteens and passed them around.

Peters took a long gulp of water before saying, "Is there any truth to the story that Indians won't attack at night? Something to do with their belief in spirits bringing bad luck?"

"Depends."

"Depends on what?"

"Depends on the Indian. Most of them I'd say no, they won't attack after dark. It all depends on how much the particular Indian believes in his spirits. They're human like us. And some of us believe in some things more strongly that others do. But these renegades... Who knows what they believe?"

Now they waited.

Peters leaned his back against the boulder, hat tilted down over his eyes, and dozed. Laramie had to marvel at him anew. Seeing the Pinkerton man for the first time like this, Laramie would have put it down as pure bravado, but he knew better now.

Rigney sat tensely, now and then peering around the boulder. Every few minutes he took a swallow of water from the canteen, his throat working convulsively.

"Better take it easy on that, Marshal," Laramie drawled. "It may have to last awhile. If you drink yours, don't expect any from us."

Rigney bared his teeth in a snarl, eyes glinting wolfishly, but he capped the canteen and put it down. He was far from dapper now. His clothes were dusty, sweat-stained, his boots dull, and a day's beard stubbled his cheeks.

Laramie moved closer to Elizabeth. "You all right?"

She pushed the hair out of her eyes and managed a smile. "I'm fine, Laramie. I'm just sorry I led you into this."

"Not your fault. We'll get out safe and sound, don't fret," he said with far more confidence that he felt. He found her hand and squeezed it. She turned her hand over and returned the pressure fiercely. Then her hand loosened, and she put her head back, eyes closing.

They waited.

The sun dropped out of sight, the swift twilight descending. Laramie began to think the Indians weren't going to attack again.

Then a hoarse shout came from Rigney. "They're coming!"

Laramie got to one knee and looked around the boulder. They charged in a ragged line this time, several yards separating each rider. The far side of the draw was in deep shadow, and they seemed to boil up out of the ground, like yelling demons out of some black pit.

"Fire at the four in the center," Laramie said tersely. "Starting with you, Marshal, left to right. But wait until they're close. We can't afford to miss."

Laramie leveled his rifle at the third Indian from the left of the center four, got the man in his sights and waited, bullets pinging off the boulder around him, until the oncoming Indian seemed about to ride down the rifle barrel. Then he squeezed the trigger. The Indian screamed piercingly and flew off the pony backward. The pony came on, veering aside just in time to avoid crashing into the boulder.

Laramie looked quickly left and right. Two more Indians down. Score one each for Peters and Elizabeth. But how about Rigney? Laramie didn't have time to look. The others were bunching up now, very close. He fired into them rapidly, trying for firepower more than accuracy.

Most of the attackers had started to turn back, but one rode in, driving his pony between the two boulders shielding the marshal and Peters. The Indian had lost his rifle in the charge, but he had a tomahawk in his right hand. He wheeled the pony in behind Peters, who seemed totally unaware of his danger.

Laramie raised his rifle, triggered it and heard a click. Empty! The Indian rode at Peters, leaning far out, the tomahawk ready to cleave through the bowler hat and into Peters' skull.

Lamamie dropped his Winchester and leaped, his arms reaching. He caught the Indian around the waist, and they tumbled into the dust together.

The Indian's body was greased and slippery. He stank

of rancid fat and the odor of cooking fires. They rolled over and over, first one on top, then the other, Laramie desperately trying to retain his grip. Then his hold was broken, the Indian on top, astraddle him.

Laramie saw the lethal glitter in the man's eyes, saw the tomahawk raised and start down with the speed of a striking rattler. Laramie heaved mightily and twisted his head aside just in time. He heard the tomahawk thump into the ground alongside his head, and he continued his roll, throwing his assailant off.

They came to their feet at the same time. From the lack of pull on his hip Laramie knew he'd lost his sixgun in the struggle. They circled each other warily. Laramie maneuvered the Indian until his back was to the boulder. Then he feinted right. The tomahawk whistled down, Laramie barely avoiding the slashing blade.

Then he drove in, shoulder low, caught the Indian around the waist and slammed him up against the boulder. The Indian grunted sharply, the breath sighing from him, and Laramie heard the tomahawk clatter against the rock as it fell from the Indian's hand.

Laramie slammed him against the boulder again and yet again. He heard something crack, the Indian went limp, and Laramie loosened his grip, letting the lifeless body fall to the ground.

It wasn't until then he noticed how quiet it was, no screams, no shots. Elizabeth, Peters and Rigney were all staring at him.

Peters whistled through his teeth. "Nelson, you're some man, you know that? I wouldn't want to get you riled at me." He pushed his hat back on his head. "I guess I owe you my life. Thanks."

Laramie gestured in some annoyance and looked around for his gun. He picked it up off the ground, spun the cylinder to check if it was free of dust, then holstered it. "They're all gone?" He looked around the boulders, but it was full dark and he couldn't see a thing.

Elizabeth said, "They're all gone, Laramie. At least for the time being."

Laramie plucked his hat out of the dust, slapped it twice against his leg and said, "Then let's make a run for it."

Elizabeth stared. "Now?"

"This is the best time."

Rigney said, "But they're probably laying for us out there!"

"Not this soon. They're either scattered, given up, or disorganized. And it's dark. They can't see us any better than we can see them." He peered at the marshal. "What's wrong? A bit ago you were bellyaching about pinned down here."

"But suppose he's right, Nelson?" Peters asked. "Suppose they *are* waiting out there?"

"We shoot our way through. We have a choice...wait out the night in the hope they're gone for good. If they're not, we're pinned down here another day and we may not be so lucky. Or else we ride out!"

6

They rode out slowly, keeping everything as muffled as possible, the men removing their spurs. Laramie put Elizabeth and Rigney in the middle, while he and Peters bracketed them on each side. The night was dark, quiet except for the slow, muffled cadence of their hoofbeats and an occasional creak of saddle leather.

One hundred yards, two hundred yards...

Laramie sensed rather than felt the ground become steeper, and he knew they were climbing up out of the draw. Suddenly his alert ears detected a sound to his right, and a rifle roared. Laramie, expecting it, fired at the splash of flame and heard a high-pitched scream as his bullet hit home. The others had their instructions. At the first hint of trouble they were to ride and ride hard. Laramie waited a couple of minutes, listening, until he was sure there were no sounds of immediate pursuit, then set Wingfoot after them.

There was an element of danger riding pell-mell in the dark. A horse could step in a hole or just plain stumble and break a leg. It was a risk they had to take.

After about two miles Laramie overtook a slowing horse.

Elizabeth's voice came at him out of the dark. "Laramie?"

"Yeah," he said roughly. "What if it hadn't been me?"

"I was worried. Are they after us?"

"Not as far as I can tell."

Another horse loomed up. "Nelson . . . is that you?"

"Why not let the whole countryside know?" Laramie grumbled. He raised his voice slightly. "Yes, damn it, it's me!"

"We're just worried about you, is all." Elizabeth's voice was ever so faintly reproving.

"Yeah. Well . . ." As always, when danger had passed, Laramie felt disgruntled, melancholy. He sighed, scrubbing a hand down across his face. "Sorry. Guess I'm not used to people worrying about me."

A few miles farther on, they made a cold camp for the night. Without risking a fire, they unsaddled the horses in the dark, hobbled them and rolled up in their blankets on the ground, all except Laramie. "We'd better keep watch all night, just in case. I'll stand the first one. I'll wake you for the second, Marshal. You take the third and last, Peters."

Laramie had selected a small rise for their camp. Although there wasn't any moon, there was a certain amount of light, and he depended on Wingfoot to alert him if they had company. The horse was good as any watchdog.

Soon the only sounds were the snorting of the horses

and a soft snore from one of the men. Laramie smoked sparingly, always shielding the match flame behind cupped hands held a few inches off the ground.

The night moved on without incident, and Laramie could give free rein to his troubled thoughts. He was troubled on several counts. First, of course, was their crazy mission. It was insane for three men and a woman even to think of capturing at least a dozen hardcases like the Taggert gang holed up in what, from the little he'd been able to glean from Elizabeth, was a hideout just about impregnable to attack. He had gone along with idea originally in the hope that Peters and Elizabeth would see how senseless it was and back off.

But he knew that their resolve was hardening with every passing day. The Pinkerton man didn't seem in the least daunted by what faced them. And Elizabeth, spurred by guilt and her thirst for vengeance, was obviously bent on going ahead no matter what the odds.

Elizabeth... She troubled Laramie more than anything else. Five years ago, he'd been younger. What he'd felt for Elizabeth was a boy's casual interest. After the fire of his love for Hallie Lindsay, and the surging passion of her response, he had an understanding of women that he'd lacked before. And he knew that Elizabeth, after a decent interval had passed, would welcome a serious courtship. She was all woman, and quite a woman at that, and would make some man a fine wife. But Laramie sensed, deep down, that that was not what he was seeking.

He sighed heavily, crossed to where Rigney was sleeping and nudged him with a toe. "Marshal?"

Rigney sat up with a startled snort. "Nelson? Is it time for me to...?

"Yeah."

"Anything happen?"

"It's been quiet as a church. And I don't expect anything. But don't go dozing off. There's always an outside chance."

41

The only answer was a surly grunt as Rigney got to his feet. Laramie rolled up his blanket and was asleep almost instantly.

He awoke to a cool dawn, to birds singing, and to the smell of fresh coffee. For a moment he felt good, then he remembered where he was and what he was doing there, and he cursed himself for seven kinds of a fool.

He turned his head and saw Elizabeth bent over a small fire. Several days of the trail, wearing men's clothing, she still managed to look wholly feminine.

She glanced up and saw him watching her. Faint rose color touched her cheeks, and she looked suddenly shy. "Good morning, Laramie."

Laramie felt good again. "Good morning." He rolled out of the blanket and approached the fire. Peters was hunkered down by it, small cigar smouldering, a tin cup of coffee in his hand.

"Anything happen?"

Peters said cheerfully, "Not a peep. Those redskins are long gone."

"Yeah." Laramie accepted a cup of steaming coffee from Elizabeth and squatted down to blow on it. He watched her for a moment as she sliced salt pork into a small skillet. "Elizabeth, how much farther?"

"We'll get there tomorrow some time," she said guardedly.

He let his irritation surface. "You'd think you knew the location of a lost mine or some such!"

She flared up. "If I told you, you'd probably ride on without me, maybe even tie me up, while you brave men did the job all on your own!"

Laramie was silent. She was right. If he could find the canyon without her, he would arrange something like that. He heard footsteps and glanced around as Marshal Rigney came up. His face was scrubbed, hair slicked down and he had shaved.

Peters answered Laramie's unspoken question. "Yes,

42

there's a creek down there. But how the marshal could shave, I'm sure I don't know. That water is just like ice."

As Laramie made his way down the slope to the creek, the sun poked up in the east. He looked west. Yes, the Rockies were clearer this morning. He knew they'd disappear in the heat haze later in the day, but now they vaulted up like a long, jagged line of mighty cathedrals reaching into the heavens.

Laramie shucked his shirt and washed. Peters was right; the creek was icy.

After a quick breakfast they saddled and rode on before the sun had climbed very high. The country grew more broken as the day wore on. They rode through a series of shallow valleys rich in grassland and dotted with grazing cattle. They met no one. Now and then a cowpuncher could be seen riding in the distance. The Rocky Mountains loomed ever closer.

"It's my first sight of the Rockies," Peters remarked. "Looks like everything they say. Is there snow up there all the year round, Nelson?"

"In the high places."

"You've been up that high?"

"A couple times, hunting. Big-horn sheep."

In mid-afternoon they topped a ridge and saw a small town set in a grove of cottonwoods. Elizabeth reined in. "This is the last town before we get there. Do we stop or ride on through?"

Laramie thought about it while he rolled a cigarette. A small breeze of caution blew across his mind. Why risk it? If they could pick up a posse now... "I don't think it's a good idea."

Rigney challenged him. "Why not? We could all use a good night's rest in a hotel." His voice took on a sneering edge. "I'm not used to sleeping on the ground like some line rider."

Peters said easily, "A cool beer would be real good about now, Nelson."

43

"If you think we shouldn't . . ." Elizabeth watched him with barely concealed eagerness. "But I could certainly use a hot bath. And we'll still get to where we're going before dark tomorrow."

Outvoted, three to one. But it was Elizabeth's vote that decided him. She was, after all, a woman. He shrugged. "Why not?"

The town was little more than a wide place in the road, a straggle of buildings: a general store, livery stable, two saloons, stagecoach office. The town had no hotel, but there was a rooming house that would rent them rooms for the night and provide supper.

Rigney disappeared as soon as the horses were stabled. Elizabeth disappeared also, happily on her way to a hot bath. Laramie and Peters had to be content with a horse-trough washing and a shave.

When they were finished, Peters said, "I'll buy the beers, Nelson. I figure I owe you a couple."

They left word they'd be back in time for supper, then walked up the street to the Watering Hole Saloon. It wasn't crowded, a half-dozen men at the bar, a lackadaisical poker game at a table in the rear. There wasn't even a dancehall girl in the place.

Peters grimaced. "Sure a busy place, this one."

"I'd guess most of their trade comes from cowhands. Town's probably treed every Saturday night."

They ordered two beers from a portly, sweating bartender.

Peters raised his beer glass. "Here's to our success." He drank thirstily without stopping until the glass was empty.

"Yeah." Laramie drank more slowly. The beer was faintly bitter and far from cold.

"You still don't think much of our chances?"

"I think we stand about as much chance as a cottontail caught in a bear trap."

"All I want are the Taggerts, dead or alive. We get them

44

and the gang will break up."

"And just how do you figure on doing that? Tell the Taggerts to ride out and we'll take 'em on, one at a time?"

"We'll find a way," Peters said with maddening confidence.

"Oh, sure we will."

"Nelson? Laramie Nelson?"

Laramie tensed, turned slowly. A tall, slim man of about twenty-five, with cold gray eyes and long blond hair stood spraddle-legged a few feet away. His hands were long and slender, white as a woman's, and there was a worn Colt strapped low on his thigh.

A gunfighter.

Laramie sighed. "Yes, I'm Laramie Nelson."

"I've heard of you."

"Well, happy you!"

"I mean, I've heard you think you're good with that iron you're toting."

"And so?"

"So I aim to find out just how good you are. I'm calling you out, Nelson!"

7

The men at the bar scrambled out of the way, leaving only Brock Peters ranging alongside Laramie Nelson.

Laramie spread his hands. "Look, friend, I have no beef with you."

The gunfighter's thin lips peeled back in a wolfish grin, his right hand, fingers spread and working, hanging by his gun. "That makes no never mind. Make your play!" \

A thumping sound from the bar brought Laramie's head around. The bartender, sweating heavily now, held a wicked-looking shotgun braced on the bar. "Not in here, gents. You're not going to shoot up my saloon. Outside!"

Laramie felt a spurt of relief. Maybe he wouldn't have to go through with it.

45

But the gunfighter laughed shortly. "That's fine with me. I'll wait for you outside in the street, Nelson."

Without hesitation he turned his back and strode out. The men inside fought for vantage points at all the front windows.

Laramie drained his glass of beer. For a moment he contemplated staying right where he was. Maybe the gunnie would give up and leave. But he knew it was a futile hope. How many times had this happened to him? Too many times, far too many.

Besides, something was nagging at him. How had the man known he was in town? He wasn't that easily recognized here.

Apparently the same thought was in Peters' mind. "How did he . . . ?"

"You tell me." Laramie thumped his glass down on the bar. "You'd better stay in here, out of the way of a stray bullet."

He started off. After a moment he heard Peters' footsteps behind him. Laramie strode on, pushing through the batwing doors. The gunfighter stood a distance up the street, his back to the sun which was low in the west.

He's not stupid, Laramie reflected wryly; he's taking every advantage open to him.

Laramie walked across the warped planks and stepped down into the dust. He risked a glance at the saloon. Peters stood just outside the doors, eyes bright and watchful.

Laramie looked at the gunman, squinting into the glare of the sun. "There's still time to call this off. I don't even know your name."

"And you're not about to live long enough to find out!"

Laramie shrugged. So be it. He considered trying for an arm or a leg, yet he knew it wouldn't do. This kind of a man was like an enraged rattlesnake. So long as he was alive and thrashing, he was deadly. Laramie stood easily, relaxed and waiting, hands hanging loosely.

Time stretched. A full minute passed, the street silent as a graveyard.

A muscle twitched in the gunfighter's cheek, his eyes blinked rapidly, and he snarled, "Draw, damn you!"

"It's your play, friend. You call it."

The words weren't out of Laramie's mouth before the man clawed for his gun. He was fast, very fast, his gun out and coming up before Laramie's cleared the holster.

But speed wasn't as important as accuracy. Speed was often a handicap, especially when the gunman was nervous, as this one obviously was.

The Colt spat lead, and Laramie felt the bullet pluck at his sleeve in passing. Then his own bullet gun bucked in his hand. His bullet slammed into the other man, blood immediately blossoming like a red flower over the heart. He flew backward, arms windmilling, his gun going off once more, the bullet going wild.

Laramie walked over, holstering his gun. The man was sprawled on his back, lifeless eyes staring directly into the last rays of the sun glinting off a peak far off in the distance.

They poured out of the saloon now, gathering around. People came from the other buildings as well. Laramie saw Marshal Rigney pause on the outer fringe of the crowd without venturing closer. The marshal's gaze was on him, his eyes bleak, unreadable.

Peters crowded in. He was excited as a small boy. "He was much faster on the draw than you! And yet—"

"It isn't always the quickest. You've got to hit what you aim at," Laramie said, his glance still on Rigney. "You've been reading too many of those dime thrillers." He gestured sharply. "I think supper'll be on the table by the time we get back to the rooming house."

As they walked away, Peters said, "Is that true, it isn't always the fastest gun who wins?"

"That wasn't exactly what I said. It depends on who it

is. Some, like John Wesley Hardin or Ben Thompson, were damned fast, but they were cold as ice, never got rattled, and always made that first shot count."

Nothing was said at supper about the shoot-out. Elizabeth had undoubtedly heard the shots, but shots weren't uncommon, so she would have no reason to suspect Laramie was involved in any shooting.

Her hair was tied up in a scarf, her face scrubbed until it shone. Apparently the bath had revived her good spirits, and she talked constantly as they ate. Rigney ate in his usual sullen silence. Elizabeth had never been east of the Mississippi River, and she was full of questions about the east. Brock Peters seized the opportunity and talked wittily and at length. Laramie, having come west from the southeast, knew that much of what Peters told her was an exaggeration. But Elizabeth was obviously enchanted, so Laramie didn't comment.

After supper Laramie sat on the rooming house steps and smoked a cigarette. Elizabeth joined him. "Brock told me about what happened this afternoon, Laramie."

So it was Brock now, was it? Aloud he said, "Brock has a big mouth."

"Does that happen to you often?"

"Too often." He scrubbed a hand across his mouth. "When a man gets a reputation with a gun, even a small rep, there's always some young gunnie around afire to prove himself better."

"Can't you avoid it?"

"How? I can't just turn my back and walk away. I'd never be able to hold my head up again. Stop wearing a gun? Others have gone down that road. Sooner or later they're forced to strap it on again or be shot down in the street like a dog."

Silence fell for a few moments. The house behind them had settled down for the night, creaking faintly as it cooled from the day's heat. A burst of laughter came from one of the saloons up the street. Laramie stirred restlessly and said, "Elizabeth, don't you think it's about time you told me about what's facing us tomorrow?"

She was silent for a moment more, then said in a low voice, "All right. I do know more than I told you. I was actually inside their canyon once, that time with Ned."

Laramie's breath escaped him in astonishment. "How did that happen? What were *you* doing?"

"Well, it was when we were camped out there, when Ned was trying to join up. They half-promised he could and he was happy. Happy, he was proud!" she said with a harsh laugh. "He wanted me to meet them. I didn't want to, I was scared stiff, but I thought I should have some idea of what he was getting into. I'd never met the Taggert brothers. To Ned, they were heroes, robbing the rich, land-grabbing railroads to help the poor.

"Help the poor! All they ever helped were themselves, spending their loot on whiskey and saloon women until it's all gone. They even had some fancy women with them the day I rode in there with Ned."

"That explains a few things," Laramie said slowly. "They know then that you know about their hideout?"

"Yes, they know."

"I suspected as much. And they won't rest easy as long as you're alive."

"They'd like to kill me or something worse."

"Something worse?"

"Lyle Taggert. He frightens me. He has the cold eyes of a snake. He even looks like one. He's tall and skinny. He walks, rides, sort of bent or humped over. I understand he was shot in the back once, injured his spine."

Laramie remembered the masked bandit, bent across his saddle at a buzzard's crooked-neck angle, riding back to finish off Ned with a bullet.

Elizabeth was going on, "When I saw him that day, looking at me with those snake eyes, I was absolutely terrified. He undressed me with his eyes. Everyone else had a dancehall woman, even his brother, Cal, who is fat and looks like a pig and was wallowing drunkenly with one. But not Lyle. He told me he didn't care for saloon women. He likes respectable women or married women who are unhappy with their husbands. Ned had wandered off to take a drink with someone. Laramie, I just about died of shame!"

She shivered, hugging herself. "I got Ned out of there as soon as I ever could. He didn't believe me when I told him. He laughed at my fears."

"All right, Elizabeth, all right," Nelson said soothingly. He took her hand and held it tightly. "Now tell me about the canyon."

"It's a dead-end canyon, the way in very narrow and hidden by brush. It's almost like riding into a cave. Inside is a small valley, good grazing for their horses. They even have houses in there, a main house and a sort of bunkhouse. Oh, yes, they always have two men on guard at the entrance, day and night, even when they're not there."

"Then there's only the one way in and out?"

"So far as I know. And that's what Ned said they told him. But one man with a rifle could hold off an army in that narrow pass."

"How about water?"

"There's plenty, a small lake on the back slope of the canyon, fed by spring run-offs. The water's held back by a natural earth dam."

Laramie sighed. "And I suppose they always have a good supply of food on hand?"

"I even saw a small herd of beef cattle."

"You're a big help," he said glumly. "Sounds to me like they could hole up in there forever, just about. And we're supposed to somehow get them out. You think of any bright ideas, I'll be glad to listen."

"Laramie . . . I'll never get a good night's sleep again so long as the Taggerts are running loose!"

"Yeah, I know. Don't fret. We'll think of something."

50

She leaned close, her breath warm, and brushed her lips across his cheek. Then she was gone, running lightly into the house.

Laramie didn't make a habit of worrying. If a situation didn't offer an immediate solution, he believed in sleeping on it. Often, a solution would come with a new day. It didn't this time. He slept very little that night. Of course, he rarely slept well in a house and on a soft bed the first night after sleeping on the trail for several days. He dropped off to sleep just before dawn without the least inkling of how they were going to lure the Taggerts out of their stronghold.

As a result, he was irritable when they rode out of town the next morning After a few tries at conversation, Peters and Elizabeth gave up and galloped up ahead together, talking in low voices. They rode hard all morning. They were in the foothills before noon, making their way through deep draws and shallow canyons and across pinon-studded slopes. The country was beautiful, but it was wild, desolate. There were no ranches now. They saw plenty of game but little cattle.

The hard riding softened the edges of Laramie's bleak mood. He rode up beside Peters and Elizabeth. "Seems to me they could have picked a much closer place to hide out."

"They're safer out here. There's almost no law and fewer people," Elizabeth said.

"Outlaws are like animals, Nelson," Peters said. "They like to hibernate and lick their wounds far removed from people. Look at that bunch up in Jackson Hole. They had to ride a long way to their jobs, too."

Laramie looked at him curiously. "What do you know about the Jackson Hole bunch?"

"I had a hand in capturing them," Peters said with some pride.

"I thought you'd never been west before?"

"I didn't say that. You just assumed it, because I looked

51

like an Eastern dude," Peters said with biting sarcasm.

Laramie eyed the man sourly, his irritation mounting again. Finally he said, "Yeah," and let Wingfoot fall back several paces.

It was about two hours before sundown when Elizabeth reined in, holding up a hand. When Laramie Nelson rode up alongside her, she pointed to a rise up ahead. "We'd better not get any closer. Over that hogback is a wide wash leading right up to the mouth of their canyon. The men they have posted can see us if we ride any nearer."

"Can we leave the horses here and go on foot for a looksee?"

"We can crawl up behind those bushes on top there and see all there is to see."

They tied the horses and started up the incline on foot. A few yards from the top Laramie waved them down, and they crawled the rest of the way. The brush was thick along the top of the ridge. Carefully they parted the lower branches and peered through. The wash was deep and wide, the bottom pebble-strewn; it had been scoured by a flash flood at some time or another.

Elizabeth nudged Laramie and jerked her head toward the mountains. About a mile from where they squatted, the wash veered away from a slope so steep it was almost a cliff. Pines grew thick on the slope and at one place a profusion of brush grew right down into the wash. As Laramie squinted into the sun, he glimpsed the glitter of something bright. He judged it to be a rifle barrel.

Elizabeth nudged him again. "That must be one of the guards," she whispered. "That brush you see coming all the way down, that's the way in. The bushes are so thick in there you have to lead your horse in."

"And to get out they have to ride down that wash?" She nodded.

Laramie slid back down the slope a few yards and leaned his back against a stunted pine while he rolled a

52

cigarette. They all gathered around him. Marshal Rigney squatted to one side, face morose, idly tossing pebbles down the slope. Peters and Elizabeth looked at Laramie expectantly, hopefully.

As though they expected him to pull a ready-made answer out of his Stetson! He wrenched it off, slapped it against his leg and said wrathfully, "If we had a posse with us, we could string everybody out on both sides of that wash and starve 'em out. If they tried to ride out, we could pick 'em off one by one."

"But we don't have a posse," Peters said calmly.

"Yeah, and without one we don't have a prayer," Laramie said quietly.

"I think we should forget the whole stupid thing," Rigney said, "and ride back to Cottonwood Springs."

Laramie glared at him. What was it about this man that rubbed him the wrong way? If one of the others had said that, Laramie knew he would have fallen over his own feet in agreeing.

"Yeah. You would say that." Nelson stood up abruptly. "Is there a decent place to camp around here?"

Elizabeth said, "Yes, a very good spot. A pine grove, a cold spring... where Ned and I camped when we were here."

"Then let's set it up." Laramie plunged down the slope without waiting for them.

The campsite was ideal. The tall pines grew thick, forming a sort of arbor, and it was shady. The spring bubbling up out of the ground gave them water as cold as ice, and the flow of water downhill made a small brook, spreading out into a shallow pool in a small meadow, providing good grazing for the horses. Someone had once made a crude fireplace out of stones.

Laramie didn't care to risk a shot, possibly alerting the bunch in the canyon, so they had beans and salt pork for supper instead of fresh game.

After supper they sat around the fire, and Peters and

Elizabeth discussed possible ways of rooting the Taggerts out of their hole. Rigney contributed nothing, and Laramie said very little. He listened with only a part of his mind, smoking, staring moodily into the fire.

Suddenly Peters said, "Maybe we could stampede a herd of cattle in there."

Nelson stared at him. "Now there's a great plan! First, where would you get the cattle? Have you seen any all day? I haven't. And second, you don't stampede cattle *into* a tight place. They always run for the open range. It'd take two cowpunchers to each animal and then some to drive a herd into that canyon."

"It was only an idea," Peters said.

"Some idea!" Laramie got to his feet. "I'm going to bed down before you two come up with any more ideas!"

Rigney was gone when Laramie awoke the next morning.

8

It was shortly after daylight when Laramie Nelson opened his eyes. As was his habit, he looked first for the horses and found only three.

He glanced over to where he'd seen Rigney bed down and saw he wasn't there. Elizabeth and Brock Peters were still sleeping.

Laramie put on his boots and prowled around. The marshal was gone, no doubt of it. It was getting light rapidly now. Laramie searched until he found the tracks of Rigney's horse. He followed on foot for a half mile. The tracks led across the ridge, down into the wash and turned west.

Rigney had ridden into the canyon.

Laramie returned to camp, routed out the others and told them what he'd found.

Peters swore without apology to Elizabeth. "He's going in to warn the Taggerts?"

"It sure looks that way," Laramie said grimly.

Elizabeth said, "I told you he'd be no good to us!"

"It looks a little worse than that. I'd say he's a member of the Taggert bunch. Or at least he's a paid spy for them. That would explain some things. Like who took a shot at me in Cottonwood Springs. Marshal Rigney. And I'd say he told that gunnie about me back in that town day before yesterday. He may even have hired him to gun me down."

Peters jumped up in alarm "They may have already ridden out! We've got to—"

"Ridden out? Why? Because they're afraid of two men and a woman?" Laramie laughed shortly. If anything, they would have sneaked in here last night and shot us in our sleep. No, they're about as worried about us as a horse would be over a pesky fly. But I reckon it'd be safe to say they now know we're here, so we'd better keep an eye peeled." He looked at each in turn. "Unless you want to give up the whole thing now and ride out?"

They shook their heads from side to side.

Laramie sighed. "Well, it was too much to hope for, I reckon."

They found a good location about two hundred yards from the canyon entrance. Trees growing on the side of the wash and several big rocks provided good cover. Both Elizabeth and Peters were with him, and Laramie knew they would have to divide the time into shifts if they were to set up an effective vigil. Time enough for that later.

"I don't know what good it'll do anyway," he muttered. "They can stay in there until we're nothing but bleached bones out here. Or if they come boiling out, we can't hope to get them all."

"Just so we get the Taggerts," Peters said.

"You think they'll personally lead a charge like that? Not on your life! They'll be the tail of the dog."

Peters moved restlessly. "We're not even sure they're still in there. Just because *you* think they are..."

Laramie squinted at the canyon entrance, his gaze

raking the hillside foot by foot. He detected no movement, saw no glitter of sun on metal. Quickly he levered two random shots at the hillside. Then he stuck his sombrero on the rifle barrel and inched it up above the rock he crouched behind. Instantly a rifle shot rang out, and the hat spun around. It was impossible to tell the exact location of the rifleman.

Laramie lowered the rifle, removed the hat and ruefully poked his little finger through the neat hole.

He asked dryly, "Satisfied now?"

"Well, yes, I suppose so."

Laramie leaned back against the rock, hat slanted down over his eyes. He rolled a cigarette and smoked thoughtfully. Peters and Elizabeth moved a few feet away and began a conversation in low tones.

Laramie smoked, gazing out from under the hat brim at the dry wash bed. A nebulous thought began taking shape in his mind. It was a long shot, completely wild, but it was better than nothing. Certainly it was better than roosting here until they grew roots.

Suddenly Elizabeth was at his side, her fingers digging into his arm. She said urgently, "Laramie, look!"

Laramie peered around the boulder. A man rode toward them, carrying a white rag elevated on a stick. The rider was tall and thin, and rode hunched over.

Elizabeth confirmed what Laramie had already guessed. "It's Lyle Taggert!"

Laramie watched the man ride up, holding his rifle steady on him. Then he saw he wasn't wearing a gun, and there was no rifle in the scabbard, so Laramie lowered his weapon and stood up in full view. "You stay out of sight, Elizabeth, until we find out what he wants."

Taggert's face was very narrow, with the shape of a blunted axe blade, his nose prominent. His eyes seemed lidless, colorless. And Elizabeth was right. Taggert had the unblinking stare of a snake.

He was dressed in a black broadcloth suit and a pleated

white shirt, with a black bow tie. He was so clean-shaven that his face had the pink flush of a sunset. He could be on his way to church. Or going courting.

Taggert reined in at the bottom of the slope. In a nasal voice he said, "You're Nelson, I take it?"

"I'm Nelson."

The man nodded. "That's what Claude told me."

"Rigney's your man, then?"

"You might say that." Taggert's thin lips drew back over yellowed teeth in what could be taken for a smile. "I've rode out to parley."

"About what?"

"First, is Mrs. Cooper with you?" He held up a long-fingered hand. "Don't bother lying. Claude told me she is and we've been watching. She hasn't left."

Elizabeth stood up beside Laramie, her head held high. "Yes, I'm here."

Taggert swept off his hat, revealing a head as hairless as an egg. "Right pleased, Mrs. Cooper. I'm sorry about Ned, but those things happen.

"Yes, I'm so sure you are sorry," Elizabeth said acidly, not looking at him.

Laramie spoke, "You killed him, Taggert. I saw you."

Taggert was unruffled. "Did you, now? Well, it couldn't be helped."

"What do you want with us?"

"Well now, I could ask what *you* want here. But to tell the truth I'm glad you're here. At least I'm glad Mrs. Cooper is. Saves me a lot of trouble." He wiped sweat from his forehead with the edge of his hand and replaced his hat. "Mrs. Cooper rides back with me and I'll let you and your Pinkerton friend go without a scratch."

"So you can kill her?"

Taggert's eyes widened in an innocent look. "Kill her? Now why would I want to do that? I'm right taken with the lady and now that she's a widow, she'll be needing a man to look after her."

"I can take care of myself, thank you," Elizabeth said tartly.

"And besides," Taggert continued as though she hadn't spoken, "if we'd wanted to kill anybody, we could have done that while you were all sleeping last night. But I figured Mrs. Cooper losing her husband and all would hardly look kindly on losing her friends."

Laramie said, "You come riding out here carrying a white flag and laying down terms to *us?*"

"I didn't want to get gunned down before I said my piece. And if you think you've got us treed, think again." Taggert laughed harshly. "We can take you any old time."

"We'll get some of you."

"Maybe so, but not enough." The man's voice hardened. "Now about Mrs. Cooper . . ."

"She stays here."

"You're making a mistake. You'll all wind up buzzard meat. Play it my way and you'll all live. It's too late now for you to ride out. My boys'll be watching you and we'll ride you down if you try it."

"I'd rather be dead than live with you," Elizabeth said in a shaking voice.

"Now that ain't good sense, ma'am. I ain't all that bad." Taggert's face crinkled in what Laramie supposed was intended to be an ingratiating smile. "You'll have a good life with me. I have a fine house in there, all furnished, just waiting for a woman like you."

"Parley's over," Laramie Nelson said. He was having a hard time keeping his anger under control. "Turn your horse around and ride back."

"Now wait a minute—"

"I said ride!"

Firing from the hip, Laramie sent a rifle bullet thudding into the dirt in front of Taggert's horse. The animal reared, whinnying, pawing the air. It took Taggert a little while to get the horse under control.

When he spoke again, Taggert's voice was ugly, his

eyes flat and hard. "You'll be sorry for that, sorrier than you'll ever know!"

Then he turned his horse and rode back toward the canyon at a walk.

Some time during the confrontation Brock Peters had stood up alongside Elizabeth. Now he said tightly, "I should have shot him down like a cur. I don't know why I didn't. A dead Taggert would be better than a live one!"

"We don't do things that way out here, Peters. He came under a white flag. Besides, I'm sure they're watching. If we'd've gunned him down, the others would have been right on top of us."

"Maybe I should have gone with him," Elizabeth said miserably.

Laramie rounded on her. "Hush up with that kind of talk!"

"But it's my fault you're here, Laramie! I don't know why I ever thought the three of us could carry this off. If you're killed, I'll never forgive myself!"

"It's too late to talk about blame. We've got to figure a way out."

"There is no way out."

9

Two hours later Laramie Nelson was hunkered down in the shade of a rock on the lip of the wash. It was edging toward noon now, the sun hotter than at any time since they'd reached the high country. Elizabeth had gone back to camp to prepare their lunch, and Brock Peters was a few yards up the wash toward the canyon, keeping watch.

In his mind Laramie had gone over and over the plan he had devised. The chances of it working depended on a number of factors, not the least of which was pure luck. He also had to gamble on the bandits being overconfident to the point of laxness in their vigilance.

He heard the scuffle of footsteps and looked around as

Elizabeth slipped in beside him with a canteen of water and a plate of heated beans.

"Laramie," she said in a low, soft voice, "maybe after dark . . . couldn't we just ride off? How would they know?"

Laramie shook his head, chewing, and swallowed some water before answering. "It's too risky. They may send some scouts out after dark, looking for us to do just that. We'd be outnumbered, about five to one."

He wasn't being entirely honest. Earlier, he would have agreed with her. In the night their chances of getting away would be better than fifty-fifty, especially if they scattered, setting up a rendezvous point. But the brief encounter with Lyle Taggert had altered his thinking considerably. So long as the bandit chief was either alive or running free, Elizabeth wouldn't be safe anywhere. The very thought of Elizabeth in Taggert's clutches made Laramie's blood run cold. It had to be resolved one way or another in this place, here and now.

He said, "Tell me again about the lake and the dam."

Her gaze sharpened. "What about it?"

"Well, you said it was in the *back* of the canyon?"

"Yes. Oh, I see what you mean. Not exactly. Inside, the valley curves, running at an angle to us. Like this." Using a stick she sketched outlines of the canyon in the dirt. "You see, the lake is actually here." She drew a rough circle and jabbed it with the stick. "It should be right over about here, right over that ridge."

Laramie said slowly, "That makes it a little easier."

Her face lit up. "Laramie, you have a plan!"

"Now don't get all excited," he said cautiously. "It depends on whether or not I can climb that ridge without being seen. You call it a ridge, actually it's a cliff. But a man on foot should be able to work his way up there without being spotted."

"You're not going in there alone!"

"I'm certainly not taking anyone else along. Elizabeth,

it's the only way. Alone, I might have a chance. Having to watch after somebody else . . . well." He scooped the last of the beans from the plate, gave it to her; then leaned around the boulder. "Peters?"

Peters came over at a crouching run, squatting on his heels beside them.

"I'm going in, over the top," said Laramie Nelson.

The man looked baffled.

Laramie allowed himself a grin. "In my saddle bags there just happens to be half a dozen sticks of dynamite, fuses, and blasting caps."

"Dynamite," Brock Peters said unbelievingly. "Were you figuring on blasting out some stumps?"

"No—but when I was buying ammunition in Cottonwood Springs, I didn't much like the idea of coming all this way with just the guns we had, and I wished we had a troop of horse artillery coming with us. Then I saw the dynamite and caps, and figured they'd come in handy in the right kind of tight place."

"Well, looks like you're right about that," Peters said. "But how come you didn't use it when those Indians had us pinned down?"

Laramie looked at him pityingly. "They were coming *down* on us—and before you start making yourself a bomb with this stuff, you'd best be darn sure it won't roll back on you. Not to mention that it'd be a little uncomfortable if one of them hostiles was to pick it up and throw it back. From the top of the canyon, I figure there's not much chance of *that*, anyhow."

He squinted up at the sun. "The problem is getting back out fast, in time to help out here. "It's close to noon, It'll take me at least two hours in and out."

Elizabeth said, "I don't understand, Laramie."

"I'm going to blow up the dam. At least I'm going to try. It'll be like pulling the cork from a bottle. The water pouring down that canyon should panic them. I doubt there's enough water to do them any real harm, but they won't know that and they'll spook and come pouring out. But with the panic they should come out one or two at a time, not all at once. Anyway, that's what I *hope* will happen."

She clapped her hands together, her smile brilliant. "I knew you would think of something!"

"Don't get carried away," he growled. "It's a long shot, but the only one I can see." He leaned around the boulder, pointing. "Peters, you work your way across the wash and down the other side to a good spot. You go down this side, Elizabeth. I hate to do this to you, but there has to somebody on each side of the wash. If things go well, I'll join you before they can come out in force."

"I'll manage, Laramie, don't worry."

"Worry? Why should I worry?" he said sarcastically. He climbed to his feet. "Well, here goes nothing."

Nelson started toward the camp. He looked back once, in time to see Peters duck down into the wash and disappear from sight and Elizabeth moving carefully from rock to tree toward the canyon. He didn't feel right about placing her in jeopardy, but there was no other way. He knew she was good with a rifle, yet she *was* a woman. If she became rattled and they located and rushed her . . .

Laramie pushed the thought from his mind and continued on to the camp. He removed his boots and donned a pair of moccasins. Boots were of no use in scaling cliffs. He made two bundles of dynamite, tying the sticks together with cord. He was particularly careful with the blasting caps, wrapping them separtely in old rags.

Then he put the two bundles of dynamite and the caps into a flour sack and tied it around his neck, letting it hang down his back. With regret he left the rifle behind, he was burdened enough as it was, and wore only the Colt.

It was a little over a mile to the bottom of the cliff. There was cover—rocks, trees, bushes—but he had to make it across open spaces here and there. He snaked along on his belly across these spaces, afraid that any sudden movement might catch the attention of the guards, his skin crawling in anticipation of the shock of a bullet. He didn't know how alert they were, but they could spot him easily if they had binoculars.

It took him an hour to reach the bottom of the cliff. The cover on the cliff was almost non-existent, a few stunted pines, no large rocks. But there was a sort of slanting chimney that had eroded out of the cliff face about a half mile from the canyon entrance. He had noticed it earlier but hadn't been able to tell how deep it was. Up close, it was about two feet deep and extended as far up as he could see. He could only hope it didn't end before he reached the top. It should hide him from prying eyes, and he could certainly come back down in a hurry, like sliding down a sled run, although it would probably be rough on the seat of his pants.

Picking his spots, Laramie started up the chimney. It was slow going. Every few yards he would lose a handhold or his foot would slip and he would slide back, small rocks cascading down with the sound of an avalanche. Each time he finally managed to stop his slide, he waited a minute, two minutes, for a shout of alarm, but he heard nothing. Long before he reached the top his nails were broken, fingers bleeding, and both knees of his trousers were torn, one knee bleeding profusely.

Trees grew thicker on the spine of the ridge. After pulling himself up the last few feet, Laramie lay for a time regaining his breath and getting his bearings. Finally he got to his feet and picked his way carefully, using the pines for cover. It was very quiet, only the chirping of birds and the soughing of wind in the pines breaking the silence. It was less that a hundred yards to the other side of the ridge. Laramie approached cautiously and peered over the edge.

It was easy to see why the canyon was close to impregnable. Here the walls fell away steeply. Even a fly would have trouble climbing up from the floor of the valley two hundred feet below.

The valley was long and narrow and very green. Laramie saw the buildings at the far end, and a corral holding a few horses. The other horses were scattered across the valley, grazing. If he succeeded in panicking them as he hoped, most of the bandits wouldn't have time to catch their horses and would have to flee on foot.

But what pleased him even more was the lake itself. It lay, a circle of blue about a hundred yards in diameter, almost directly below him. The valley narrowed there even more, like the neck of a bottle, the earthen dam stretching from canyon wall to canyon wall.

All he needed was to be sure that his aim was good and it would be like dropping eggs.

Laramie took the dynamite and caps from the sack and arranged them on the ground. Then he rocked back on his heels, rolled a cigarette and lit it. He drew on it until the coal was burning evenly, took a deep breath and stood up with one bundle of dynamite.

The caps were attached, the fuse ready. It was time.

He started to touch the cigarette to the end of a fuse when a harsh voice said behind him, "Freeze, friend. Hold it right there!"

10

Laramie Nelson froze as instructed, scarcely daring to breathe. To get this close and have this happen...!

"All right, you can turn around now, But slow and easy. Don't make any sudden moves."

Laramie turned.

The man holding a gun on him was a big one, shoulders barndoor wide and legs like stumps, with a heavy, drooping moustache and a two-day growth of beard. His clothes were filthy, his face smeared with dirt, and even from ten feet away Laramie caught a strong whiff of a sour smell.

"Now just what are you doing here?"

Laramie's initial despair had receded, and his mind was working coolly, weighing his chances. They weren't good. Even if he could get to his gun, he couldn't risk a shot. It would alert those down below and spoil his plan. He said slowly,

"Well, that's a long story."

"First . . ." The man motioned with his gun. "Unbuckle your gunbelt and let it drop."

"You know what this is?" Laramie held the bundle of dynamite up before him, the fuse only an inch from the burning cigarette.

Even under the dirt the big man's face paled visibly. "What the hell! Dynamite!"

Laramie nodded. "You know what will happen if I touch this cigarette to the fuse?"

"You wouldn't!"

"Try me." Laramie moved the cigarette closer. "Throw your gun away."

"You're bluffing! You'll go sky-high too, if you light that fuse!"

Laramie touched the coal to the fuse, and it began to sizzle. The other man stared in fascination and growing horror, bloodshot eyes bulging. Then, in a convulsive movement, he threw his gun away from him. Laramie pinched the burning fuse between thumb and forefinger, bent and gently placed the dynamite on the ground.

Then, straightening, he was on the big man in two strides. He slammed his fist into the other's mouth before he came out of shock. The blow sent the man crashing back into a tree. He grunted in sudden fury and swarmed at Laramie with both fists swinging wildly. Laramie absorbed a stunning blow on shoulder and turned his head aside to let the other fist whistle past. Then he closed with the man, crowding him back against the tree, pummeling the soft belly unmercifully with both hands.

Laramie hoped to put him away before he could yell a warning, but he soon realized, regretfully, that it wasn't to be. The man was soft, slow-witted, but he was bulky, strong, and could absorb a lot of punishment before going down—if Laramie could take him at all.

Laramie hit him again in the face, this time on the jaw, the blow jarring his arm all the way up to the shoulder. The other man shook his head like a wounded bear, falling back. And Laramie, as though reading the man's thoughts, knew he was about to yell his head off.

In one blurring motion Laramie drew his Colt and laid the barrel alongside the man's head. The other, mouth half-open to yell, reeled back and toppled, slowly, the strangled shout turning into a snort of pain.

He wasn't unconscious, only dazed. Working quickly, Laramie stripped him of his belt and lashed his hands together behind the tree. Then he tore a piece of flour sack and made a gag.

There was less than an inch left of the burned fuse. Laramie quickly replaced it with a fresh one, rolled and lit another cigarette, then hurried to the edge of the canyon wall.

He lit the fuse, aimed carefully for the dam and let the bundle of dynamite go. He stooped, picked up the other one and touched the cigarette to the fuse. He heard a muffled boom and glanced over the edge. His heart sank as he saw a geyser of water settling back into the lake. He had missed the dam entirely.

He corrected his aim as best he could and let the second bundle drop. He didn't wait around to check on his accuracy. Either he had missed the dam or he hadn't. In either case, he had to get out of here.

He was halfway to the other side of the ridge when he heard the second explosion. It was impossible to tell from the sound how successful he'd been.

Laramie made no attempt at concealment on the way down. He had to get back to Elizabeth as quickly as possible. He went down the chimney on his backside, catching at a rock or a shrub now and then and digging in his heels to slow his descent.

Halfway down, he heard gunfire, the rapid clatter of handguns and the echoing crack of rifles. He let himself go and slid down the last few feet without trying to check his fall. He hit the bottom, lost his balance and fell headlong, then was up and running, the Colt in his hand. He had about fifty yards to go to Elizabeth, and he covered them in a matter of seconds.

She was kneeling behind a rock, firing the rifle calmly, as unruffled as though baking bread. Laramie slid in beside her and raked the wash with his glance. There was about a foot of water running swiftly along the bed of the wash. Men were splashing up the channel on foot, firing at random. Laramie saw three riderless horses, three still bodies on the ground.

"We decided to get those on horseback first," Elizabeth said as though in answer to an unspoken question.

"Good thinking," Laramie said between gasping breaths. "The Taggerts or Rigney?"

"I haven't seen either. Not yet "

They were within easy range of the canyon entrance and could have picked off the men one by one as they came out. And now Laramie saw several women running out. He placed his hand on Elizabeth's arm.

"Hold up, we might hit one of the women. We want the Taggerts and Rigney. They'll be coming out soon. If some of these get away, let them." He raised his voice. "Peters?"

"Ho!"

"Hold your fire!"

After a brief pause Peters replied, "All right, Nelson."

"Laramie!" Elizabeth cried. She pointed. "Cal Taggert!"

Riding bareback on a big palomino, heels thumping the animal's sides furiously, was short, plump man, wearing nothing but pants and boots and carrying a sixgun in his free hand.

67

"He's mine! I'll take him!"

Laramie glanced across the wash in time to see Brock Peters leave his cover and plunge halfway down the slope.

"The idiot!" Laramie thought aloud. "Who does he think he is, Wild Bill Hickok?"

He swiveled his head and saw that Cal Taggert had spotted Peters. He began firing, but his bareback perch on a running horse was too precarious for any kind of accuracy.

Peters stood patiently, ignoring the bullets whistling around him as though they represented no more of a threat than buzzing hornets. Slowly he raised the Winchester to his shoulder and waited until Cal Taggert was almost abreast of him before he fired once. Cal Taggert flew off the palomino. The horse raced on, but Cal Taggert lay still, the water swirling around him turning pink from his blood.

Laramie noticed, without giving much thought to it, that the level of the water was falling. The lake must be close to empty.

The sound of another shot jolted him. He looked again at Peters and saw him totter and fall, clutching his shoulder. He rolled down the slope and splashed into the water.

"It's Lyle Taggert!" Elizabeth cried.

Laramie glanced up the wash and saw Lyle Taggert riding hard on the big black horse. He was fully dressed, all in black, and Laramie thought of a vulture swooping in to feed on a carcass.

Rage flooded Laramie. If Taggert's shot had killed Peters...

He stepped out in full view and called out in a loud voice, "Over here, Taggert!"

Although raging, his mind was cold and clear, and a tiny part of it jeered at him. He was being as much a show-off as Peters. This man, this Taggert, with the snake

68

eyes and the buzzard stoop, was deadly and could better have been shot from ambush and without pangs of conscience.

As these thoughts sped through his mind, Laramie Nelson saw Taggert's head turn, saw the black horse veer and head straight for him.

Laramie stood tall, feet planted firmly, waiting. He waited until Taggert got off a shot, the bullet pinging off the rock by Laramie's shoulder. He waited until the rider was close enough for Laramie to see the wolfish grin.

Then he drew and fired. His shot sounded an instant before Taggert's second. Taggert lurched in the saddle, and the black horse reared high, but Taggert stayed in the saddle. At the same time Laramie felt a streak of fire brand his right thigh and his feet went out from under him. Falling, he fired again. He tumbled over and over, finally ending up at the bottom of the wash. The thirsty earth had soaked up all the water now, leaving a scum of mud.

Laramie raised himself on his elbows. He had lost his gun on the way down. He steeled himself for the shock of another bullet. But it was all right. He saw the black horse, riderless, standing a few yards away nuzzling the still figure of Lyle Taggert on the ground.

Then Elizabeth was there, all concern. "Laramie! Are you hurt bad?"

He examined his thigh. "It's nothing, a scratch."

With her help he got to his feet, took a couple of tentative steps. It would soon stiffen up, but he could walk all right. He nodded across the wash. "I'm all right, you'd better check on Peters."

Elizabeth uttered an exclamation and hurried away. Laramie looked around. As suddenly as it had begun, it was all over. There were a few horses milling about aimlessly, but the men were all gone. Up toward the canyon entrance was a huddle of women looking his way, plainly frightened.

That was going to be something of a problem, herding a bunch of scared dancehall girls back to the nearest town.

Laramie searched around for his Colt, found it and holstered it, then limped across to where Elizabeth was tending Peters.

The Pinkerton man was sitting up, in the act of lighting a small cigar. Elizabeth had his shirt stripped away from his shoulder and was sponging up blood with a handkerchief.

Laramie squatted down beside them. "Is it bad?"

Peters exhaled a cloud of smoke with a gusty sigh. "A flesh wound. I think the bullet went clean through. Soon as it's bandaged, I'll be fine. Say, we did it, didn't we?" He was exuberant. "It's all over!"

Laramie started to nod, then remembered. His face hardened. "Not quite. There's one more to go. Rigney. He has to still be in the canyon."

Peters shrugged. "The hell with him. The Taggerts were the important ones."

"He's important to me. He tried to get me killed. Twice. I owe him for that. And if there's anything I hate, it's a crooked lawman."

He stood up and started to limp away.

Elizabeth turned a stricken face up to him. "You're not going in there alone?"

"Alone." He grinned sardonically. "Like Peters said, this one is mine."

11

If he hadn't known where to look, Laramie Nelson could have walked within six feet of the canyon entrance and never have seen it.

He pushed his way through thick bushes, thorns plucking at his clothing. He reflected that he'd certainly need new duds after it was all over. His shirt was ripped in several places, his trousers practically in shreds.

The narrow canyon walls pinched together overhead, and it was almost like entering a cave. It must be a real job forcing a horse through, he thought.

After about thirty yards the opening widened, and he stepped cautiously out into the valley. The main house and the bunkhouse were about fifty yards from the entrance. There wasn't a soul in sight, only a few horses and several head of cattle.

He was fairly sure Rigney was lurking somewhere about, probably in the main house and probably watching him, and there wasn't a bit of cover between where he was and the house.

He had a choice of either going ahead or turning back. He started toward the house, limping more noticeably now, every sense alert. The ground was spongy, muddy where the water had soaked in. He could see the dam at the far end of the canyon, a great gap blown in it.

He had covered over half of the distance to the house when he heard the crash of glass as a window smashed outward and saw a gun barrel poke through.

Laramie threw himself down and to one side an instant before the gun spat at him. He rolled over twice and came to his feet. He got off two quick shots at the window, then went in a crouching, zigzag run toward the corner of the house, ignoring as best he could the pain in his thigh. The man in the house managed two more shots, but Laramie made it to the house safely.

It was a log structure, but quite large, two stories, and very well-constructed.

There was only one window in the side of the house where he flattened himself out. While he got his breath back, Laramie quickly reloaded his Colt. He saw that the floodwater had risen about two feet up the side of the house.

He shouted, "Rigney? Throw your gun out and come on out. You backed the wrong hand and you've lost the game."

71

"Go to hell!"

"Don't be a fool! There have been enough killings."

"You want me, come in and get me. But you'd better come shooting!"

Laramie sighed and hunkered down with his back against the wall. Let the marshal sweat a little. Let him wait and wonder until he was jumpy as a cat on a hot stove lid. Then would be the time to go in.

The minutes dragged. Laramie yearned for a cigarette but that might give his position away. More time passed, a quarter hour. Laramie squatted with the patience of an Indian.

Finally, from inside, came Rigney's outraged roar, "Damn you, Nelson! Where are you? Come on!"

Laramie smiled slightly, but he didn't move.

Then he heard the sounds of furniture being kicked over. Window glass shattered, and Rigney fired at random through the broken windows, going all the way around the large house. Laramie waited quietly.

Then it was quiet again, and Laramie made his move. He went down the side of the building, ducking under the window. There should be a door on the back side of the house.

There was.

Laramie inched along, back to the wall, until he reached the door. He tested the knob. It was unlocked.

It had the smell of a trap.

He had a sudden, vivid picture of Rigney inside, waiting, desperate—crazed into a kind of courage by the shattering of all his plans. . . .

He hesitated for a moment more, then drew his gun, turned the knob with his left hand and sent the door crashing in with a hard kick. He was inside the door in two strides, leaping to one side, his back flush against the wall.

He had steeled himself for the blast of a gunshot, but nothing happened. After a little the silence became slightly unnerving.

He stood where he was until his eyes became accustomed to the dimness, his gaze probing every foot of the room. Furniture was overturned and shards of glass glinted on the floor like icicles. Rigney had been as wantonly destructive as a child throwing a tantrum.

Laramie advanced warily into the room. There were several doors opening off the main room, all closed, and a staircase leading up.

He heard a small sound overhead and realized his mistake, almost too late. He whirled, crouching, as a gun roared loud in the room. Splinters flew up from the floor at his feet. The stairs led up to a small balcony. The bedroom were probably up there.

Rigney was crouched behind a balcony post, only his gun and part of his arm visible. Laramine snapped off a quick shot and saw a chip fly from the post. Rigney also fired again but he was shooting blind and the bullet went wild.

Laramie steadied his aim and fired his second shot. Rigney screamed like a woman in agony, his gun thudding to the floor. He staggered out from behind the post and leaned over the balcony rail, clutching his arm, which dripped blood on the floor below.

Laramie gestured with the Colt and said quietly, "We'll ride back to Cottonwood Springs and tell the good people there what you've been up to."

12

Two hours later they broke camp and rode out. They had found a buckboard hidden in a side canyon. The saloon women had been loaded onto the buckboard and now led the procession. Close behind them rode Rigney, the man Laramie Nelson had tied to the tree on top of the ridge and one other man they had found wandering around. The three men had their hands lashed to their saddle-horns. The others had all vanished. The bodies of both

Taggerts were draped over their horses, the other dead bandits buried back in the wash.

Laramie and Brock Peters brought up the rear. Elizabeth was riding alongside the buckboard, deep in conversation with the women, something that both surprised and pleased Laramie. It was rare indeed that a *nice* woman in this part of the country would admit that dancehall girls even existed, much less talk to them.

"We look like the walking wounded left over from an Indian massacre," Peters said with a laugh.

"Yeah, we do at that."

Laramie wore the same torn garments; he hadn't brought extra ones along on the trip. In addition to the other rips and tears, his trousers were split where Elizabeth had bandaged the thigh wound. And she had torn away most of Peters' shirt to bandage his shoulder and had placed his arm in a crude sling. The round hat had been crushed some time during the melee and would never be the same again. Yet it was perched on the man's head at the usual cocky angle, and a slim cigar fumed between his lips.

Only Elizabeth looked reasonably presentable. Somehow she'd found time to scrub her face and hands and remove the dust from her clothes.

"Laramie, I want to thank you for helping out, especially since you didn't want to come along," Peters said. "It would have been a different story without you."

Laramie glanced at him in surprise. It was the first time the Pinkerton man had called him by his first name. "I told you, I didn't do it for—"

"I know, I know, you did it for Eliza—for Mrs. Cooper." Peters gestured impatiently with his cigar. "All the same..."

They rode in silence for another mile. Laramie saw Elizabeth glance back at them and pull her horse in to wait for them.

Peters said, "What now, Laramie?"

74

"I haven't thought much about it." Laramie shrugged. "Something will come along, It always does."

"The agency could use a man like you. We're always short of good men."

"A Pinkerton agent?" Laramie scrubbed a hand across his mouth. "I don't know—"

"The pay is good, you're pretty much your own boss as long as you do your job." They were close to Elizabeth now, and Peters spoke rapidly. "It's exciting work—"

"Yeah, I can see that."

"—and it's worthwhile. Will you think about it? I can put in a good word for you. In fact, I think I can promise you a spot if you want it."

"Well, sure, I'll think about it."

They were even with Elizabeth now. Peters clucked his horse and rode on ahead.

Elizabeth said curiously, "What was that all about, Laramie? Think about what?"

"I was just offered a job with the Pinkertons."

"You? A Pinkerton agent?" she said in quick dismay. Then, as he scowled around at her, she added hastily, "I don't mean you wouldn't make a good one. But I was hoping you'd stay around."

"Why?"

"Well..." She was flustered and refused to meet his gaze. "I thought we..."

"Elizabeth," he said gently, "you've just lost a husband. It's not the right time for us to think about the future."

"Then you're going to take Brock's offer?"

"I think so." And even as he spoke, Laramie knew he would. The prospect excited him. This could be the life he'd been looking for since he'd left Spanish Peaks.

"I'll never see you again!"

"Now I didn't say that, did I? I'll be riding back this way again some time. Brock said a Pinkerton man travels all over."

They rode for a little without speaking, Elizabeth with

her back held ramrod-straight, staring straight ahead.

Then Laramie asked, "What will you do, Elizabeth? Stay in Cottonwood Springs?"

"No, I'll go to Dodge. I can get a job there," she said evenly. Then she relented slightly. "Don't worry about me, Laramie. I'll be fine."

"Sure you will." He reached across to touch her arm. "Sure you will."

Elizabeth raised his hand to her lips, briefly, then let it fall and drummed her heels against her mount and sent him surging ahead until she was riding alongside Brock Peters.

Laramie watched her with a sense of melancholy, yet it wasn't very deep, and he knew it wouldn't last.

He would be back. He would see her again. Something might develop between them. Or it might not. That was in the future. Now was now, he wasn't ready to settle down, and there was the prospect of a new and exciting job before him.

He stood up in the stirrups, stretching. He was sore from head to toe, but it had been a good day, all things considered, and there would be other good days.

Laramie Nelson looped the reins around the saddle-horn, rolled and lit a cigarette, then spoke to Wingfoot and rode at a lope to catch up to Elizabeth and Brock Peters.

Showdown
at Lone Tree

1

Laramie Nelson rode out of the timber and reined Wingfoot in atop the rise of land. The horse he was leading pulled up alongside. To the east the low hills stood up like bruised knuckles. The sun would be up shortly. From where Laramie sat his horse the ground sloped sharply away. The valley lay like a watering trough between the two ranges of hills. The town was a straggle of buildings at the bottom. The giant oak that gave the town its name was a brilliant splash of autumn color.

The morning was cold; the breath of both horses rose in clouds of steam. The only signs of life from the town below were a few pencil-thin streamers of smoke rising straight up in the chill air.

Finally Laramie stirred. He threw a long leg over the saddle horn and eased his rangy body to the ground. He opened his mackinaw and took out a sack of tobacco, then rolled a cigarette. He held a match to the cigarette, drawing in a lung full of smoke. He stood thus for a long time, his legs set wide apart, his brooding gaze on the town of Lone Tree. The horse grazed half-heartedly.

Laramie was tall, lean as a whipcord, sandy-haired. His face, lightly dusted with freckles, had a melancholy cast, his smile rare and sudden. His gray eyes were slightly squinted from so many years of staring into the glare of the sun.

Now he tossed the cigarette to the ground, grinding it out under his bootheel. He turned to Wingfoot, feeling the pull of the worn Colt strapped to his thigh. He threw a leg across the saddle and mounted. Leading the sorrel, he allowed Wingfoot to pick his way down the slope.

Riding loosely in the saddle, the rising sun warming his chilled blood, he felt a mounting distaste for the job he had to perform. Once more he reviewed the circumstances leading up to it, his thoughts slipping back to a day two weeks ago in Denver in Brock Peter's office....

He had glared at Peters in outrage. "A woman! I'm not hunting down a woman!"

Peters faced Laramie's fury calmy. "You're a Pinkerton man now, Nelson, and you'll damned well do what you're told. It's a job like any other."

Laramie glowered at him. Peters was immaculate in Eastern clothes, including a bowler hat. And with his round, innocent face and short height, he looked about as dangerous as a rabbit. Laramie, having ridden with him, knew differently. The man was one of the Pinkerton Agency's most effective operatives. More to the point, he was Laramie's immediate superior.

"A man has to live with himself," Laramie grumbled. Then he sighed gustily. "What did this woman—Sarah Knight, is it?—what did she do that's so bad?"

"She killed a railroad land buyer, man named Bronson."

"Why? I expect she had a reason?"

"The reason doesn't matter," Peters said, somewhat stiffly. "The thing is, the railroad wants her, and the Pinkertons work for the railroad. She's living in a town called Lone Tree down in New Mexico."

Laramie stared. "You mean you know where she is?"

"We know where she is."

"Then you don't need me. Telegraph the local law to arrest her."

"The marshal in Lone Tree won't co-operate," Peters said angrily. "He seems to think she's one of God's angels. I've sent a couple other men down after her, and this blasted marshal ran them out of town."

"Suppose he runs me out of town?"

"If I thought he could, I wouldn't send you." Peters grinned suddenly. "But don't think it'll be easy because she's female. If you get by that marshal, you'll still have to face her and she can shoot better than most men I know!"

Laramie said gloomily, "I've yet to see you hand me an easy job. Why should this one be any different."

So now Laramie was on the last leg of his mission. The huddle of buildings that was Lone Tree was a half mile up ahead. He rode in at a canter, following the wagon tracks into town. Although the sun was well up now, he saw little sign of life along the dusty main street. From the livery stable at the far end came the sounds of hammer on anvil, bell-like in the still air.

As Laramie reigned Wingfoot in at the hitching rail before the Trail's End Saloon, a burst of drunken laughter spilled out into the street. He saw four more saloons along the street, all open and doing business even at this early hour. Laramie wondered, idly, where they got the trade to survive. That was a large number of saloons for a town the size of Lone Tree. Few trail herds of any size passed through the area. True, the country was rich grazing land, and he had seen a number of prosperous ranches along the way.

And there were several mines in the hills to the east. Still, it seemed doubtful that a few cowpunchers and miners could supply five saloons with enough customers.

Laramie shrugged. What did it matter to him where Lone Tree's saloons got their trade?

His gaze settled on a small building adjacent to the Trail's End. A small sign over the door proclaimed it as *The Ladies' Emporium*. Behind the window was a full-sized dummy decked out in a full-length dress of dark velvet and a large hat, with a saucy feather atop it like a defiant flag.

Laramie Nelson grinned faintly to himself, amused at the intimate juxtaposition of the two businesses.

A roar of outrage from the Trail's End brought his head around. He was in time to see a man catapulted backwards through the saloon doors.

A hulking bartender with an apron knotted around his barrel waist stepped through the doors and sailed a battered hat after the cowboy he had just tossed out. The cowboy had landed on his back in the dust at the end of

80

the hitching rail. The bartender waited a moment, hands on his hips, then turned and went back inside.

It was not until then that the ejected cowboy climbed to his feet, swaying on high heels. He shook his fist at the door and loosed a string of oaths. Laramie slid from the saddle and stood watching with an amused smile.

Finally the cowpuncher ran down. He spotted his hat. He bent over to pick it up, almost lost his balance but managed to right himself, hat and all. He clapped the hat on his head and started to turn away.

He saw Laramie and lurched toward him, bristling. "Hey! What're you grinning at?"

Laramie silently swore at himself for being stupid, for calling attention to himself. He said quietly, "Nothing, friend. Nothing at all."

"Friend! Who the billy-be-damned you calling friend?"

"No offense. It's just a manner of speaking."

"It it now?" His eyes had the glitter of drunken rage. He pointed at Laramie's worn and dusty boots. "I wonder if they'd stand up to a littly spry dancing? Let's have a little gun music and find out!" His hand clawed for his gun and missed.

Laramie said mildly, "I wouldn't, cowboy."

The puncher's lips peeled back in a snarl, and he took two steps forward, reaching for his gun again.

Laramie moved in, his Colt out and coming up before the cowboy's gun cleared the holster. Laramie raked the barrel of his Colt down across the man's temple. Blood spurted. The blow knocked the cowboy back against the watering trough. Laramie poked him in the belly with the Colt, with just enough force to tumble him in the trough with a splash.

Laramie turned away to his horses, intent on leading them up the street to the livery stable.

A yell of pure rage disturbed the morning quiet. Laramie Nelson dropped the reins and spun around, falling into a crouch. As his hand flexed toward his gun, a shot rang out.

2

Laramie saw the cowpuncher, dripping wet, leaning against the water trough, staring in disblief at his bleeding hand. His gun was sill spinning in the dust a few feet away.

A voice said cheerfully, "How many times have I told you, Laramie, never to turn your back on a snake until you make damned sure he's defanged?"

Laramie Nelson swiveled his head. That voice had aroused long-buried memories...

There were several men on the wooden sidewalk before the Trail's End now. One was coming toward Laramie, holstering his gun. He was tall and lithe, with shoulders barndoor wide and star-black hair. A star glittered on his vest.

"Luke? Luke Cole?" Laramie said hoarsely.

"Who else?" the big voice boomed. "Ain't I always around, amigo, when you need a leg up?"

Luke Cole had a round, dimpled face, with merry black eyes. Now he stuck out a hand, a hand remarkably small and slender for a man of his size. But it had the same wiry strength Laramie remembered.

They measured one another, two men remarkably alike in size and weight. But Laramie was fair while Cole was dark. And Laramie rarely smiled, while he had seen Cole kill more than once with that boyish smile on his face.

Each assessed the other for the signs of time, for the relentless erosion of the years. Laramie found little change in Cole's face. He said, "How many years, Luke? Ten?"

"Give or take a month or so amigo."

"Chihauhua, wasn't it?"

"It was."

"And her name was...?"

"Dolores."

"Never forget a lady's name, do you, Luke?"

Cole's laughter exploded. "She was no lady, Laramie. And I think you knew that. I think that's why you rode off and left me with a clear field."

Laramie said solemnly, "I had some such suspicion."

And then Cole fell on him with a whoop, pummeling his shoulders. "Ten years, Laramie, ten years! Man, it's good to see you again, amigo! This calls for a drink!"

Laramie held back, "It's a little early for that, Luke. I could use some breakfast, though."

"Then come along! The Palace serves the best whiskey *and* the best grub in town."

Laramie still held back. "First, I have to look after my horses."

Cole laughed. "You haven't changed there, at least. The horses always come first."

"And what was it you used to say, Luke? 'Horses and women... there'll always be another one along'?"

A change came over Cole's countenance. His eyes darkened as he said soberly, "One thing *has* changed, Laramie."

But Laramie wasn't listening. Two men had come up and now stood nearby looking at the wounded cowboy. One was a big man, well over six feet, and very broad, with a great shock of red hair bared to the morning sun. He wore a black broadcloth suit, with a black string tie and highly polished boots. His attire was that of a gambler, but his manner was not quite controlled enough. Bright blue eyes blazed with contempt as he glared at the cowpuncher clutching his wounded hand. And the big man wasn't wearing a gun, unless there was a derringer snugged in his armpit.

Normally Laramie Nelson could gauge a man's

83

occupation at a glance, yet this one baffled him.

But there was no doubt about his companion. Small, slight, with slim, dainty hands and feet. His hair was wheat-blond, his face as delicate as a woman's. He was also dressed mostly in black, but he was natty, while the big man had a slightly rumpled look. The smaller man wore two bone-handled guns strapped low on his thighs.

And his eyes, as they met Laramie's gaze, were the chill gray of a winter sky. The impact of the glance struck Laramie like a dousing of ice water.

No, there was no doubt in Laramie's mind. This one was a professional gunfighter. As always in the presence of the breed, Laramie felt his nerves go taut.

The big man was speaking. "A little too much of the grape, Marshal?" His voice was deep, resonant.

"I guess you could say that, Mr. Pike." Cole chuckled. "And he tried to throw down on Laramie here from behind. I had to . . . take steps."

"You know what I always say, Marshal. A drink in itself is not harmful, but excess in any form is sinful in the eyes of God."

"Yep, I know," Cole said, just loud enough for Laramie's ears. "You've said it often enough."

At the water trough the injured cowboy straightened up and, holding his wrist, staggered up the street without picking up his gun.

Laramie said, "Luke, I'll be back as soon as I stable my horses."

Cole nodded without looking at him. "I'll wait for you inside the Palace, amigo."

Cole seemed somewhat in awe of the big man named Pike, Laramie thought as he led the horses away. And that would mean that time *had* wrought a change; the Luke Cole he had once known had stood in awe of no man.

But what was even more unsettling was the fact that Cole was the marshal of Lone Tree. For that meant he was the man who had fought off all the men Peters had sent to bring the Knight woman back to Denver!

Laramie turned the horses over to the man at the livery stable and went back up the street to the Palace Saloon. Cole sat alone at a table against the rear wall, a bottle on the table before him.

Even at this early hour there were a number of people in the place, several men at the long bar, two poker games going, a roulette wheel whirring, a woman with black net stockings in attendance, her rouged face gray with fatigue.

Cole glanced up and saw him, lifted one hand to motion him over. Laramie threaded his way through the crowd to Cole's table.

Cole toasted him with a raised glass. "Sure you won't have an eye-opener, amigo?"

Laramie started to remark that it would hardly be an eye-opener since he'd been riding all night. But he knew that would bring on the questions, and he wasn't ready yet to tell Cole his purpose in Lone Tree. Time enough for that when he learned which way the wind blew.

He sat down. "All right, Luke. Just one, for old times' sake."

The liquor started a spreading warmth in his empty gut. He glanced over at Cole. "Who was the big man outside talking to you when I walked away?"

"Pike. Jeremiah Pike."

"He a gambler?"

"A gambler? Hardly!" Cole laughed with his head thrown back. "He's a preacher."

"A preacher! But that fellow with him..."

"A gunnie. That's right." Cole sobered. "Chris Gunderson. Gunner. You must have heard of him. He's Pike's bodyguard."

"Gunner? Yes, I've heard of him. Who hasn't? But a *preacher* with a bodyguard?"

"You don't know Lone Tree, amigo." Cole threw a

drink down his throat with a toss of his head. "We've got an odd situation here. Any minute it's liable to break out into war, with blood running in the streets. Me, I'm in the middle. I feel like I've swallowed a stick of dynamite with a slow-burning fuse."

"War? Between who and who?"

"You noticed the number of saloons along the street out there?"

"Yeah, It's hard not to. I wondered about that in a town this size."

"Well, if the Merchants' Association has its way, there'll be more right soon."

"But where do all the customers come from?"

"Mostly from the mines to the east. A new vein of silver has been discovered. Two new mining companies are coming in. And from all the ranches for a hundred miles around. The Merchants' Association has hired a couple of drummers to call on all cattle drovers and try to get them to route the trail herds this way. Lone Tree's been clean as a whistle for several years, Laramie. I was a part of that."

"I was wondering."

"You mean how I come to wear a star? That was a funny thing." Cole scrubbed a hand down across his face in a rueful gesture. "Oh, I tamed down considerable a couple years after you saw me last. Then one day five years ago I rode in here. Lone Tree was pretty woolly in those days. A local guntoter had the town treed. He saw me as another notch on his gun and I had to take . . . steps. The next thing I knew I was the marshal here, with orders to clean up the town. Well, that didn't take too much doing. For the next four years things were pretty peaceful hereabouts. You could sleep all day out there on Main Street and never be disturbed."

Cole paused to take a drink. "Well, all that was fine for a while. Then the merchants began to slowly starve to death. Everybody avoided Lone Tree like the plague. That's when the Merchants' Association was formed.

They came to me and asked me to ease up a little. I could see the way they felt. If Lone Tree kept on the same way, the town was going to dry up and blow away.

"I agreed to take it easy. But things got out of hand, Oh, nothing too bad at first. But a new saloon opened up, another, then another. It got worse and worse. Games going full blast, night and day. Women and gamblers drifted in, like flies to the honey pot. But that was what the Association wanted, so I strung along. After all, they pay half of my salary now."

"And just where does Pike enter the picture?"

"He's on one side, the Association the other."

Laramie said slowly, "I guess that needs a little filling in, Luke."

Cole helped himself to another drink. "Pike rode in here about six months ago, right around the time the Association was getting organized. He started holding services. When the town began to open up, he was dead set against it. The town split right down the middle. The folks who didn't agree with the Association lined up behind Pike. He's the leader of those who want Lone Tree clean, back like it was once."

"And Gunner?"

"Some of the new people who drifted in, saloonkeepers, gamblers and suchlike, have joined the Association. They're not as particular about how they get their way as they might be. I reckon they figure they can have things pretty much their own way with Pike out of the picture. A couple of tries have been made at killing him. That's when he hired Gunner."

Cole grinned sardonically. "Preacher Pike believes in fighting fire with fire."

"And that leaves you in the middle?"

"Right smack, amigo,"

"I'd say you'd be smart to hand in your badge and get the hell out."

"You think I haven't thought of doing just that? And I

would have, only—"

Cole was interrupted by the arrival of a fat man wearing an apron. He was carrying a tray on which rested a platter and a steaming mug of coffee. The platter held calf liver, browned to a turn, fried potatoes, two fried eggs and three hot biscuits.

Laramie glanced over at Cole. The man was grinning widely. "Yep, I remembered you favored calf liver and eggs for breakfast, when you could get them."

"Like I said, Luke, you've got a good memory. Thanks all to hell." Laramie attacked the food with a lusty appetite.

Cole said, "I recollect a lot of things, amigo. Those were the good days, remember?"

Laramie Nelson had reservations about that. There were many things about those wild days when he rode with Luke Cole he would just as soon forget. But he contented himself with a noncommittal grunt and went on eating.

Cole was speaking. "Remember that time I got full of hooch and treed that little border town? I can't even remember the name—"

Cole was interrupted again, this time by the sound of angry voices. Both men turned to look. A space was rapidly being cleared at the bar for two men who were backing away from each other, hands hovering near their guns.

Cole sighed. "See what I mean? A thing like this would never have happened in the old Lone Tree. Not at this hour of the morning, anyways." He sighed again and got to his feet, cold sober all of a sudden. "'Scuse me, amigo, while I go and keep the peace. Can't have your breakfast being ruined."

One thing about Cole certainly hadn't changed. It was still a pleasure to watch him in action. Light-footed as a big cat, he made his way through the tables and approached the two men, who had stopped backing when a distance of about ten feet separated them. Except for in their immediate vicinity, activity in the saloon was going on as before.

Cole stepped in between the two men, stopping quite close to the one who was bald as an egg. He said lazily, "Boys, ain't it a little early in the morning for getting all riled up?"

The bald man said in a high voice, "You get back, Marshal! This ain't none of your business!"

"Now that's where you're wrong, friend," Cole drawled. "You're forcing me to . . ."

Without warning Cole's knee came up, slamming into the man's stomach. The bald man's breath left him in a whistling grunt. As he folded forward, arms clutching at his midsection, Cole gathered a handful of his shirt collar and propelled him into the second man, who was caught unprepared.

As the two bodies collided, falling against the bar in a tangle of arms and legs, Cole moved in smoothly. He disarmed them, dropped their guns on the bar and then calmly cracked their heads together.

It had all happened within seconds, but Cole had accomplished the head-cracking as easily as though the men had been a pair of scuffling schoolboys. Now, a hand hooked into each shirt collar, Cole dragged them to the door and tossed them out into the street, one after the other.

Smiling to himself, Laramie Nelson glanced around the room. Except for the men who had moved back out of the way at the bar, the fracas had attracted little attention. And even now the space earlier cleared was filling up again.

He had finished his breakfast and was rolling a cigarette when Cole returned to their table.

"You notice that one bird?" Cole chortled. "He didn't have nary a hair between him and Heaven!"

"You've gone soft, Luke. Time was, you wouldn't have

just cracked their heads together."

Cole sat down with a grin. "Bullets cost money, amigo. And I have to pay for mine out of my salary. Which ain't a great deal." He sobered, leaning forward. "I just remembered, Laramie. There's a box supper at the church tonight. They're raising some money. Come along. There's somebody I'd like you to meet."

"Oh, I can't, Luke. I didn't bring any clothes along for socializing." He indicated his trail-dusty clothes with a gesture.

"No problem," Cole said with an airy wave of his hand. "Don't you recollect how we used to wear each other's duds? Neither one of us has changed all that much. You can wear a suit of mine."

Laramie had forgotten about that. He looked at Cole in speculation, as a question rose to the surface of his mind. Why hadn't Cole asked his purpose in Lone Tree? Or did he already know? But that couldn't be. How could he know?

"Amigo?"

Laramie came to a sudden decision. A box supper usually drew a large number of women. Maybe Sarah Knight would be there. "All right, Luke."

"Good!" Cole popped to his feet. "Come on down to my office and we'll dig out the duds. I bunk in a room behind the office."

3

The marshal's office was also the jail, with three narrow cells in a row along the rear wall. The office was divided by a waist-high wooden railing, Cole's desk and gun rack on one side, two hard benches and a stove on the other.

Laramie Nelson borrowed one of Cole's three suits. As he started to leave the office, Cole said wistfully, "It'll be just like old times, huh, amigo? Come back around seven and we'll walk over to the church together."

It was now noon, and Laramie was weary. It had been his intention to find Sarah Knight and ride out with her at once. But the fact that Luke Cole was the marshal in Lone Tree had changed his plans. Laramie decided to proceed cautiously until he learned if Cole intended taking a hand.

In the hotel room Laramie removed his clothes, took a bath as best he could in the wash basin, and stretched out across the bed. But, tired as he was, sleep didn't come immediately. He found his thoughts swinging back to those wild days ten years ago with Cole. They hadn't been owlhoot days, not exactly. Yet some of the things they had done had certainly been outside what law there was.

They had first met on a cattle drive and had become friends at once, Laramie attracted by Cole's devil-may-care attitude toward life, his habit of viewing everything, even personal calamity, as amusing. And Cole had been apparently drawn by Laramie's steady influence. They had been close to the same age, both just past twenty, Laramie a few months the elder.

Neither had been particularly fond of the hard work and low pay of a cattle drive. As Cole had put it, "There has to be an easier way to come by some dinero."

At the end of the drive they had, with very little discussion decided to ride together. Both were far above average with a gun, and they discovered they could make top money hiring out their guns. They didn't hire out for killing, although it sometimes came to that. Their guns were used by nesters against cattlemen, cattlemen against nesters. They hired out to protect towns against outlaw raids. They always tried to hire out to the side with the most right, at least Laramie did. In the main Cole left the selection of their employers up to him.

For five years Laramie and Cole were names to command fear and respect, and big money. The years were wild and carefree. They made good money and spent it freely.

But somewhere along the way things began to pall for

Laramie. It came to a head in Chihauhua. For once they had been on a losing side and had thought it prudent to reside in Mexico until the victors had had time to savor their victory and become a little more forgiving.

It was there that Laramie decided to ride on alone. It hadn't been because of the fiery Dolores, desirable as she had been. It had been Laramie's growing conviction that the wild streak in Cole was ungovernable. Sooner or later, if they continued to ride together, Cole's wildness would get them into serious trouble that spending a few months in Mexico wouldn't solve.

Apparently he had been wrong about that. Laramie's thoughts were drowsy now. But imagine Luke Cole a marshal!

Laramie Nelson chuckled, turned on his side and squirmed down until he was more comfortable and drifted into sleep.

It was growing dark when he awoke. He folded Cole's suit over his arm and went downstairs to the barber shop. He had a real soaker of a bath, and a shave and a haircut, then put on Cole's suit. It wasn't a bad fit. He took the clothes he had been wearing back to his room. After some hesitation he decided against wearing a gunbelt and stuck the Colt down in the waistband of the trousers.

He strolled toward Cole's office. The Trail's End Saloon was located halfway between the hotel and the marshal's office.

As he crossed the mouth of the alley alongside the Trail's End, Laramie saw a bulky figure standing at the corner of the building. There was nothing menacing about it, but something prompted Laramie to break stride. He struck a match as though his cigarette had gone out.

In the match flare he recognized the man standing in shadow. "Evening, Reverend Pike."

"It's Mr. Nelson, I believe the marshal said?" The alley behind Pike was dark as a mine shaft.

"That's right, Reverend. Laramie Nelson."

The man laughed, a deep rumbling sound. "The term reverend is rarely heard in Lone Tree, Mr. Nelson. Preacher seems to appeal to the good people here more."

Laramie glanced about. "Where's your...?"

"You mean Gunner, Mr. Nelson? He's inside the Trail's End." The big man's voice was still amused. "Even watchdogs must—"

Laramie sensed rather than heard a movement in the alley. Instinctively he threw himself at Pike.

As they hit the ground together, gunfire flared in the alley darkness, like a night-blooming flower.

Laramie pushed himself away from Pike, rolling over twice, clawing for his gun. He came up on his elbow, Colt in his hand, waiting for the gun to blast again.

When the second shot came, he fired twice at the splash of flame, aiming high and to the right. Three sounds came in rapid succession—a chopped-off scream, a groan, and then the thud of a body against the building.

Laramie said, "You all right, Reverend Pike?"

"It would seem so, Mr. Nelson. It would also seem I'm in your debt."

"He was either a rotten shot or only trying to frighten one of us." Laramie got to his feet and strode toward the building. His toe hit a body. He struck a match and leaned down. The man was small, with a narrow face and a scraggly beard. "Either way, he won't be bothering us again."

"The wages of sin are death," Pike said in his deep voice.

There was a yammer of voices from the street, spilling over into the alley. Laramie recognized Cole's voice. A lantern bobbed down the alley as Laramie said, "Over here, Luke."

Cole bulled his way through the men. He took the lantern and swung its rays onto the dead man's face. He grunted explosively. "Ed Harker." He held the lantern up

93

to peer at Laramie. "What happened here?"

"All I can tell you is, Reverend Pike and me were talking in the alley entrance. This fellow took a potshot at us. The reverend and me hit the dirt. When he fired again I was ready for him. Which one of us he was aiming for, I haven't the least idea. He missed both of us by a country mile."

"Pike, most likely." Cole's gaze sharpened. "No reason for anybody to be gunning for you, is there, amigo?"

"None that I can think of. You're the only one in town knows me." And yet there was the woman, Sarah Knight, the one he'd come to Lone Tree for. Could she, by some remote chance, have learned of his purpose here and hired Harker to kill him? It seemed unlikely.

Cole's attention had already returned to the dead man. "It figures he was only out to scare the preacher. I doubt we've reached the killing stage yet."

"I don't follow you, Luke."

"Harker worked for Joel Pardee. Pardee owns the Trail's End and is a member of the Merchants' Association. In fact, he rides herd on it. And he's the one pushing hardest to open up Lone Tree."

Cole raised his voice. "A couple of you men take the body over to the undertaker's. The rest of you get back to your drinking."

The body was taken away, and the crowd slowly broke up. Soon, only Laramie, Cole and Pike were left. They moved out of the dark alley and into the street.

Laramie was slapping the dust from his clothes when the slight man named Gunderson burst out of the Trail's End and came down to them with cat-like strides. "You all right, preacher? They told me somebody tried to gun you down. Did this galoot . . .?" His lethal gaze came to rest on Laramie, and one small hand hovered by the gun low on his right thigh.

Laramie went tense, then forced himself to stand loose and easy. His dislike for the gunman overrode his good

94

judgment. He drawled, "You accusing me of something, Gunner? Why not just spit it out and quit horsing around?"

The man in black fell into a crouch, hand hovering near his gun, thin lips drawn back in a wolf-snarl.

Laramie waited for him to make his move.

4

"That's enough, Chris!" Reverend Pike's voice curled like a lash. "This man did your job for you—he saved my life!" He gestured curtly. "Come along, I'm due at the church."

Pike strode off. Gunderson, after a last measuring look at Laramie Nelson, swung in behind him.

Cole chuckled. "I'd watch it with the Gunner, was I you, amigo. He's deadly as a rattlesnake, more so since he doesn't bother to rattle first."

Laramie knew that Cole was right. He had made a mistake in nettling Gunderson unnecessarily. He might have to face him later, and that was the last thing he needed, a showdown with a hired gun. His nerves still taut, he said testily, "Ain't we supposed to be at this box supper?"

"Right, amigo. But I have to make a stop first. Come on, there's somebody I want you to meet."

He started toward the Trail's End. Laramie followed reluctantly. He had the feeling that Cole was trying to get him involved. Unless the man had changed drastically, he had a talent for doing just that.

The saloon was packed. It throbbed with raucous life like a raw nerve. A balding piano player thumped at a rickety piano. Several poker games and a faro game were in progress. Dance-hall girls, faces weary and hard under layered rouge, moved to and fro, exchanging vulgarities with the customers. The men lined up two deep at the long mahogany bar, keeping two bartenders hopping.

Laramie followed in Cole's wake as the marshal plowed a path toward a table in the rear. A man sat alone at the table, an untouched glass of whiskey before him, a long cigar smoldering between strong teeth. The man was dressed in a neat, black business suit, with a snowy-white linen shirt and a black string tie. He was a slender man and had a tubercular look. His gaze settled on Cole as the marshal approached. His eyes were black, hard, opaque as colored glass. Yet his lips formed a smile, and his deep voice was pleasant as he spoke. "Hello, Marshal. You look riled."

"Maybe not half as much as you'll be, Pardee, when I tell you the news."

Pardee shrugged and placed both hands flat on the table. "I don't get upset all that easy, Marshal."

"Ed Harker's dead. He tried to gun down the preacher and Laramie here." Cole jerked a thumb at Laramie. "And Laramie shot him stone cold dead."

Pardee's cold gaze moved to Laramie. "A lawman?"

Ignoring the question, Cole said, "The thing is, Ed Harker worked for you, didn't he?"

"Marshal, if you're going to accuse me of something, do it! Don't jump on your horse and ride off in three different directions at once."

Dark color flooded Cole's face, and Laramie sensed just how close to the edge the man was. In the old days it would have taken a lot more to get under his skin.

Tight-lipped, Cole said, "All right then damn it! Did you order Ed Harker to take a potshot at the preacher?"

"I did not." Pardee tapped the long ash from his cigar, making a contemptuous gesture of it. "Any other stupid questions, Marshal?" he asked.

"You've been pushing me pretty hard of late, Pardee! Watch you don't get pushed back!"

"Thanks for the warning, Marshal. I'll watch it very carefully."

Cole whirled away, eyes blazing. "Come on, Laramie.

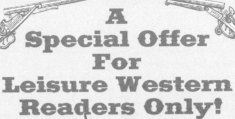

GET YOUR 4 FREE* BOOKS NOW— A VALUE OF BETWEEN $17 AND $20

Mail the Free* Books Certificate Today!

FREE* BOOKS CERTIFICATE!

YES! I want to subscribe to the Leisure Western Book Club. Please send me my 4 FREE* BOOKS. Then, each month, I'll receive the four newest Leisure Western Selections to preview for 10 days. If I decide to keep them, I will pay the Special Member's Only discounted price of just $3.36 each, a total of $13.44 ($16.35 in Canada). This saves me between $3 and $6 off the bookstore price. There are no shipping, handling or other charges.* There is no minimum number of books I must buy and I may cancel the program at any time. In any case, the 4 FREE* BOOKS are mine to keep—at a value of between $17 and $20!

*In Canada, add $7.50 US shipping and handling per order for first shipment. For all subsequent shipments to Canada the cost of membership in the Book Club is $16.35 US plus $7.50 US shipping and handling per order. All payments must be made in US dollars.

Name _____

Address _____

City_____ State_____

Zip_____ Telephone_____

Signature_____

Biggest Savings Offer!

For those of you who would like to pay us in advance by check or credit card—we've got an even bigger savings in mind. Interested? Check here. ☐

If under 18, parent or guardian must sign. Terms, prices and conditions subject to change. Subscription subject to acceptance. Leisure Books reserves the right to reject any order or cancel any subscription.

Tear here and mail your FREE* book card today!

Get Four Books Totally
F R E E* –
A Value of between
$16 and $20

Tear here and mail your FREE* book card today!

Let's get the hell out of here!"

Without waiting Cole plunged through the crowd, pushing men out of his way. Laramie nodded to Pardee, received a curt nod in return, then followed in Cole's wake. He found the marshal waiting for him on the saloon veranda.

Laramie took out the makings, rolled a cigarette and lit it before saying, "Luke . . . you deliberately let him think I was a lawman, siding you."

Cole drew a deep breath and faced around, his old smile flickering. "You see how it is in Lone Tree, amigo? I *do* need your help. Together, you siding me, we could ride herd on this town."

"No dice, Luke. I'm not about to dodge bullets on a lawman's thirty dollars a month."

They started walking up the street, boots sending up puffs of dust. Laramie felt the weight of Cole's curious gaze, and he knew what the man's next question would be.

"Come to think of it, amigo, you never did tell me what you're doing in Lone Tree."

Laramie wanted to confide in him, but he felt a nudge of caution. Not yet. It would be better to wait until he'd had time to find out how things were. He said carefully, "Just passing through. I'm on my way north and decided to stop off and rest a spell."

"On your way north to where? And to what?"

"I have some money put away. I'm thinking of buying a little spread in Wyoming."

Cole snorted. "Laramie Nelson settling down?"

"You have, haven't you?"

"Yeah. Yup, I guess you could say that. But why not a last fling first, Laramie, something to remember . . . ?"

"No, Luke," Laramie said flatly.

Cole sighed. "You're right. Why should you mix into something that's none of your never-mind?"

Laramie seized the opportunity to move away from the subject. "You've changed in more ways than one, Luke. In the old days you'd never have let what happened back there with Pardee get under your skin."

"Circumstances have changed more than me. Like I said, I'm thinking of settling down, too. Here in Lone Tree. And I don't want it to turn into a stinkhole."

"Thinking? I thought you'd already settled down?"

"More than that. I'm thinking of getting married. You'll meet her at the church tonight."

The church was at the north end of Front Street, dividing the street into two roads, in the same way an island divides a river. The church was a one-story structure, with a steeple, and had been recently painted.

"The church hadn't been used in years until Preacher Pike came to town last year," Cole explained. "He started preaching there and has been raising money for it ever since, holding box suppers and things like that. This one tonight is to raise money for new pews and benches."

The one-room building was close to full, about equally divided between men and women, with children of all ages running about and yelling. The adults seemed rather solemn for a gathering supposed to be festive. The bidding had already started. Jeremiah Pike was the auctioneer. He stood at the pulpit with a table close at hand stacked high with boxes. Gunderson stood a few feet behind him, cold black eyes jumpy as birds, his watchful gaze constantly raking the crowd.

Laramie and Cole found seats near the back. The benches were old and splintery.

Laramie rolled and lit a cigarette and settled back to watch the proceedings.

Pike would hold a box to his nose, sniff audibly, then announce his guess as the contents of the box. Pike was good at the task, scorning low bids, and able to get a number of men involved in spirited bidding on most of the boxes. In Laramie's estimation, Pike had all the wheeling talent of a good confidence man.

Many of the boxes had large ribbons of different colors

tied around them. From past experience at such affairs, Laramie suspected that this was ruse used by the women to let the men of their choice know which box was theirs.

After a time it struck Laramie that Cole was unusually quiet. He glanced over at the man and found his gaze intent on a woman a few benches to the front and to the right. Laramie had a strong hunch it was the woman Cole had talked of marrying.

She was about twenty-five, very good-looking. But then Cole had always had an eye for a handsome woman. She was well-dressed. Most of the women present wore long cotton dresses. This one wore a green dress that, to Laramie's unpracticed eye, seemed to be made of some silken material. And on her head was a wide-brimmed hat, decorated with artificial flowers and fancy gewgaws. Laramie knew that the hat had come from the east at considerable expense to somebody.

As though feeling the weight of his gaze, the woman half turned, the light striking reddish glints from her long chestnut hair, and Laramie got his first good look at her. Her nose was small, delicate, over a wide mouth soft and curving in amusement as she followed the bidding. Her chin had a shape that suggested firmness as well as stubbornness.

Abruptly Laramie realized that Cole had switched his attention to the pulpit. Laramie glanced that way. Pike was holding to his nose a round hat box.

"I smell...fried chicken. Yes, fried chicken! And peach cobbler. The Good Lord only knows where the lady got the peaches." Pike held the box aloft with a flourish. "What am I bid for this box, gentlemen?"

"One dollar," Cole said immediately.

"I'm bid a dollar! Do I hear two?"

The box belonged to the woman with the chestnut hair, of course. And from the silence following Cole's bid it was obvious everyone in the church knew it and had no intention of bidding against their marshal.

Almost without thinking, Laramie said loudly, "Two dollars!"

Cole twisted about to give him a startled look. Out of the corner of one eye Laramie saw the woman also looking at him.

"Marshal Cole, do I hear three dollars?" Pike's deep voice held laughter.

"Two-fifty," Cole said grudgingly.

"Three dollars," Laramie shot back.

Laughter was general throughout the room now. Under his breath Cole said, "Damn you, Laramie! What are you trying to do to me?"

"Why I'm bidding for a box supper. Ain't that what we're here for?" Laramie said, all innocence. "Besides, I'm hungry."

"I'm bid three dollars," Pike said. "Do I hear four?"

"All right!" Cole's face reddened. "Four!"

"Five!" Laramie said promptly.

Cole was frantically searching his pockets. "I didn't bring more money. I didn't think I'd need it . . ." He raised his voice. "I didn't bring more'n four dollars with me. I'll bid against this galoot all night if you'll give me credit!"

"I'm sorry, Marshal. You know the rules. No credit. And we can't make exceptions, much as I'd like to."

Cole bent a fierce glare on Laramie. "Laramie, you trying to rile me?" All of a sudden he grinned broadly. "But of course you are! Just like old time, huh, amigo?" He slapped Laramie on the shoulder.

Pike was intoning, "The bid was five dollars, gents. Going once . . . twice . . . three times. Sold to Mr. Nelson for five dollars!" He slapped his hand down on the pulpit with a loud report. "Come up here and get your supper, Mr. Nelson."

Laramie rose and started up the aisle. He avoided looking directly at the woman. He now regretted the impulse that had prompted him to bid on the box. She probably thought him some kind of a fool.

100

At the pulpit he gave Pike five silver dollars and accepted the box.

Pike said, "You have to share the supper with the lady who cooked it. That's part of the deal. Sarah?"

Laramie froze. Sarah?

"Sarah? Sarah Knight, come up here!"

5

Many things were all at once made clear to Laramie Nelson. Learning that the woman with the chestnut hair was Sarah Knight explained why all the others sent to Lone Tree to bring her back had been stopped. Cole was in love with her and was protecting her.

Keeping his face expressionless as possible, Laramie turned to face Sarah Knight.

She was taller than he had reckoned her. Her face was tanned but surprisingly unwrinkled in this country where most women had skin the texture of old leather by the age of thirty. The eyes were gray and friendly, her mouth full and curving now in a warm smile for him.

Despite the pressing knowledge of his mission, Laramie found himself responding to the smile. There was something about this woman that was outgoing, warm, yet she was no simpering female, turning coltish in the presence of a man. Her eyes were intelligent, frankly appraising him.

Laramie didn't know what he had been expecting. A hardened dance-hall type, he supposed. She was nothing like that. At least not on the surface.

Something of what he was thinking must have been mirrored in his face, for her voice held a hint of laughter as she said, "You needn't worry, Mr. Nelson. You didn't buy a pig in a poke. I'm a very good cook."

He cleared his throat. "I wasn't worried about that."

Sarah tilted her head to one side, her smile growing. "What then?"

He was saved an answer by Pike's voice. "Here's your supper, Mr. Nelson."

Laramie took the box from Pike. Turning back, he let his gaze rake the room. "Where do we eat?"

She nodded toward the rear of the church. "One of those benches along the back wall should be a good place."

As they fell into step, she put her hand on his arm. It was done naturally, not at all contrived. "You're either a very good friend of Luke Cole's, Mr. Nelson, or a stranger in town."

"How did you arrive at that?"

He glanced down in time to see her make a wry face. "Luke is a very nice man but he gets a little... over-protective at times. Sometimes he treats me like a China doll that would break in rough weather. So either you're a very good friend he trusts or a complete stranger who doesn't know any better."

"If I'm a stranger, that means I'm in for some rough weather, then?"

He felt her hand tighten on his arm. Her glance came up to meet his. Temper clouded her face, briefly, and then her eyes began to dance. "You're thinking I'm the type of woman who'd enjoy two men fighting over her?"

It was exactly what Laramie had been thinking, but he didn't say so.

Sarah shook her head, long hair rippling like water. "No, Mr. Nelson, if you think that, you're wrong. And you'll have to forgive me. It so happens I *knew* you were an old friend. How many times has Luke mentioned his amigo, Laramie Nelson, to me?"

Laramie was absurdly pleased that Cole had remembered him to that extent down through the years. And, oddly, it made him feel that he was an old friend to the woman by his side.

They reached an empty bench along the rear wall. They sat down, Sarah taking the box from him and spreading a

102

linen napkin on the bench.

Laramie said lightly, "Just what did Luke tell you about me?"

Sarah had removed a plate from the box and was arranging pieces of golden fried chicken on it. She glanced up at him, her expression roguish. "Some pretty wild tales."

Laramie cleared his throat. "Probably..."

"I know you're going to tell me they're all lies!"

"Well...no. I was going to say they probably weren't as wild in his telling as they really were."

Cole said, "Amigo, if I could think of a charge, I'd toss you into the hoosegow. That'd get me even!"

Cole had approached unnoticed. He stood before them, hands on hips, rocking slightly on his feet. Despite the fierceness of his voice, his black eyes were snapping merrily.

Laramie said innocently, "Get even for what, Luke?"

Cole snorted. "You know what! We used to make a game of it, Sarah, taking each other's gals away. But this ain't the old days." He sobered, his glance skipping to Sarah, and his manner became possessive.

Sarah colored slightly. "Luke, I wish you'd..."

Cole ignored her. "But I'll shut my eyes to it this time. *This* time, mind you! At least it's in a good cause. And you probably ain't had cooking like Sarah's in a coon's age. Enjoy yourself, amigo." He lifted his hand in a magnanimous gesture and moved off.

"That man! Honestly!" Sarah said between her teeth. "Sometimes I could—" She clamped her lips shut and went rummaging in the box as though rooting out insects.

Laramie was uncomfortable. Despite Sarah's annoyance with Cole, Laramie sensed that she was more than fond of him. He had a hunch he'd come in on the heels of a lover's quarrel. Watching her, he found himself wondering what it would be like to have a woman like this love you. She was beautiful, wholly feminine, yet she seemed more than capable of handling herself in any situation. And that brought home to him that she could, indeed, handle herself, at least according to Brock Peters. And she had killed a man.

Self-derision washed over him, and it was all he could do to keep from laughing at himself. He saw Sarah looking at him quizzically. She had just taken two thick slabs of peach pie from the hatbox.

He said quickly, "Where *did* you get the peaches?"

"There's an old abandoned farm in a little canyon a few miles outside of town. Somebody started an orchard there a long time ago, with a couple of peach trees. I ride out sometimes on nice days. I picked the peaches yesterday."

"Peaches in *this* country?"

"The trees don't bear fruit every year. This year they had only a few peaches but they're real good, what were on the trees."

She held the plate of chicken out to him, and Laramie selected a breast piece and bit into it. Still chewing, he said, "Luke's right. You're a wonderful cook." He swallowed. "Is that what you do here in town, cook? Or run a boarding house maybe?"

Sarah shook her head. "Neither. Did you happen to notice the Ladies' Emporium next to the Trail's End? That's mine." Her lips quirked. "I understand some of the men use my place as an excuse. They claim the hats they see in my window drive them to drink."

Laramie laughed. He liked her sense of humor. "I've heard of snakes and pink elephants but ladies' hats are something new. Of course some of the toots Luke and I went on in the old days..."

Sarah paused with a chicken leg halfway to her mouth and said, "I'd like to hear your side of those yarns."

"They're hardly fit for a lady's delicate ears."

"This lady's ears aren't all that delicate, Nelson."

Between bites of chicken he related some of the less rowdy episodes of the old days with Cole. Sarah's laughter was frank and hearty, clear as a bell.

6

"And sometimes we'd be away from anything but cattle, horses and unwashed cowhands for months at a stretch. When we'd finally hit a town we'd really tree it. One thing I will say, we usually paid for all the damage we caused. I remember some little town in Kansas. We'd just come off trailing a herd up from Texas. Luke got sore at some storekeeper, I can't even recall why now. Outside of town we rounded up about a dozen half-crazy Texas longhorns, drove them down the main street and right into his saloon. It took us a year to get paid up on the damages for that one!"

Laramie took the last bite of pie. "This is not only the best peach pie I've ever tasted but also the first in I don't remember when." He leaned back with a sigh, got out the makings. "Mind if I smoke?"

"Not at all. Go right ahead."

Sarah busied herself putting what was left back into the hat box. Laramie lit his cigarette and glanced around the room. While he'd been talking to her a change had taken place. The boxes had long since been auctioned off, the suppers eaten; and the meeting had taken on a different, grimmer character.

Pike was at the pulpit again, leaning on it on his hands. Cole and a couple of other men sat on the platform behind him. The crowd had thinned considerably, down to about half its former size. Most of the women and all the children were gone. One other thing Laramie noticed. Gunderson wasn't anywhere around.

For a moment Laramie thought Pike was about to deliver a sermon. But if that were the case, why was Cole up there with him?

Laramie glanced around at Sarah Knight. She answered his look with a short nod. "You're right, Nelson. There's more to this than a box supper. We're here to try and settle, again, what to do about Pardee and his henchmen. A couple of times we've had meetings for just that purpose and his men have always managed to break them up. Doing it this way, we thought maybe we could meet without his getting the wind up."

Once again Laramie Nelson had the feeling of being caught in the middle, a foreboding of being drawn into something that was none of his business. Cole had known about this, yet hadn't told him. Laramie had the urge to seize Sarah by the hand and haul her out and back to Denver, throw her over his shoulder if necessary, and deal with Cole if he had to. It was exactly what Peters would expect him to do. But Laramie knew he couldn't do it, not in that way and at this particular time.

He sighed and looked away from Sarah in time to see Gunderson edging out the front door.

As though reading his thoughts Sarah said near his ear, "The townspeople don't much like Gunderson. They know he's necessary, but he makes them feel uneasy during these meetings, especially when tempers get a little short as they're bound to do. They're a little afraid he might gunwhip them if they get heated up and talk back to Reverend Pike. The reverend knows this and always sends Gunderson out."

Laramie nodded absently, his glance still on the door. Then he sent his gaze sweeping the room. Several men were on their feet, all trying to talk at once. Pike seemed to be listening patiently.

"It's always like this," Sarah said wryly. "Pike will let them work off steam, then he'll bring about some sort of order? Did Luke tell you about the situation here?"

"A little."

"Poor Luke. He's caught smack in the middle. The Merchants' Association pays a part of his salary, the town the rest. Which means the Association pays him, since they practically run the town. Luke can't please both sides at once. He would have given up long ago but for me. He wanted me to go away with him. Well, I won't do it! This is my home now. I have a business here. Nobody runs me off!"

Looking at the set of her jaw, Laramie could well believe it.

"But the lawless element in Lone Tree is slowly driving the rest of us out of business," Sarah went on. "And that's what this is all about. The Reverend Pike is trying to clean things up. Luke wants to help him—wants to, with me prodding him, that is. \

"But he doesn't have the money to hire decent deputies and he's always on the edge of getting fired himself. He would have long since, if Reverend Pike didn't have strong support in town. A couple of the Association members are having second thoughts about turning Lone Tree over to the rowdy crowd. There's one of them now."

She nodded to a tall man with a shock of gray hair and shoulders barn-door wide.

"Tom Burns. Owns the livery stable and is the town's only blacksmith."

Burns' voice had the rumble of distant thunder. Clearly he was angry at something that had just been said, something Laramie had missed. "Guess you all got a right to say that about me. I did vote along with Pardee to open the town up. Well, I was wrong. I can see that now. I didn't think ahead to what would happen. The town's full of gamblers, gunmen, painted hussies. It ain't safe for our decent women to walk the streets, day or night. I say it's time to stand up and be heard, time to tell Pardee that he don't own our town!"

A murmur of agreement swept the room. Then a voice in the crowd said, "I'd be careful was I you, Tom. It ain't healthy to talk like that. Yancey Holmes was walking

107

around saying that very same thing last week. Now he's dead and buried six feet underground!"

"I know about Yancey but I still say it's time to speak out!" Burns smacked a huge fist into his open palm. He raised his voice. "I'm behind you, Marshal Cole, and I think most of the folks in this room are as well."

Cole stood up and ranged alongside Pike. He seemed uncomfortable as the focus of attention. "I appreciate that, Tom. I need all the backing I can get. But it ain't enough. I need deputies. I hire one and one of Pardee's gunnies runs him out of town if he steps on toes. The ones Pardee don't scare off, he buys off. You volunteering to hire on?"

Burns shuffled his feet. "I'm not a gunfighter, Marshal. I've never handled a gun in my life."

Pike spoke up, "What the Marshal is trying to say, folks, is that he can't do it alone. All he can do is keep the peace as best he can until such a time as he can hire competent deputies that can help him get the job done. And that means, Tom, that you're going to have to enlist more members of the Association on our side. Get them to ante up enough money to hire good men. Get them to pass better laws. About the only thing against the law in Lone Tree these days is murder and failing to pay for drinks at the Trail's End!"

"And it ain't murder if one of Pardee's men does the killing," said a voice from the audience.

Pike nodded solemnly. "That's pretty much true, I'm afraid. We've got to win more support, especially from the Association." His voice took on a sonorous note. "They must be made to see the error of their ways. Then we must rise together in concerted wrath and smite the wicked, cause the sinners to repent!"

"You tell 'em, Preacher!"

"Amen, Brother Pike!"

Burns said grimly, "I'll do my best, Reverend. You

108

have my word on it. Some of the Association members have told me they aren't too happy the way things are going."

Pike said, "We will be grateful to you, Tom Burns."

Burns nodded and looked around, as though getting his bearings before heading for the door.

Laramie, his gaze tracking Burns, asked Sarah, "How many members in this all-powerful Association?"

"Twelve. A round dozen."

"Twelve? Why so many—oh, I see."

"Yes, Nelson. Everybody wants a piece of the pie. We had a nice little town before. Nobody made a lot of money, true, but nobody starved either. Now too few are making it all. Marcus White, for instance, one of the Association members I'm sure Tom was talking about. He owns the General Store. Up until last week he was doing fine. Then a drunken cowhand broke into his store one night, shot out all the windows and poured coal oil over most of his goods. It's a wonder he didn't set it on fire. And now Marcus is stuck with the loss. Who can he collect from? The cowhand is in jail. He had a dollar and fifty cents in his jeans and doesn't even have a job."

Tom Burns was almost to the church door. Laramie was dimly aware that the meeting was breaking up. He said, "Isn't there a town council? A mayor?"

"The Association *is* the town council. And Pardee is the closest to a mayor we have."

Tom Burns had reached the door. He opened it and stood in it for a moment, outlined sharply against the night by the light spilling from inside the church. Suddenly two shots rang out, so close together as to sound almost as one, and Tom Burns was hurled back inside as though a giant fist had slammed into him. His body hitting the floor shook the whole building.

7

Without thought Laramie Nelson was on his feet, his gun out of his waistband before he'd taken a full step. He ran past the man on the floor without a single glance. He knew Tom Burns was dead.

The street outside the church was deathly quiet. Laramie saw no one, but there were shadows everywhere into which the killer could have melted. Laramie strained his ears for the sound of hoofbeats. He heard nothing. The killer had to be on foot then.

Then Cole came boiling out of the church, Colt in his hand. "See anything, Laramie?"

"Not a thing, Luke."

"It had to be one of Pardee's men," Cole muttered. "Who else?"

Others were crowding the church door now. Cole turned, holstering his gun. "All right, folks. Back inside. There's nothing to see out here. Whoever it was might just decide to take another potshot."

He started back inside, Laramie following. People were clotted around the body of Tom Burns. Cole forced his way through. Pike was kneeling beside the body, the cold-eyed Gunderson beside him.

Pike got to his feet. "Tom is dead, Marshal."

Cole nodded. "I figured that."

"This is the last straw. This will split the town right down the middle."

"It'll bring things to a head all right."

"This lawlessness has to stop!"

Cole spread his hands. "What can I do, Preacher? I'm only one man."

"We've got to rid Lone Tree of Pardee and his like." There was a rising murmur of agreement from those around him. "We'll get you more money, Marshal, for deputies. You have my word on it." Pike held up his hands for attention. "You folks go to your homes now. The meeting is over."

"Money for deputies. I hope he means more than thirty a month," Cole muttered to Laramie. "You be interested then, amigo?"

Laramie wasn't really listening. His gaze was fastened on Gunderson. He was remembering where he'd last seen the man. "Gunner, where were you? You stepped outside just before it happened."

"I walked up the street." Gunderson's pale eyes burned. He fell into his lethal crouch. "You accusing me of something, mister?"

Pike stepped in front of him quickly. "All right, Chris, that's enough!"

Cole said in a low voice, "You're really scouting for trouble, ain't you, amigo? You'd better go. I'll see you in the morning."

With a curt nod Laramie Nelson started out, brushing rudely past Sarah on the way. He kept on going. He was furious with himself. Again he had the feeling of being boxed in. But even worse, what had prompted him to twist Gunderson's tail again? He seemed drived to involve himself in the town's troubles. He realized that part of his irritation came from his reluctance to arrest Sarah, thus forcing the inevitable showdown with Luke Cole.

Lone Tree was buttoned up for the night, except for the saloons and they were going full blast. Yet there wasn't a soul on the street, as though they'd all been warned to stay inside.

Laramie spent a restless night and got up early the next morning feeling tired. The hotel dining room wasn't yet open for breakfast. He went outside into the crisp morning air, rolled a cigarette and smoked it leaning against a verandah post.

The streets were deserted, even the saloons muted and still. There was a *feel* about Lone Tree this morning, a tenseness in the air, a sense of waiting as though everyone had chosen his side and was waiting for the first shot to be fired. It was a fanciful feeling, Laramie realized, but very real.

Now he heard a rather strange sound. Cattle bawling. He shook his head in bafflement before he recalled seeing cattle pens when he had ridden into town. He stepped down the street, toed out his cigarette and strolled toward the corrals.

The corrals were full of bawling cattle, about two hundred head in all. Laramie vaulted to the top rail and hooked his bootheels on the one below. He rolled a cigarette and smoked it thoughtfully. Some of the tension left him. He always felt more at home around cattle than in towns.

The corral railings creaked as a figure climbed up beside Laramie. He glanced around at Luke Cole.

Cole grinned. "It'd be a lot simpler dealing with cattle than a bunch of town mavericks, wouldn't it, amigo?"

"This part of a trail herd?"

"Not exactly. Belongs to the Running W spread out west of town. A cattle buyer came through here, bought two hundred head. He told them to pen 'em up here for a couple days. He'll be back through with another herd and move 'em over to the railhead."

Cole lit a cheroot and stared moodily down at the milling steers. He glanced up and caught Laramie's inquiring look. "I got fired this morning, amigo. I told Pardee that he had Tom Burns killed, so he fired me in the name of the Association."

"Then Lone Tree's without a marshal?"

"Wrong. It has two."

"Two!"

"Yep. Preacher Pike and his crowd want me to stay on. They'll pay my full salary and I understand Pardee has already appointed *his* marshal. A gunnie by the name of Devlin. I'm one up on them, however. I've still got the office and the jail and I'm staying there until they smoke me out."

Laramie heard himself saying, "Still want that deputy, Luke?"

"You mean . . . ? Damn right I do, amigo!" Cole let out a whoop and clapped Laramie on the back. "You and me together, we'll tree this town like hound dogs after a coon." He jumped nimbly down to the ground. "Come on up to the office, I want to swear you in before you change your mind!"

So, a half hour later, Laramie Nelson entered the hotel dining room wearing a deputy's badge. He received some curious stares and was given a wide berth as he ate his breakfast. Afterward, he stood on the hotel verandah, smoking. He was conscious of the star pinned to his shirt as though it weighed ten times as much. He was, in a way, a law enforcement officer with the Pinkertons, yet he had no badge of office, seldom even carrying proper identification papers. Most Pinkerton agents worked under cover.

He thought of Brock Peters and laughed aloud. If Peters could see him now, wearing a star, he'd have a loco-weed fit.

On impulse Laramie walked along the wooden sidewalk past the Trail's End and to The Ladies' Emporium. The door was unlocked. He pushed it open and went in to the accompaniment of a bell tinkling overhead.

The interior of the store was small, dim, cluttered with women's garments of every description. There was a mixture of sweet odors of perfumes, scented soaps, leather. Laramie felt ill at ease, out of his element. Sarah Knight was busy behind the long counter, an older woman helping her.

Sarah saw him and came immediately, a smile of pleasure lighting her face. "Good morning!"

"Good morning." Laramie cleared his throat. "I'm

113

sorry about last night. I was rude..."

Sarah brushed his apology aside. "It's all right, with everything that happened, I understand. Oh, you're wearing a badge! I'm so glad!"

"Yeah," he drawled. "Suddenly Lone Tree has all sorts of law."

"I heard about that. This Devlin is a notorious gunfighter, isn't he? That will mean trouble, won't it?"

Laramie shrugged. "I expect so. Luke thinks he can handle it. And who am I to argue with Luke Cole?"

The impulse that had propelled him into the store now prompted him to say, "Sarah...I'd like to shake the town stink off me for a bit. How about riding out with me? Maybe out to that peach tree you mentioned. I have an extra horse that needs exercise. Or are you too busy here?"

Her hesitation was brief. Her smile came again. "I'd love to, Laramie. Anne can take care of the store. There's nobody out this morning, anyway. It'll just take a minute for me to change."

She disappeared into the back of the store, leaving Laramie alone under the curious gaze of the other woman. He fidgeted. Without thinking he reached out to touch something on the counter. Then he jerked his hand back as though he had poked it into a flame. He had started to pick up a woman's corset! The woman turned away, shoulders heaving with laughter.

His face burning, Laramie stalked outside to wait for Sarah. She came out in less than ten minutes, wearing boots and a riding habit with a divided skirt.

There was nobody at the livery stable.

"Poor Tom," Sarah said. "He didn't have a family. Maybe that's a good thing. I don't know who'll end up with the livery stable. Probably Pardee." Her voice stung with bitterness. "He's taken over everything else in town."

Laramie saddled Wingfoot and the sorrel, and they rode out of town at a canter. Both horses were well-rested and frisky. Sarah was an excellent rider. She rode easily and gracefully, yet kept a strong hand on the reins to hold the sorrel under control. They rode west for about a mile. The wooded draws were brilliant with autumn splashes of color, orange and gold and red. There wasn't a cloud in the sky, and the distant mountains stood out as distinctly as though snipped out of tin. It was noon now, and the day had warmed up considerably.

Sarah turned off on to a faint trail leading up a canyon. A brook, water clear as glass, trickled along-side the trail. After about two hundred yards the canyon opened up, and they rode out into a meadow. A small house, windows gone, roof sagging, crouched in a small grove of trees, some shade trees, a few fruit trees. The only one bearing fruit was a gnarled peach tree, with a few peaches left on the topmost branches.

Laramie kneed Wingfoot up under the tree. Standing up in the stirrups, he could just reach three peaches. He plucked them, tossed one to Sarah and dismounted. He helped her off, letting the horses graze in what little grass there was.

Laramie munched on a peach. It was ripe and juicy. "It's peaceful here."

"Yes, it is," Sarah agreed. "That's why I ride out here alone now and then."

She sat on a fallen log nearby, tucking her skirt around her ankles, and Laramie sat down beside her.

"You born and raised around here?" he asked tentatively.

"As a matter of fact, no. I came from Colorado originally. My father owned a small ranch out of Denver. Then the railroad came through and wanted to buy him out. My father was a stubborn man. He fought them, in court and out, until he died of a heart attack. I'm not saying he was right, necessarily, but that was the way he was. After his death I refused to sell, too. Out of stubbornness and because I blamed them for his death. In fact . . ." She faced him squarely.

"I'm a fugitive, Nelson," she said. "I killed a man, the railroad's land buyer. It was in self defense, he was going to kill me because I accused him of being responsible for my father's death, but nobody believes that."

Laramie Nelson was astounded. Why was she telling him this? Did she know why he was here? But how could she?

A smile tugged at the corners of her mouth. "Oh, I'm not telling any great secret. Everybody in Lone Tree knows, Luke most of all. They don't care much for the railroad here. And poor Luke! They've sent men down after me and Luke keeps running them off. I'd go back and face it, only . . ."

She looked away, her face melancholy. "I wouldn't get a fair hearing. I know I wouldn't. The railroad just coming through, benefiting so many people . . ." Her voice trailed off. After a moment she glanced at Laramie again. "Did you come to Lone Tree just by chance?"

Laramie was relieved to be able to change the subject. "You might say that. I was on my way north."

"I suppose you dream of having a ranch of your own some day?"

"Why, I reckon," he said, startled. "I hadn't really thought much about it."

"I thought all men wanted that. It's all Luke talks about. He's a nice man, a sweet man, but he takes too much for granted." She was gnawing on her lower lip, and her eyes had the glitter of tears. "I don't love him, you see."

Laramie had never claimed to understand women, but this one had him completely baffled. He failed to see what she was getting at, jumping like a grasshopper from one thing to another. And the intimate revelations about her relationship with Luke Cole were as acutely embarrassing to Laramie as though he'd suddenly glimpsed her naked.

He got to his feet abruptly. "We'd better be getting

116

back. Luke may be wondering about his new deputy."

Sarah didn't demur. She seemed withdrawn, her thoughts far away. Laramie brought up the horses, helped Sarah on the sorrel, then mounted Wingfoot. They started back for town, Sarah riding three lengths ahead. Laramie was content to hold the pace without trying to catch up.

Luke Cole burst into the livery stable as Laramie was unsaddling the horses. Cole was highly agitated. He skidded to a stop when he saw Sarah, then wheeled on Laramie. "Where the devil have you been? All hell's broke loose here just when I needed you!"

"All right, Luke, simmer down," Sarah said soothingly. "What's happened?"

"While I was having breakfast, Devlin broke into my office and took over, that's what happened! He's holed up in there with a half-dozen of Pardee's men!"

8

Laramie Nelson said softly, "So it's started."

Cole glared. "Maybe it wouldn't if you'd been here. Where have you been, anyway?"

"The question is, what can we do about it?"

"Do about it? Why, we go down there and take back my jail, what else?"

Jeremiah Pike had stepped into the stable in time to hear Cole's last words. "Do you think that the wisest course, Marshal? It seems to me that you should arrest Pardee. That man is Satan incarnate, the acme of wickedness. When fighting Satan, Satan should be the prime target!"

Cole turned about. "If I arrest him, Preacher, where do I hold him? They've got my jail."

"Use the church, Marshal. It shall be a symbol of goodness triumphant! We can lock him in the vestry room and have several of the good townspeople help guard him."

"I hate to let them take over my office."

"That building is like a fort, Marshal. To storm it would cost lives needlessly. And arresting Pardee may succeed in breaking the back of his gang of cutthroats."

Cole heaved a sigh. "Yeah, I guess you're right."

"What do we arrest him for?" Laramie asked.

"Murder, what else? He had Tom Burns killed, didn't he?"

"You keep saying he did, Luke, and maybe he did, but where's the proof?"

Pike's gaze came to rest on Laramie in speculation. Cole bristled. "He took over my jail, didn't he? Ain't that a crime?"

"I don't know, Luke. Is it?"

"Whose side are you on, amigo? You're my deputy, for hell's sake!"

"It's right he should be concerned about justice, Marshal," Pike said smoothly. "But there's always suspicion of murder. That should be enough to hold him."

And it was left at that.

Laramie didn't like it. Everything seemed to be moving too fast, slipping out of control. He glanced over at Sarah, who hadn't spoken a word since Pike came in. She shrugged, returning his look.

So, a few minutes later, Laramie was striding alongside Cole on their way to the Trail's End.

As they paused outside the batwing doors, Cole said, "If Devlin's in there and tries to horn in, leave him to me. He's mine!"

They went in together, side by side, pausing again just inside. There were only a half-dozen men in the place. Pardee was at the same table as last night. Sitting with him was a tall dark man of around forty. He had a heavy moustache and was wearing a star.

"That's him, amigo!" Cole hissed. "Remember now, he

118

belongs to me!"

They started down the room, separating until they were about ten feet apart when they finally reached Pardee's table. Devlin got to his feet as they stopped. A bone-handled gun was strapped low on his thigh.

"I'd've thought you'd be gone by now, Cole," Pardee said.

"You're under arrest, Pardee."

"Arest! You can't arrest anybody." Pardee sneered. "You ain't marshal anymore."

"You say I'm not. There're other people in Lone Tree aside from you."

Pardee shrugged. "Those people don't count, far as I'm concerned." His voice hardened. "You're on my property, Cole. Get out while you can still walk out."

"When I leave, you're going with me, under arrest, Pardee!"

Pardee jerked his head at the man beside him. "Devlin!"

Laramie hadn't once taken his gaze from Pardee since he'd entered the saloon. As Devlin made his move and Pardee hunched forward, one hand dropping below the table, Laramie took one step, raised his foot and slammed his bootheel into the table, tumbling it into Pardee. The table knocked the gambler to the floor, chair and all, as two guns boomed almost as one.

Laramie, gun out, risked a glance. Cole was unhurt, smoke eddying lazily up from the snout of his Colt. Devlin was stumbling back toward the wall, one hand clutching at his heart, blood leaking through his splayed fingers. He slammed into the wall and crumpled slowly to the floor.

Laramie glanced back at Pardee in time to see the gambler reaching across the floor for his gun, which had been knocked from his hand. Laramie brought his gun to bear. "Hold it right there, Pardee."

Pardee froze, eyes suddenly alive with fear. Laramie

119

took two steps and booted the gun out of reach. Then he turned, back against the wall, his glance raking the room. He saw at once there was nothing to be concerned about. The few men in the barroom were all very still, hands carefully in sight and away from their guns. Laramie's gaze jumped to Cole.

Cole's cherubic face split wide in a grin. "You see, amigo? Just like old times. They ain't a chance against us together!"

"It's not over yet, Luke," Laramie muttered. He bent down, seized Pardee's arm and hauled the man to his feet. "Like Luke said, you're under arrest."

He gave the gambler a hard shove toward the door and followed him, gun centered on his back, Laramie didn't look to the left or right, confident that Cole was covering him. They got out of the saloon and headed up the street toward the church without further incident.

Cole fell into step beside Laramie. In a low voice he said, "Where did you go with my girl?"

"Your girl?" Now that the danger was over for the present Laramie's spirits had lightened considerably. "I'm not sure she knows she's your girl, Luke."

"Well, I say she's my girl and I don't take kindly to some galoot coming in here and riding out with her!"

"All right, Luke, all right. Pull in your horns. It was nothing. I wanted to ride for a little and asked Sarah to come with me. We rode out to the place where she got the peaches for the pie. What's wrong with that?"

After a few steps, just before they reached the church, Cole said grudgingly, "All right. This time. Just see to it that it doesn't happen again."

There were four armed men in the church. Neither Pike nor his bodyguard were there.

One man, a stocky, middle-aged redhead, spoke up, "The preacher said for us to do what we could to help, Marshal."

Cole nodded absently. "Thanks, Red. I surely do

appreciate it."

The vestry was a small room off the pulpit. "I don't know why the preacher calls this the vestry, whatever it is," Cole grumbled. "It ain't nothing much that I can see. It's just a room, not even finished yet, not even a window."

"Then it should make a good cell," Laramie said.

As they started to lock Pardee in the room, he turned on them. "My men'll be coming for me, you know that, don't you? And they outnumber you four to one. You let me go now, Cole, and I'll let you two ride out of town with a whole skin."

"Why don't you shut the hell up!" snarled Cole. He shoved the gambler into the room and locked the door.

Laramie said slowly, "He's probably right, Luke."

"You don't think the preacher called it? They won't break up now he's under lock and key?"

"I doubt it, Luke, not without a try or two anyway. They've been having it too good with Pardee."

"Yeah, I guess you're right, amigo." Cole scrubbed a hand down across his face, sighing. "Maybe I'd better see if I can scout up some more men. I don't think they'll try anything until dark, do you?"

"I wouldn't think so."

"You stay on top of things here. I'll be back long before sundown." Cole told the others that Laramie Nelson was in charge and left.

Laramie stationed the men at the windows and the back door, taking the front door himself. Then he settled down for a boring wait. The town was very quiet. Main Street, stretching away from the front of the church, was as deserted as a ghost town. Nothing stirred under Laramie's gaze, not even a stray dog.

His thoughts were caustic. Well, he'd gotten into it with his eyes wide open. He had asked for it, nobody had forced him into anything. Right now, he could be twenty miles away, headed for Denver, with Sarah Knight in tow.

And that sent his thoughts in another direction, one

he'd been avoiding. Sarah Knight. Why had she talked so freely to a man she'd only known for a few hours? Why had she made it clear she didn't love Luke Cole? He mulled over the questions without receiving any clear answers.

The afternoon dragged. Shadows lengthened along the street as the sun dropped westward. One by one, armed men approached the church, identified themselves as being sent by Cole and were let in by Laramie. By sundown they numbered a full dozen.

Then Laramie saw Cole hurrying toward the church. He stood aside for him to enter. Cole leaned against the wall by the church door while he caught his breath, his glance sweeping the church as he counted.

"Twelve and us two make fourteen," he finally said. "They're coming all right. They've got about thirty men ready to move in."

"That cuts Pardee's estimated odds down to less than three to one."

"That cheers me up no end." Cole took out a cheroot, bit the end off and lit it.

"Where's Pike and his shadow?" Laramie asked. "They coming?"

"You know, that's a funny thing. I didn't run into them anywhere and nobody seems to know where they are. But they all said the preacher'd left word to help me. Do you suppose they've got him over at the Trail's End, holding him as a hostage or something?"

"I wouldn't know, Luke." Laramie's attention was caught by a flicker of movement in the street. He tensed, peering into the gathering dusk, expecting the vanguard of the attack. Then he saw a billow of skirts and relaxed with a muttered curse. It was Sarah. She was headed directly for the church, carrying a small satchel.

"What?" Cole demanded. "What is it?"

"Sarah. She's coming here."

"What the hell!"

Cole shouldered Laramie aside and started through the door. Sarah was already mounting the church steps.

"What are you doing here, Sarah?" Cole snapped. "There's going to be shooting here any minute!"

"You think I don't know that?" Sarah came on. "That's why I'm here."

"What do you mean?"

She stepped around Cole and entered the church, smiling at Laramie. She hefted the satchel. "There'll be shooting, somebody will be hurt. I've got bandages and what medicine and instruments I could beg off Doc Whittaker. I tried to get him to come, but he said it wasn't his fight. I've done some nursing, Luke."

Cole was palely furious. "You get out of here right now! You've got no business here!"

"Oh, but I have, Luke" she said calmly. "It is my fight, too. I even thought of bringing along my rifle, I can use it, you know. But I knew you wouldn't stand still for that."

"You could be shot! I won't have it!" Cole seized her by the arm and started to wrestle her through the door.

Down the room a man shouted, "Here they come!"

9

A shot rang out from the street, and a window shattered. Laramie pushed Cole and Sarah back out of the way, then slammed the door and bolted it.

To Sarah he said, "Now you're here, stay down." He smiled without humor. "You get hit, who'll tend you?"

Sarah obeyed without argument, crouching down behind one of the rear benches.

Drawing his gun, Laramie ran to the closest window. It was nearly dark outside, just enough light left to show figures moving like shadows. He snapped off a shot at one and was rewarded with a yelp of pain. As though this were a signal, gunfire became general.

Cole dropped to one knee beside Nelson, gun barrel

resting on the windowsill. He was still furious and muttering under his breath, "Damm fool woman! Stubborn as a pack mule!"

He fired twice rapidly, and Laramie saw a running figure stumble and fall, then roll out of sight behind a building.

For the next half hour firing was brisk. The attackers were on both sides of the church now, and they poured a steady stream of bullets through the windows, while those on the inside fired at the gun flashes.

During a brief lull, Cole said, "The preacher ain't going to be happy, all his windows busted this way."

"If that's all he's got to worry about—" Laramie broke off to raise up and snap off a shot.

All at once the firing stopped. The sudden silence was almost eerie.

"Think they've given up?" Cole whispered.

"You know better, Luke. My guess is they're regrouping, counting their wounded. I wouldn't advise sticking your neck out a window."

"Yeah." Cole raised his voice. "Sarah? You all right?"

"I'm fine, Luke." Her voice was steady as a boulder.

"Anybody hurt?" Cole shouted down the room.

"Man down here got a bullet in his shoulder, Marshal," a voice answered.

Another voice said, "I've got a glass splinter in my cheek. Hurts like the devil."

"I'll be right there," Sarah said.

"Now keep down, Sarah, don't stick your head above window level." Cole moved off at a crouch.

Laramie rolled a cigarette, ducked his head below the windowsill to light it, then smoked with his hands cupped around it. He glanced down the room and saw the faint glow of a lantern burning behind the altar and Sarah's shadow as she worked over the wounded men. Cole stood off to one side, gazing down at her.

Abruptly the thunder of hooves broke the silence

outside. This time they were attacking on horseback. For the next quarter hour Laramie was busy firing and reloading until the Colt grew hot to the touch. The riders ringed the church, like Indians attacking a wagon train, firing and shouting. Twice, bullets struck a horse and the animal went down with a womanish scream.

And then, as suddenly as before, they ceased firing, and it was quiet again. The church reeked of gunpowder.

"Did you get any, amigo?" Cole asked hoarsely from beside him.

Laramie hadn't even realized the man had returned. "I don't know. How can you tell in the dark? It's all blind luck. They have a target, the church. They can keep us pinned down here forever."

"Yeah."

A man groaned somewhere behind them. Laramie said, "And I'll tell you something else. They've got food, water, guns and bullets. Everything's on their side. Sure, we can hold them off for a while, but they'll wear us down in the end. If they pick us off one at a time, sooner or later they'll be coming in."

"I know, amigo, I know." Cole pounded his fist on the windowsill. "Where is Preacher Pike?"

"I don't think we'd better depend on him for anything." The wind was rising, blowing cold through the shattered windows. Laramie thought longingly of his mackinaw back at the hotel. "It's going to get damned cold in here before morning."

"That's what Sarah said. She said it's going to be tough on the wounded."

"Then why not a fire? There's a stove back there and I saw a box of wood. That won't offer them any more of a target than they've got already."

Without waiting for a response from Cole, Laramie went at a crouching run toward the pulpit. As he clambered up onto the platform, Sarah turned about from where she was working, shading her eyes from the

125

lantern's glare. "Luke?"

"No, it's Laramie."

He dropped to one knee beside her. Sarah brushed the hair out of her eyes and smiled wanly. There were three men lying on blankets now.

"Anyone bad hurt?"

"No, we're lucky so far. The worst one has a bullet in his shoulder. I can't get the bullet out. I can only make him comfortable until we can get him to a doctor."

"I'll start a fire going."

"That'll help."

Laramie had a fire going in the potbellied iron stove in short order. Then he helped Sarah move the wounded men close to the stove. He sank down on his haunches, leaned wearily against the wall and lit a cigarette.

After a moment Sarah joined him. "There's nothing more I can do at the moment. Will they be coming again?"

"They'll be coming again," he said grimly. "You can depend on it."

She sat down beside him, gathering her skirt around her ankles. "It doesn't look good, does it?"

"It doesn't look good." Laramie toed out his cigarette. "Sarah, something you said this morning has been bothering me. You said you shot this railroad land buyer in self-defense? Was he trying to kill you?"

"He was. He had a short fuse, I guess. I was still grieving over my father's death and full of hate. I taunted him, called him all kinds of names, the least of which was a murderer. And I guess he was under a lot of pressure from the railroad to get the deed on the ranch. He drew his gun, he even got off a shot at me before I could get to my Winchester. I only intended winging him, but my aim was a little off."

"Did anyone see it? Any witnesses?"

"Two of his men were with him. They saw it. But do you think they would testify for me against the railroad?"

Laramie Nelson was silent.

"Why are you so interested?"

He roused. "Oh . . . just curious. It's unusual to hear of a man throwing down on a woman."

It was a lame explanation. Laramie realized, but just then one of the wounded men groaned, capturing Sarah's attention. She got to her feet and hurried off as the man groaned again.

Laramie started back toward his window post. On the way he stopped at the window guarded by the red-haired man. "Anything stirring?"

"Nope. It's still quiet, Nelson, but they'll be coming again any minute."

Cautiously Laramie peered out the window. It was quiet. Then he heard a distant sound. It took him a moment to recognize it. The cattle, the cattle in the corrals.

He walked on slowly, an idea nudging his brain. He found Cole by the glow of his cheroot. "Luke, I've got an idea. It may work, it may not. It'll all depend on us getting out of here without being spotted."

"Anything's better than waiting here like this," Cole growled.

Quickly Laramie outlined what he had in mind. Then he said, "I figure the best time to try to get out will be during an attack, the next one if we're ready. The noise and confusion should help us."

"I'm with you amigo," Cole said without hesitation.

"All right, let's get going."

Laramie called softly down the room for one of the men to take over their post. Then he and Cole went quickly to the platform and to the stove, collecting Sarah and the man called Red on the way. Scrubbing soot off the inside of the stove door, Laramie and Cole blackened their hands and faces.

As they worked, Cole explained their plan to the other two. "We're going out during the next attack. We shouldn't be more than a half hour, if it works. If it doesn't, it won't much matter anyway. The thing is, you're going to be a little thin here."

"We'll manage," Red said stoutly.

"I can shoot, better than most men," Sarah said. "Give me a rifle and I'll cover a window."

"No!" Cole's reaction was immediate and explosive. "Sarah, I won't have you getting into—"

"Luke," Laramie broke in, "this is no time to be gallant. Sarah's here, she's already involved. Let them break through while we're gone and get in here, they're going to gun down anything that moves, without checking first to see if it's male or female."

"He's right, Luke," Sarah said. "You know he is."

Cole's shoulders slumped. "Yeah, I guess so. Damn it, why did you have to stick your—"

A voice shouted, "Here they come!"

Shots sounded, bullets whined in through the windows, and the men inside began returning the fire.

Laramie took charge. "Red, we're going out the back door. Cover us!"

He glanced at Sarah, started to say something then changed his mind and merely nodded. Sarah's lips formed two words: "Good luck!"

Laramie held back for a moment at the door and said in a low voice, "We've got one thing going for us. They're not expecting anyone to try breaking out."

Cole said impatiently, "All right, let's go, let's go!"

Laramie said, "Red, you fire over our heads, make them keep under cover. We should be across the street and behind that feed store in about five minutes. After that, we're home free"

Laramie opened the door. Too impatient to wait, Cole went first, down the two back steps on his hands and knees, then squirming on his belly in the dirt of the street. Laramie followed right on his heels. Behind them Red opened fire.

The night was only slightly lighter than the inside of the

128

church had been before they lit the lantern. The darkness was broken only by orange splashes of light as the guns fired. But after a few minutes, Laramie's vision adjusted and he could make out the bulky shadow of Cole crawling along the ground.

Cole made it to the feed store building and disappeared around the corner. Laramie followed him around, waiting until he was well past the corner before standing up.

As he reached his feet, a gun was jammed into his back and a taut voice said, "Hold it right there, whoever you are!"

10

Laramie swore under his breath and froze, his thoughts racing. Where was Luke Cole? If he turned on the man and managed to take the gun away somehow, he could cry out before he could be silenced, alerting everyone within hearing.

"Now just who are you and what are you doing here?"

"Like the rest of us, I'm trying to get Pardee out of the church," Laramie drawled. Where the hell was Cole?

"It won't wash, mister! I saw you crawling across the street. Now, are you going to tell me who you are or do I blast a hole through you?"

Laramie sighed. It seemed he had little choice. He let his knees sag ever so little and started to turn.

Then he heard a crunching sound, a groan, and the pressure of the gun left his back. He completed his turn in time to see a figure slump to the ground. He whispered, "Luke? That you?"

"Yeah."

"Where have you been?"

"Sorry, amigo. I was halfway to the livery stable before I realized you weren't behind me. We'd better tie this hombre up and gag him, else he'll be setting the dogs on us. Have to use our belts, I reckon."

Laramie whipped off his belt. They knelt and tied the man's wrists and ankles together with their belts. Then Laramie fumbled for the bound man's face and crammed his bandana into the slack mouth.

Cole's soft chuckle sounded. "Hope my pants stay up. I wouldn't cut much of a figure of a marshal riding down Main Street with my pants down around my ankles."

"Well, I'm glad you've cheered up some!"

"Oh, we're going to make it now, amigo. I just know it!" Cole stood up. "Let's go!"

They moved along behind the buildings, always alert, guns drawn, but nobody challenged them. The gunfire was sporadic now. By the time they reached the livery stable the only gunshots came at spaced intervals. Laramie felt a tightening of apprehension. That could mean they were closing the net tighter around the church, perhaps even getting ready to crash in. A mounting sense of urgency drove him on.

As they neared the livery stable, Laramie realized something strange. Although it was only a little after nine, there wasn't a light to be seen anywhere. Even the saloons, at least the ones he could see, were shuttered and dark.

They ducked into the livery stable through the back door. Laramie hurried toward the front, calling back, "I think we can risk a light here, Luke. See if you can find a lantern."

Looking out through the front door, Laramie saw Main Street stretching dark and empty. Only the Trail's End, two blocks up, was ablaze with light.

A lantern flared behind him, and Laramie turned back. "The Trail's End is all lit up like a Christmas tree."

"That's probably where they're holding the preacher and Gunner," Cole said.

Wingfoot whinnied as Laramie approached. Apparently the gunfire had spooked him. Laramie patted the animal, spoke to him soothingly for a moment. By the

130

time he had Wingfoot saddled, Cole was already astride his horse. Laramie blew out the lantern and mounted up.

They rode out the back door and turned left toward the corrals, walking the horses slowly, minimizing the noise as much as possible. It was less than two hundred yards to the corrals. The penned steers were restless, in constant motion, clearly disturbed by the sound of guns.

As they reined in, one on each side of the corral gate, Cole laughed suddenly. "Hey, amigo, do you remember when we drove that herd down the street of . . . what was the name of that town I should remember but I don't."

"How do you think I got the idea?" Laramie hooked the toe of his boot in the gate bar. "Ready?"

"Ready, amigo! Let 'er rip!" Cole cried exuberantly.

Laramie drew his Colt, jerked the bar and kicked the gate wide. He fired once into the air, Cole firing right behind him. The cattle broke, stampeding through the gate like a raging cataract.

Laramie and Cole fanned out, riding herd on the leaders, heading them right down Main Street and toward the distant church. Cold wind whipped at Laramie's face like stinging sleet as he rode, guiding Wingfoot skillfully with a touch of his knee. The ground shook with the thunder of hooves.

All of a sudden Laramie threw back his head and yelled in pure delight. It had been a long time since he had ridden at the head of a stampede.

Now the street was a solid sea of moving steer backs. Laramie rode Wingfoot up on the boardwalk and reined him in. The herd didn't need guiding; there was no way they could be turned back now. As the stragglers pounded past, Laramie fell in behind, as did Luke Cole on his horse.

A crackle of gunfire could be heard now over the noise of the hooves, and Laramie knew that some of Pardee's men had been caught out in the open street. They were being run down by the stampeding cattle. Laramie throttled back any feeling of compassion for them. After all, that was the purpose of the whole plan, wasn't it?

A random shot was occasionally directed at them from the dark buildings. Without slacking their pace, they fired back at the flashes.

Then the church loomed up, the cattle splitting, flowing on each side of the church like a river at floodtide dividing around an island. Laramie and Cole reined in at the church steps. The last stragglers stumbled past them, and the cattle were gone, the sound of their passing receding in the distance.

Laramie and Cole sat their horses, alert and tense, waiting for the first gunshot out of the dark. None came.

"Think we cleaned them out, amigo?"

"Cleaned them out or scared them away. "Either way, I'm sure it took the heart out of them."

"You know something?" Cole chuckled. "There's going to be one sore cattle buyer when he comes riding in here and finds his cattle scattered to hell and gone."

"Thank him for me, Luke. Without his cattle we'd have been dead by morning."

A voice called softly from the church door, "Luke? Nelson?"

"Yeah, Sarah, it's us." Cole swung down to the ground with a creaking of leather. "Everything all right? Any more get hurt?"

Laramie had also dismounted. Sarah met them on the church steps.

"One man was killed, another wounded. They came close to getting in, Luke. They were attacking when the cattle came. Just in time."

"That's why we got so many, then. They were mostly out in the street," Cole said in satisfaction. "Well, it's all over now."

"Not quite, Luke," Laramie said. "We still haven't located Jeremiah Pike."

"By God, that's right! I plumb forgot about the

preacher!" He strode to the door and bellowed, "Red! Get out here!"

Sarah moved closer to Laramie. "You weren't—were either of you hurt?"

"Not a scratch." Laramie remember the man behind the feed store. "Thanks to Luke."

Red came through the door. "Yes, Marshal?"

"Send a man for Doc Whittaker to come tend the wounded. Have another man stable our horses. And I'd appreciate it if a couple of you men would stay here and guard Pardee for a little while longer."

Cole turned to Sarah. "And you, go home, Sarah. That's an order, damn it! We're going after the preacher, if he's still alive. Which I very much doubt. Let's go, amigo!" He plunged down the steps and started up the street.

Laramie lingered a moment. "Do as he says, Sarah. Go home. Get some rest. You've earned it."

She took a tentative step toward him, hand coming up. Laramie nodded shortly, wheeled about and hurried after Cole. He caught up with the man just outside the Trail's End. It was still ablaze with light, yet a pall of silence hung over it. They went in shoulder to shoulder.

Cole stopped short with a grunt of surprise. For a moment out of time Laramie thought it was the night before and Pardee and Devlin were at the rear table.

Only it wasn't Pardee and Devlin, it was Jeremiah Pike and Gunderson.

11

Pike and Gunderson were the only people in the barroom. There wasn't even a bartender. Gunderson was leaning indolently against the wall, small, slight, deadly as a coiled rattler.

As they started down the room, Laramie Nelson

glanced at Cole. His face screwed up in a scowl, his brows knitted together.

Pike nodded cordially to them. "Marshal, Mr. Nelson. We've been waiting for you."

Laramie saw the gun on the table, close to Pike's big hand.

Cole plowed to a stop. "I thought you were dead, Preacher! They turn you loose? Pardee's men, I mean?" His voice was puzzled, but it was edged with anger, as though he was slowly beginning to comprehend that something was wrong.

"Nobody had to turn you loose, did they, Pike!" Laramie asked, his gaze never leaving Gunderson.

Cole demanded, "What do you mean, amigo?"

"I mean, Luke, that they were never being held. They've been directing all those guns against us. Am I right, Pike?"

The big man said easily, "You're telling it, Mr. Nelson."

"There was something about the whole set-up that smelled to me the minute I rode into Lone Tree. I kept remembering tales I'd heard of a fire-eating preacher with a bodyguard who rides into certain towns, gets the folks all riled up against the sinners and the corrupters, sets them at each other's throats. When the battle is over, both sides weakened, this preacher moves in and takes over, runs everything wide open and milks the town dry before moving on. Doesn't that about tell the story of what happened here, Preacher Pike?"

"You mean this Bible-thumper has been setting me up all along?" Cole's voice throbbed with outrage. "Why, I could've been killed out there tonight!"

"That was the whole idea, Luke. We were all supposed to be killed tonight, including Pardee. Then Pike has everything his own way."

"But a *preacher*!"

"But he's not a preacher, Luke. Don't you see? He's no

134

more a preacher than you are."

"I underestimated you, Mr. Nelson," Pike said sauvely. "I should never have let you get involved. With only the marshal here to contend with, my plans would have worked."

"I might never have suspected if your gunfighter hadn't pulled that stupid blunder killing Tom Burns. When I got to thinking about it, I knew it had to be him. Oh, I'm sure he was acting under orders from you. By killing Burns you hoped to set Luke and Pardee at each other's throats. Which is exactly what happened."

"That was, as you say, a blunder. Chris may be depended on to carry out orders, but he is sometimes a little crude about it."

There was nothing of the sin-fighting evangelist about Pike now, yet he was still smooth, glib, unruffled. He could have been sitting down to dinner.

A roar came from Luke Cole. "I've been made a fool of in this whole thing!"

"That's right, Marshal, you have indeed been made a fool of. And now . . . Chris?"

Laramie had made a mistake taking his gaze from Gunderson. It almost cost him his life. At the signal from Pike, Laramie reacted instinctively. He threw himself down and to the left, clawing for his gun.

Gunderson was fast, faster than any man Laramie had ever faced. His hand was a blur as it streaked for his gun. He got off two shots before Laramie hit the floor, rolling. Both shots missed, one whistling harmlessly overhead, the other thudding into the floor.

Which didn't say much for his accuracy, Laramie thought with a tiny corner of his mind.

Laramie rolled over once, then got off two quick shots as he came up on his left elbow. Both shots struck Gunderson around the heart, in an area no larger than a silver dollar. The impact drove Gunderson back against the wall. Laramie was sure the man was dead before his body hit the floor.

Somewhere in there Laramie had heard another shot. He darted a glance at the table. Cole stood where Laramie had last seen him, Colt in his hand, and Pike apparently hadn't moved.

Puzzled, Laramie climbed to his feet. Then he saw Pike holding his gunhand with his left. The right hand was smashed, bleeding profusely. Pike was staring at it as though it didn't belong to him.

Laramie glanced at Cole.

Cole interpreted the look correctly. "Yeah, he went for his gun, but I couldn't bring myself to kill him," he said somewhat sheepishly. "I can't help thinking of him as a preacher. And I can't gun down a preacher any more than I can a woman."

"I'll include you in my prayers, Marshal," Pike said with a wry twist of his full lips.

"You just shut the hell up or I'll lay my gun alongside your head!" Cole said violently. "I'm not forgetting you made a fool of me!" Cole stood glaring for a moment, breathing wrathfully. Then, in one of his lightning changes of mood, he turned to Laramie with a spreading grin. "Well, now it's really over, huh, amigo?"

Except for the reason I came here in the first place, Laramie thought. Aloud he said. "How about Pardee? What do we do about him now?"

Cole looked startled. "Why . . . I reckon we let him go. It appears he hasn't done anything. Will you take care of that, amigo, while I take the preacher here to jail and lock him up? And tell Red and the others thanks from me and they can go home."

"Sure, Luke, I can handle that."

"Then you might as well go to bed and get some shut-eye. I sure as hell am. It's been a long, hard day."

Laramie watched silently as Cole got Pike on his feet and herded him out of the saloon. It wasn't until Cole was gone that Laramie remembered the star pinned to his shirt. He should have given it back, he wouldn't be needing it any longer.

It seemed strange walking out of the saloon and leaving it with the lamps burning, the doors unlocked and nobody in attendance. But that was Pardee's problem, and he would probably be too grateful about his release to complain about anything.

Out on the street Laramie started to smile. Lights were on in most of the buildings along Main Street now, all the saloons going full blast, and people were beginning to appear on the walks.

It was indeed all over.

But not for Laramie Nelson. There was still the problem of Sarah Knight to contend with.

Red was waiting on the church steps. "You can go home now, Red."

"What was the shooting all about, Nelson?" Red asked eagerly. "Who was killed?"

"Pike's gunfighter." Laramie rubbed at his eyes, trying to scrub the acid-burn of weariness out of them. "It's a long and complicated story, Red. Get it from the marshal."

"What about Pardee?"

"I'll let him out. Go home, Red."

Laramie entered the church. There was a single lantern burning on the altar. He told the two men still there to go home, then took the lantern down to the vestry room. He unlocked the door and called inside, "Pardee? You can come out now."

The gambler, no longer so dapper with a beard stubble and his clothes mussed, emerged from the dark room blinking. "It's about time! I thought I was going to be locked up in there forever. What's been going on?"

"Your saloon's empty up the street, Pardee, waiting for you to come back to it. Most of your men are dead or gone, but I expect you can find more. And you'll find a dead man in your place, Pike's gunfighter. No questions!"

137

He held up his hands, palms out. "Just thank your lucky stars it's all over and you're free."

The gambler hesitated a moment, seemed about to speak, then left quickly. Laramie waited until he was outside, then blew out the lantern and followed him. He trudged up the street to his hotel. He was bone-tired, but he had a strong hunch sleep wouldn't come easy.

He was right. He slept fitfully, and what sleep he got was nightmare-haunted. But out of it came a decision. He rose shortly before dawn with his mind made up. He put on his trail clothes, shrugged into his mackinaw and stepped out into the cold morning. He left his gun in the hotel room. His breath smoked, and the watering trough all had a skim of ice.

He had to knock loud and long on the door to Cole's office before the man finally unlocked it. Cole was in his stocking feet, his clothes rumpled from sleeping in them. He yawned widely, scratching at the thick hair on his chest.

"What's the problem, amigo?" He peered past Laramie. "For God's sake, it's hardly daylight! I just got to bed."

Laramie pushed past him into the room. He tossed the star onto Cole's desk. "I wanted to give this back."

"You don't have to do that! I want you to stay on . . ." He scowled suddenly. "You woke me up at daylight to tell me that?"

Laramie faced him squarely. "There's more, Luke. Luke . . . I'm a Pinkerton agent. I'm here on a job."

Cole ran the palm of his hand over his tousled hair, trying to smooth down the sleep-brushes. He chuckled. "You a Pinkerton man, amigo? I don't . . ." Then his eyes narrowed, and he snapped fully awake. "A job? What job?"

Laramie drew a deep breath. "It's Sarah Knight, Luke. I'm taking her back to Denver."

Without visible transition Cole was in the grip of a

coldly murderous rage. "Over my dead body!"

"If I have to, Luke. But I hope it won't come to that. You'll notice I'm not carrying a weapon."

"A bounty hunter!" Cole spat on the floor between Laramie's feet. "My old amigo a bounty chaser! And after a woman at that. Nothing could be lower!"

"Not for bounty, Luke. It's my job."

"Job! *Job!* What kind of a job is that. Nobody takes Sarah out of Lone Tree. Not you, not anybody!"

"Luke, she can't hide here forever," Laramie said desperately. "It's better she go back and face it now. If it was in self-defense, nothing will happen to her."

"Shut up!" Cole's face worked. "You're worse than a mongrel dog eating out of garbage pails!"

"Luke, listen to me—"

Cole hit him, a roundhouse right high on the cheek. Dots of light exploded behind Laramie's eyes, and he was sent reeling back against the railing. Still dazed, he gathered himself and pushed away. Cole hit him again.

This time the railing splintered and went with him as Laramie skidded on his back all the way across the room and up against the far wall. The second blow succeeded in clearing his head a little. Yet, before he could scramble to his feet, Cole was on him with a flying leap. One hand fastened on Laramie's throat and the other raised high, the fist descending like a club.

Laramie rolled his head just in time, and Cole's fist sailed past him, thumping hard against the floor.

Cole yelled in agony. Laramie took advantage of the other's momentary lapse and heaved his body like a bucking horse. Cole was thrown off. They both got to their feet at the same time and circled each other warily. Cole was muttering curses under his breath all the while, his eyes wild and staring.

Then he charged, fists swinging. Laramie, patience thinning, anger growing, met him head-on. They stood toe to toe, slugging it out without any attempt at finesse,

139

two men of almost equal strength and size. The blows had the sound of a meat cleaver chopping into sides of beef.

Laramie felt his lip split, a tooth loosening, and the brassy taste of his own blood filled his mouth. One of Cole's eyes was rapidly closing, and his round face was smeared with blood.

The pommeling continued. They ranged back and forth across the office. Laramie's belly began to throb from the pounding. His head reeled, and blackness came and went as Cole hammered at his head.

Something had to happen soon. One of them had to go down and stay down. Laramie gathered all his strength, awaited his opportunity, thought he saw it and lashed out with a right, catching Cole high on the head. Pain lanced up his arm, and he knew he had broken a knuckle. Then his foot slipped on something on the floor, and he staggered sideways, losing his balance.

With an inarticulate cry Cole lowered his head and charged like a bull. He crashed into Laramie, bringing his head up sharply against Laramie's chin.

It jarred Laramie to his toes. Unconsciousness battered at him in waves. He must have passed out briefly. The next thing he knew he was on his back on the floor. Pain gouged at his side. He opened his eyes and saw Cole looming over him.

Cole was putting the boots to him! Evidently his fury had swept him beyond the bounds of decency.

Laramie tensed himself, waited until the boot slammed into his side again, then wrapped both arms around it and twisted violently. Cole yelled and tumbled like a tree, shaking the building with his fall.

When they started to get up, they found themselves face to face, only inches apart and each on his knees.

Cole worked his mouth and spat right into Laramie's face.

All of a sudden Laramie had had enough. He had been angry before; now his fury exploded. He saw Cole's face as though through a shimmering red mist. He slammed his fists into the face repeatedly and slowly drove Cole back. He tried to fight back, but Laramie was not to be denied now. Neither man got off his knees.

To Laramie, it seemed to go on forever. He kept hitting out at Cole's bloody face, which kept receding; yet it always bobbed up again. Laramie's arms grew heavy as lead.

Finally, with a great effort, he climbed to his feet. He looked down at Cole, still on his knees, head hanging. Laramie locked his hands together and brought them down across the back of Cole's neck like an axe blade. The marshal grunted softly and slowly collapsed to lie curled up and still on the floor.

Laramie leaned against the wall, sobbing for breath. He had never been so tired. He wanted nothing so much as to curl up on the floor beside Cole and sleep for a week.

Slowly he became aware of a slapping sound. He forced himself away from the wall and blinked around dazedly. For the first time he realized he was in the jail corridor behind the office. Only one of the three cells was occupied and that by Jeremiah Pike. Pike's arms were poked out between the bars. His right hand was bulkily bandaged. He was slapping his left hand against his right arm, making the applauding sounds.

"Bravo, Mr. Nelson! You were magnificent! I know not why you battled our good marshal but I'm sure your cause was just. We all know that the righteous shall always emerge victorious." Pike's tone was mocking.

Laramie blinked Pike into focus. He said thickly, "Go to hell, Pike."

He started toward the office having to brace himself against the wall every two or three steps.

"Nelson, wait! Let me out of here."

Laramie continued on.

"Look, it's no skin off you. You'll be moving on, what do you care? Think how sore Cole will be if he come to

141

and finds me gone!" Pike's self-assurance had deserted him now. His tone was wheedling. "Look, I'll pay you. I have money, a lot of it. Nelson, don't go! I'll pay, I swear."

Laramie entered the office and shut the door, closing off the sound of Pike's pleading voice. Laramie was appalled at the wreckage. The office had the look of being struck by a tornado. The railing was in splinters, all the furniture was overturned, and even Cole's heavy desk stood on its side.

Laramie made it to the door and filled his lungs with the icy air, ignoring as he could the stab of pain in his ribs. Together, the air and the pain cleared his head somewhat. It was full daylight now.

Each step an agony, he trudged to his hotel, washed off as much of the blood as he could manage and tried to close some of the cuts. His lip was swollen, one tooth was loose, one eye was rapidly closing, and his nose felt as though it was broken. And the ribs Cole had kicked sent a sharp pain probing deep into his lungs each time he took a deep breath.

Laramie supposed he should see a doctor, but more than anything else he wanted to gather up Sarah and be quit of Lone Tree forever.

He packed his saddlebags, paid his hotel bill and walked to the livery stable. He saddled Wingfoot and the sorrel, then led them at a walk up the street. He left his Winchester in its scabbard and looped his gunbelt over the saddlehorn.

Cole was waiting for him in front of The Ladies' Emporium.

12

When Luke Cole saw Laramie Nelson, he took a few steps away from the hitching rail. "Hold it right there, bounty chaser!" The man's battered face was pale, the dried bloodstains standing out like grotesque freckles. His right hand hung loosely by his gun.

Laramie halted. "I'm still not packing a gun, Luke."

"You think that'll stop me? You try to take Sarah, I'll shoot you down like I would a mad dog running in the street!" His voice was lethal. "By God, I will!"

"You wouldn't shoot down an unarmed man, Luke. I know you too well for that." Laramie spoke soothingly, spoke as he would to a spooked horse. "Besides, you're the law."

"Not any more I ain't!"

For the first time Laramie noticed that the star was missing.

Cole advanced another step. "Now turn around and fork your horse and ride out!"

Laramie said quietly, "I'm not leaving without Sarah, Luke."

"You'll get her when I'm dead. If you won't ride, then strap on your Colt and let's finish this. You always did think you were faster than me."

Laramie stood perfectly still. "This isn't the time to find out."

"Then, by God, I'll shoot you down where you stand!" Cole was raging. "Dirty, sneaking, conniving bounty chaser!"

Laramie took an involuntary step forward, dropping the reins of the horses onto the ground.

Cole's hand moved in a blur of speed, and Laramie found himself staring down the man's gun barrel.

Laramie's gunfighter reflexes flinched like a raw nerve and he wondered, as he has so often during those wild days of their youth, if Cole really was faster. But it was too late now to find out. He held himself ready for the shock of the bullet.

"Drop the gun, Luke!"

The voice was Sarah's.

Cole stiffened. Laramie looked past him to where Sarah stood in the doorway of the store, the Winchester in her hands aimed at Cole's back. She was dressed in her riding habit. A hatbox was at her feet.

"For God's sake, Sarah!" Cole said in anguish.

"I said drop it, Luke."

Cole dropped the gun in the dust and turned to face her.

Sarah hefted the rifle. "You've seen me use this, Luke. And believe me, I will." Her face was pale and drawn. "I'm going back with him."

"Sarah, they'll send you to prison, if they don't lynch you!"

"What am I here but a prisoner? Am I to hide here forever with you my keeper? No, Luke, I'm going back. Now you go on along." She motioned with the rifle. "Go back to your office. And put your star back on, for Heaven's sake!"

For a long moment Luke Cole stared at her. Then his shoulders slumped and he walked away, never once looking at Laramie.

Sarah watched him go, her features shaded with regret. Then Laramie stirred and moved toward her. She leaned the Winchester against the wall and waited for him, her face composed, unsmiling.

"You knew?"

Silently she nodded.

"Luke told you?"

"Nobody had to tell me. I was sure you'd come here after me."

"And yet you didn't say anything?"

She shrugged slightly. "I was waiting for you."

"I'm sorry, Sarah. I couldn't bring myself to."

A smile broke the tenseness of her face. "I understand. And it's all right." Then she laughed aloud. "Wasn't it a little foolish of you, Nelson, coming for me without a gun? I can shoot, you know."

"Yes, I know," Laramie Nelson said soberly.

Her face spasmed with bitterness. "I had to run. I couldn't fight it out alone."

"You won't have to fight alone this time, Sarah. I'll be there. And we'll win out. Wait and see!"

She gazed at him intently for a little. Color touched her cheeks. "I believe you. If I didn't, I wouldn't have been waiting for you this morning."

She came swiftly to him. He took her hand tightly and looked down into her face, but he made no further move to touch her.

Sarah reached up to touch his face with gentle fingers. "Your poor face!"

His grin hurt. "You should see the other fellow."

"So you fought over me, after all. It did come to that."

"I guess you could say that, in a manner of speaking. But I can't say I'm sorry." He turned his head and whistled shrilly. Wingfoot lifted his head and danced toward them, the sorrel trailing behind. Laramie led Sarah toward the horses.

Then she held back, pulling free of his grip. "Wait! I forgot something!"

She ran back to the front of the store and picked up the hatbox. Returning to Laramie, she held the box up for him to see.

He scowled at it.

"Recognize it?"

"Isn't that . . . ?"

"The same." A faint flush stained her features. "I thought we might get hungry on the way, so I packed a lunch for us."

For the first time that morning Laramie smiled, then burst into laughter. She began laughing with him. Still laughing, Laramie helped her up onto the sorrel and then handed her the hatbox. He mounted Wingfoot, and they rode north up Main Street.

Once Laramie Nelson glanced back. There was no one in sight except Luke Cole, far up the street before the marshal's office. He stood, a tall and desolate figure casting a long shadow in the early morning sun, and watched Sarah Knight and Laramie Nelson ride away.

Last Stand
at Indigo Flats

1

Laramie Nelson rode into Copper Springs at noon.

It was mid-August, and the Arizona Territory sweltered in heat like the first plateau of hell. Cooper Springs was a clutch of buildings set astride the mountain trail. There wasn't a soul in sight as Laramie rode down the main street, not even a stray dog.

The heat had taken a heavy toll of Wingfoot. He plodded wearily, hooves sending up puffs of dust. Laramie reined him in before a small, weathered building with a sign over the door; *Marshal's Office*.

Laramie threw a leg over the saddle horn and slid to the ground.

Tall, slim, sandy-haired, he stood for a moment, shoulders sloping with weariness, the holstered Colt pulling at his right thigh. His lean face had a light dusting of freckles. His gray eyes were slightly squinted, giving his features a melancholy cast, and his smile was a sometime thing. His gaze idly raking the empty street, he brushed at the dust coating his clothing.

There was a water trough a few yards away. Laramie led Wingfoot over, tethering him to the hitching rail. He loosened the saddle girth.

Wingfoot sigh gustily, dipped his head and began drinking. Laramie slapped him affectionately across one haunch.

Then he strode into the marshal's office. It was dim, the dirty windows letting in very little light. At first Laramie thought the office was empty. Then he saw a fat, elderly man behind the ancient desk, hands crossed over his belly. He was sound asleep, his breath stirring the ends of his untrimmed mustache.

Laramie Nelson cleared his throat loudly.

The man behind the desk snorted and sat up, blinking. He mumbled, "Just restin' my eyes."

"Marshal Tate?"

"Nope. Marshal ain't here. Left early this morning with a jail wagon full of prisoners for the territorial prison over to Yuma."

"He take along a man named Regan?"

"Cleaned out the whole jail. Ain't a soul here but me, and I'm just holding down the office until the marshal gets back."

Laramie felt a wash if irritation. "But we got a telegram from him. I'm with the Pinkertons. The marshal was supposed to be holding this Regan for me. Regan's wanted up in Kansas for robbing trains."

The man shrugged unconcernedly.

"Don't know nothin' about that. You want the marshal, I'd suggest you hustle after him. He's got about five hours start on you, but with you horseback and him slowed down with the jail wagon, you should catch up afore long."

Laramie stared, seething in frustration. He had been riding hard for a week, a ride initiated by Marshal Tate's telegram, and now this. He spun on his heel and stalked out.

Wingfoot, thirst quenched, was half-asleep, head hanging. Laramie ran a hand down his sweaty flank. "Sorry, hoss. Looks like we have to hit the trail again."

Laramie considered holding over until morning, stabling Wingfoot for a good feed and a rest, and sleeping around the clock himself. But that would only mean the jail wagon would have that much more of a lead.

He did take Wingfoot down the street to the livery stable and told the man on duty to give the horse a feed and good rubdown.

Laramie stood outside the door, leaning against the wall and taking advantage of the sparse shade while he rolled and smoked a couple of cigarettes. He thought back to the day over a week ago when he'd first heard of Darr Regan.

It'd been in the Pinkerton office in Denver, across the

149

desk from his immediate superior, Brock Peters. Peters was a small man, with a round, innocent face, always dressed in Eastern clothes. But Laramie knew from experience that appearances were deceiving. Peters was hard as a keg of nails.

"We want this Regan bad, Nelson," Peters had said. "He's held up several trains all across Kansas. We finally broke up his gang after the last robbery, but Regan got away with a payroll, about twenty thousand dollars. We're gradually discouraging all these damn train bandits, but we need to make an example of him. The thing is, he disappeared down in Arizona Territory somewhere. We put out some flyers on him.

"Just yesterday we got a wire from this marshal in Copper Springs. Says he has a man in jail there he thinks is Darr Regan. We want him. Bring him back up here so we can hang him."

"Do you have a picture of this Regan?"

"No pictures, not even an accurate description. A dozen people have described him to us, all differently."

"How am I supposed to know him then?"

"You don't have to know him, Nelson," Peters had retorted. "You just accept delivery of this man the marshal says is Regan and bring him back here."

"How about the payroll?"

"I doubt he'd have it in jail with him, do you? It's doubtless spent by now. We'll settle for the man himself."

It had seemed a simple enough job, even without a description, but now it wasn't simple at all. It meant more riding in this infernal heat. One thing puzzled Laramie. Since the marshal knew someone was coming for Regan, why had he taken him out of town?

Laramie sighed, ground his cigarette out under his toe, pushed away from the wall and went inside. A half hour later he was riding out of town on Wingfoot.

Cooper Springs was a little mining town clinging like a flyspeck to a mountain slope. The trail began dropping

150

down almost at once, the heat growing more intense with each passing mile. There was only the narrow wagon road leading out of town, winding down the mountain like a great snake.

Laramie rode through pines diminishing in size. Wingfoot picked his way daintily. Heat rose in shimmering waves from the valley floor three thousand feet below.

Laramie didn't meet a soul, and the tracks of the jail wagon weren't hard to follow. They reached the canyon floor and more level ground in mid-afternoon. Laramie pushed Wingfoot at a good pace the rest of the afternoon and for a few hours past dark.

Finally, beside a small creek, he made camp for the night.

He let Wingfoot drink his fill, let him graze awhile, the hobbled him beside the creek. In between times Laramie chewed on dried jerky, drank quite a bit of cold creek water, and finally rolled up in his blanket on the ground.

The heat of the day was gone; the night became chill, the far-off stars like points of cold fire. Laramie rolled and smoked a last cigarette before settling down. He knew he could travel much faster than the jail wagon, so he should catch up to it some time in the morning.

He went to sleep with that thought.

He was up and on his way before sun-up the next morning. Wingfoot, well rested, was frisky, and Laramie let him step out out at a good pace. The heat was sweltering by the time the sun had been up an hour. The country opened up, the timber thinning, becoming mostly sagebrush. The land was semi-desert, rolling sand dunes occasionally showing up alongside the trail. And a low range of brown hills came ever closer as the road wound steadily west.

Wingfoot had settled down to a steady clip. The saddle motion and the heat lulled Laramie, and soon he was half dozing.

All of a sudden he was jolted wide awake by a fusillade of rifle fire somewhere up ahead. Several hundred yards in front of them the trail rose up over a slight hump in the earth.

Laramie touched Wingfoot lightly with his spurs, sending him into a gallop. The gunfire increased rapidly in sound and in intensity. Then Wingfoot topped the rise, and Laramie saw the wagon about a mile up ahead, careening from side to side, a thick dust cloud boiling up behind. It was the jail wagon, all four horses going all out, bellies low to the ground.

And pounding alongside and behind it rode two dozen or more Indians, riding low their ponies and firing at the wagon.

Without hesitation Laramie spurred Wingfoot again and headed straight for the racing wagon.

2

It was too far away for Laramie Nelson to be sure, but he judged the Indians to be Apaches. This was Apache territory and, although an uneasy truce existed between the whites and the Indians, now and then a group of renegade Apaches banded together and ravaged the countryside.

The road ran straight on ahead of the jail wagon. About two miles in the distance, like a mirage, floated a tangle of buildings. It was a small town. Evidently the jail wagon was headed for there in search of refuge.

Now Laramie was drawing up behind the wagon and the Indians. He waited until he was within easy rifle range before he plucked the Winchester from the saddle scabbard. He snapped off a shot at the nearest Indian. The bullet drove the Apache off the pinto, the little horse racing on. Laramie got off another shot, this time only wounding his target.

They had been unaware of his presence until now. One

by one they glanced back and saw him. They veered off, left and right, and Laramie rode through, pushing Wingfoot hard until he drew abreast of the wagon seat. Two men were on the seat, one tall, rangy, with a full mustache, rifle in his hands. The other was short, paunchy, the reins in his hands. He was yelling profanities at the straining horses in a hoarse voice. Both men wore stars.

The one with the rifle looked over at Laramie in a startled way as he rode alongside. The man swung the rifle around to bear, and Laramie thought for a moment he was going to fire. Then he raised the weapon slightly and fired over Laramie's head. The Indians were closing in again, and the rifle shot downed a horse a few yards away.

The town up ahead was much closer now, less than a half mile. Laramie strained his eyes, hoping to see men riding out to their rescue. Surely they had heard the gunfire. But there wasn't a horse in sight. The town might as well have been a ghost town.

Laramie gestured with his rifle to the approaching town, yelling at the top of his voice, "If we can make it there, we can get help and hold them off."

The man with the rifle nodded. Laramie let Wingfoot drop back until he was riding along at the end of the wagon.

There was a barred window set in the side, and Laramie saw a white face looking out. Then he dropped back a little more and turned his attention to the yelling Apaches, firing left and right alternately, concerned more with keeping them at a distance than with hitting anything.

Later, when he had time to think about it, he considered it a minor miracle he wasn't hit. Perhaps they were all bad shots. Perhaps the fact that Wingfoot as well as the Indian ponies were going hell for leather accounted for it. Whatever the reason. Laramie remained unscathed.

Then, suddenly, the Apaches were falling back,

153

fanning out. Laramie saw that the jail wagon was entering the town. But that didn't explain it. The single street was deserted, no gunfire from the buildings, no reception committee waiting for them.

Why didn't the Apaches follow them in?

Baffled, Laramie drew Wingfoot to a plunging halt just short of the first building and looked back at the Indians. It was obvious they were ringing the town, making sure the white-eyes were penned in.

By why had they pulled back?

Laramie shrugged, momentarily dismissing it from his mind, and rode on in after the jail wagon.

The town was small, only a dozen or so business buildings in the single block, a few residences here and there. The wagon driver was sawing on the reins. He pulled the horses in before the hitching rail of a saloon. A graying sign hung over the door. *Paradise Saloon.*

Laramie got down, looping Wingfoot's reins over the rail. The horse was flecked with lather, his sides heaving mightily. The wagon horses were also winded, leaning into the traces.

Laramie strode to the jail wagon as the man with the rifle jumped down.

"Thanks, stranger, whoever you are," he drawled. "Reckon you helped save our bacon. Sorry I almost potted you. I thought you were one of those damn redsticks."

"You Marshal Bart Tate?"

"Yep, that's me." The man's eyes suddenly narrowed in suspicion, and the rifle swung up. "How'd you know that? Who're you?"

"Never mind, I'll explain later." Laramie batted a hand at him. He glanced around. "Right now I think we'd better find out why nobody came out to welcome us. Strikes me as almightly strange."

Marshal Tate also darted a look around, squinting hard. "You know, you're right! This place could be a

154

ghost town, only it ain't. I was in Indigo Flats only last week. People all over."

Laramie was looking back the way they'd come. He saw the Apaches sitting their ponies a respectable distance out. They were watchful, but clearly they weren't coming in right away. He turned and looked the other way and saw other mounted Indians.

They had the town ringed, but they weren't prepared to attack, not yet anyway. That struck Laramie as very strange.

He stepped upon the veranda before the Paradise Saloon and pushed open the batwing doors. Inside, he stepped quickly to one side, his back to the wall.

His caution was unnecessary. The barroom was empty. Yet the place looked as though people had been there only moments before. Half filled glasses were on the bar, on the tables. On one table was a plate of half eaten meat and a mug of coffee. Laramie touched his fingers to the mug, then jerked them away with a self-conscious laugh. He had halfway expected to find the mug warm. It wasn't; it was cold.

He turned and went back outside. Marshal Tate had unlocked the jail wagon doors and was herding his prisoners outside. There were three men chained together and—

Laramie stopped short, staring.

One of the prisoners was a woman!

3

She was a tall woman of twenty-five or so, with a cloud of fiery red hair. She stepped down into the dust, the last one out, and moved to one side, shaking her long skirts disdainfully, as though disassociating herself from the others. She glanced up as Laramie Nelson approached. Her eyes were green, her lovely face pink with anger or embarrassment.

155

Laramie revised his opinion. Maybe she wasn't a prisoner. The men were all chained together, and she wasn't shackled at all.

But why had she been inside the jail wagon?

The paunchy man had the wagon team unhitched and was now leading them toward the livery stable a few doors up the street.

Marshal Tate jerked his head toward the saloon. "Anybody in there?"

Laramie shook his head. "Nobody, but it looks like they just left a few minutes ago."

"If we have to make a stand, how about in there?"

"It looks about as good a place as any."

The marshal drew his gun and prodded one of the prisoners. "Inside! And don't give me any trouble." The men started off, the marshal following. After a few steps he noticed the woman wasn't coming along. "Come on, Letty. Fall in."

"I'm not one of your prisoners, Bart!" the woman snapped in a throaty voice.

Marshal Tate chuckled. "Same difference, far as I can see. I got my duty toward you same as them."

"I've been locked up with them, putting up with all their insults long as I intend to! Besides, they could use a bath. They stink!"

"You don't smell like any bouquet of violets yourself, Letty," Marshal Tate said with a broad grin. Then he shrugged. "But suit yourself. Stay out here for all of me. That red hair of yours would look good hung in some redstick's tepee." Still chuckling, he prodded the prisoners on into the saloon.

"You'd better go along with them, miss," Laramie said mildly. "At least you'll be safer in there than out here."

The woman brushed a strand of hair out of her eye, and glared at him defiantly. "You wouldn't say that if you were a woman and had been riding penned up with them all this time. They're animals. And that includes the

156

marshal and his flunky."

"That may well be, miss, but the marshal's right about one thing. The red hair of yours would make a prize scalp for those Apaches out there."

Letty glanced up the street at the distant Indians. She shuddered and took two quick steps toward the saloon. Then she paused, looking back. Again, in a distracted gesture, she brushed the hair out of her eyes.

Her manner altered slightly, her voice softening in something like appeal as she said hesitantly, "Aren't you coming in?"

"Not right this minute. I want to look around first, see if there's anybody around here."

Her glance shuttled around the street. "There's *nobody*?"

"Doesn't seem to be."

She shivered again, hugging herself. "It's spooky."

"It's all of that," he agreed soberly.

"How about them?" She jerked her head at the circling Apaches.

"I don't think they'll be coming in. Not right away, anyhow. Whatever's strange here seems to have them spooked, too. Indians have a strong belief in spirits. Apparently they know something odd has happened here. In my opinion they'll wait, see if anything happens to us before they come in. So why don't you go along in, miss?"

"You'll be back? You won't ride out, leave me alone with them?"

"As long as the Apaches are out there, it's not likely I'll be riding anywhere," he said dryly. "I value my scalp too. I'll be back. You have my word on that."

"Well—all right."

With dragging feet she started toward the Paradise. The marshal and his prisoners had already disappeared inside.

Laramie watched her for a moment, wondering anew

why she was along. He suspected from her finery that she was a dancehall girl, but there was something vulnerable and oddly touching about her. Saloon women, to survive, had to be hard, and this woman had the veneer of one, yet there was more to her than that.

At the door she paused and looked back at him with a shy smile, then went on inside. Tate's plump deputy came up the street from the livery stable, looked at Laramie with lively curiosity, followed the girl into the saloon.

Laramie investigated the houses on both sides of the street, one by one. None were locked, and all showed signs of being recently and hastily vacated. There were a few dwellings between the stores, one rooming house. There wasn't a person around anywhere.

The last building Laramie went into was the livery stable, leading Wingfoot inside. The only animals there were the wagon team. He unsaddled Wingfoot, fed and watered him, then led him to a stall.

"Better get some rest, hoss," he murmured, stroking the horse alongside the neck. "You may need it."

Wingfoot, ridden hard that day, was recovering. He tossed his head spiritedly, neighing.

Carrying his Winchester, Laramie went outside and leaned against the hitching rail. He rolled and lit a cigarette. It was well past noon, but the heat was oppressive still. Laramie's gaze drifted out to the Apaches. They were quiet now and stood their ponies still as statues about three hundred yards out from the edge of town. There wasn't the least doubt in Laramie's mind that anybody trying to leave town would be killed.

He pulled his thoughts back to the town of Indigo Flats and the mystery of the disappearance of its inhabitants. It was certainly a mystery, a baffling one. There had been people here hours ago, probably no later than that morning, and probably fifty or more to judge from the size of the town.

What had happened to them? They couldn't be dead; there were no bodies around. They had simply fled, as though from a plague.

Could that be it? Had Indigo Flats been hit by a plague? There had been plagues in the past, Laramie knew, plagues that had wiped out the population of entire towns. But if a plague had struck here, there should be bodies. Or had they escaped in time?

Also, if some plague had chased the people away, that meant that anyone in Indigo Flats at the moment was in danger.

His breath exploded in a snort of harsh laughter.

It appeared they had a choice. They could stay and be struck down by some mysterious illness or charge the Apaches and be shot down like game running before hunters.

Some choice, he thought wryly.

Laramie toed out his cigarette, sighed and trudged through the dust up the street to the Paradise Saloon.

They were all there, widely separated. Marshal Tate and his deputy sat at one table, backs to the rear wall, a bottle and glasses before them. The three prisoners, still chained together, sat in a row at another nearby table. The redheaded woman was halfway across the room at still another table, eyeing the others warily.

At the sound of the batwing doors, Marshal Tate turned, snatching up his Colt lying on the table before him. For just an instant his black eyes were cold and hard, his mouth a thin line. He had the look of a tough man, deadly as a coiled rattler. Then, recognizing Laramie Nelson, he relaxed, amiable again.

Laramie strode down to his table.

"Find anything, stranger?"

"Nothing," Laramie said. "This place is as empty of people as a graveyard at night."

The man's jaws began to move, placid as a cow chewing, and a knot the size of a marble popped out on his

159

cheek. He turned his head and spat a brown stream at a nearby spittoon, his aim accurate.

"I find that passing strange. Like I said, I rode through here a few days ago. Indigo Flats never was what you'd call a bustling community, but there were people around, alive and kicking, just like we are now."

The deputy said nervously. "Maybe the Apaches spooked them off?"

"Naw, Monte. It don't figure. They could stand off an attack here better than somewhere else."

Laramie thought of his plague theory, but he decided now wasn't the time to bring that up.

Monte shivered. "I don't like it."

"Too damn many things I don't like. Them Apaches out there, for one," the marshal said. His gaze came to rest on Laramie. Although he was still smiling, amiable, the tough, alert core of him peeked through. "It's time we got around to you, stranger. How do you figure in all this?"

"I'm Laramie Nelson. I'm with the Pinkerton Agency. You wired us that you were holding a train robber, a man named Darr Regan. I rode into Copper Springs yesterday, a few hours after you'd left."

As he talked, Laramie moved his glance from the marshal to the three prisoners. Since he had never seen Regan, and the descriptions of him were many and vague, it was going to be difficult to pick his man out of three. *If* he was one of them. The consensus seemed to be that Regan was a man of above average height, close to forty and good with a gun. None of the three, of course, had a gun, but the other two requirements fitted them.

As Laramie mentioned Regan's name, he watched closely, but he noted no reaction from the trio. He looked back at the marshal. "How about Regan, marshal? He one of these three men?"

"Don't know, Nelson."

"You don't know? Then why'd you send the wire?"

"Let's just say I ain't so sure now. All three of these

hombres are due to start serving time at Yuma Prison. And that's where I'm taking them."

Laramie held a tight rein on his temper. "Then let's put it this way. Is one of the three the man you *thought* was Regan?"

"Reckon I can't say about that," Marshal Tate turned his head, spat a stream of brown tobacco juice, and said blandly. "You wouldn't want me to go and point a finger at an innocent man, now would you, Pinkerton man?"

Laramie measured the marshal for a moment. Something about the whole thing didn't make sense. And he discovered that he had developed a sudden and unreasonable dislike for Marshal Tate. Rarely did he ever take such a sudden dislike to a person.

"I was sent down here for Regan," he said slowly, "and I aim to take him back with me."

"Well now, that all depends," Marshal Tate drawled. "Seems to me it ain't going to be all that easy. First, how you going to know which is which? Then there's something else. He's my prisoner and I'm the law around these parts. And there's those redsticks out there."

"One thing at a time, Marshal—"

Laramie broke off—his head coming around, as a sound from the bar caught his attention.

A gasp came from Letty, and Laramie found himself gaping.

4

A man had risen up from behind the bar like an apparition.

He was redfaced, unshaven, sparse gray hair standing up in sleep brushes, eyes bloodshot and squinting.

The man was close to sixty, a harmless derelict, a bit of flotsam found around every saloon, a floorscrubber, a dishwasher, yet his sudden appearance was so startling that Laramie Nelson had his Colt half out of the holster before his mind caught up with his reflexes.

And he saw that both the marshal and his deputy had their guns bearing on the newcomer. The man gawked at them in sudden fear.

"Who're you?" Marshal Tate barked.

"I'm—." The man hawked, cleared his throat. "I'm Jed Hawkins. They call me Toddy."

"Where'd you come from all of a sudden, Toddy?"

"Why, I—" He gestured vaguely. "I've been sleeping back here." He grinned sheepishly. "Passed out, I reckon you'd say. I heard voices and—" He frowned. "I ain't seen any of you gents before."

Marshal Tate asked, "Where is everybody?"

"Where is—? I don't catch your meaning, Marshal. You are a marshal, I take it?"

Marshal Tate turned his head aside and loosed a stream of tobacco juice. "I'm a marshal."

Laramie said, "There's not a soul in town who belongs here. Except you."

"Last I remember, the saloon here had people. Tex, the barkeep, was right here." Toddy broke off to gape. "Nobody? You mean, everybody's taken off?"

"Something's happened to them, that's for sure." Laramie broke off as a shot sounded on the edge of town, followed by several ear-splitting yells.

Hawkins paled, eyes rolling wildly. "What's that?"

"Indians. They've got the town treed."

With a shaking hand Toddy groped for a whiskey bottle on the backbar and splashed a glass half full. He gulped it down, large Adam's apple bobbing furiously.

"Hell," Marshal Tate said in disgust. "Nobody in town but a barfly. What else can happen to us?"

Laramie strode to the bar and got a bottle and glasses. With all that had happened, he decided he could use a drink. Then he was reminded that he hadn't eated since an early, meager breakfast an it was now past noon. "Does this place have a kitchen?"

162

Toddy nodded. "That's my job. I cook here."

"Think you could whip us up some grub?"

"Sure thing, boss." He lowered his voice with a furtive look around. His breath reeked. "You mean there's nobody here, nobody at all?"

Laramie nodded. "It looks that way."

The man's whiskery face split wide with a watermelon grin. In an awed whisper he said, "All this free red-eye!"

He took another quick drink, wiped his mouth on his sleeve, then reached again to the backbar and tucked a full bottle under each arm.

"You just set, hoss," he said happily, "and I'll have you folks something to eat in a jiffy. All on the house."

He headed toward the rear. All at once he leaped into the air, clapped his heels together and loosed a rebel yell.

Laramie looked after him for a moment, smiling faintly, wondering if the man would stay sober long enough to cook anything. Then he turned away with the bottle and glasses, crossing to the table where the redheaded woman sat. She sat up straight, eyeing him warily, and gave the impression of drawing back from him.

"I thought maybe you'd like to join me in a drink, miss?" he asked.

"What's it going to cost me, cowboy?" she said in a flinty voice.

"Cost you? Nothing. There seems to be nobody around to pay. We've even been promised a free meal."

"That wasn't what I meant." She gestured, relaxing her guard slightly. "Sure, cowboy, I'll join you in a drink."

"I'm Laramie Nelson," he said, sitting down.

"Letty. Letty Morgan." She watched him carefully, as though wondering if the name meant anything to him.

"Hello, Letty," he said solemnly and poured two generous drinks.

She drank it neat, with a quick toss of her head, as a

man might, then sat glaring at him as though challenging him to comment.

"Why did they have you in that jail wagon?" Laramie asked. "What crime did you commit?"

"Nothing. No crime."

Laramie simply looked at her.

"The only crime I committed was just being," she said bitterly. Then she gestured. "All right! I'm a dancehall girl, a saloon woman. Does that shock you? Do you want to move to another table?" Without waiting for an invitation she poured another drink.

"I've known dancehall girls before. There are good and bad ones, like with anyone else. That still doesn't explain—"

"The good women of Copper Springs said I was stealing their husbands away from them. As if I'd have their husbands! Can I help it if a man would rather spend a little time with me that with those dried-up, don't-touch-me sticks they're married to?" Tears flooded her eyes, and she looked quickly away.

"So they told the marshal to hustle you out of town or they'd run you out."

Her head swung around. "How did you know?"

Laramie shrugged. "It's not a new story. It's happened before and it'll happen again. That still doesn't tell me why the marshal had you riding cooped up with three men prisoners."

"Because he's mean, that's why, just purely mean!" she said violently.

"I don't like Marshal Tate. He isn't the kind of a man I'd chose to ride with but—" Laramie glanced over at the marshal's table.

Marshal Tate, about to take a drink, raised his glass in a toast and grinned broadly. He sat alone now, having sent Monte out front to stand guard.

"Don't let that manner of his fool you," Letty said. "He

wears that cat-eating grin of his while he plucks the wings off butterflies."

"Do you know of the three prisoners by name?"

"By name!" Her snort was far from ladylike. "I stayed as far away from them as I could. All I know is they're all thieves of one kind or another. Bart Tate put me in there with them deliberately to shame me." Again her eyes glinted with tears. "He didn't have to do that to me!"

"I agree, Miss Letty, He didn't have to do that."

Just then Toddy came toward their table, carrying a tray. There were two plates on the tray, each holding a steak and fried potatoes. Also on the tray were a mound of bread and a pot of coffee. Toddy, beaming and exuding whiskey fumes, set the tray on the table before them.

"Here you are, mam—Mr. Nelson."

"It looks good, Toddy. I'm starved," Laramie said.

Toddy remained at the table as they began eating.

From across the room Marshal Tate called, "Hey, barfly! How about some grub for me?"

"Trash, that's what he is," Toddy muttered under his breath. "Marshal or not, he's trash." But he raised his voice to say, "All right, Marshal. You're next."

As Toddy started toward the rear, one of the prisoners sprang up. "How about us, Marshal? You going to starve us?"

Laramie looked up in time to see Marshal Tate bat a hand good-naturedly at the prisoners. "You'll get grub. Don't worry."

The food was good, and Laramie ate every bite, as did Letty. He finally leaned back with a sigh of content and rolled a cigarette. "With your permission, Miss Letty?"

"Stop with the Miss Letty, will you?" she snapped, scowling. "And of course you may smoke."

Laramie nodded gravely. "All right, Letty. And I'm much obliged."

Laramie lit up and sat smoking contentedly. Despite the danger presented by the band of hovering Apaches,

Laramie found himself in good spirits. He liked Letty, liked sitting there with her.

He had know other saloon women. Many of them, probably most of them, were hard, brassy, avaricious and depraved. This woman could possibly be all of those things, yet he didn't think so. She had spirit, and she was honest in her feelings and beliefs.

Toddy, weaving noticeably now, approached the table to gather the dishes.

"Toddy," Laramie said, "any ideas as to why the townspeople up and skeddaddled?"

The man rubbed the back of his hand across his mouth, bloodshot eyes thoughtful. "I've been thinking on it, hoss. I just can't figure it."

"Could it have been fear of some kind of plague? Anyone sick you know of?"

"Not that I know of."

"What time was it when you went to sleep back of the bar?"

"It's all kind of hazy." Toddy grinned sheepishly. "I'd taken on quite a load of red-eye. Must have been some time late last night. After midnight, I'm sure."

"Hey, barfly!" It was the marshal. Toddy faced about. "Bring some grub out for my deputy. I'm relieving him to eat."

Toddy grunted assent and gathered up the dishes, then shuffled off toward the kitchen.

Marshal Tate got to his feet, burped loudly and started toward the batwing doors. He was still several feet away when Toddy burst back into the room, wild-eyed and panting.

"Them redskins! They're coming at us four ways from Sunday! They're attacking from the rear, Mr. Nelson!"

Laramie Nelson shot to his feet, snatching up his Winchester. Marshal Tate roared through the front doors, "Monte! Back inside here and watch the front door!"

Letty also came to her feet. "I can shoot, Laramie. We'll need all the guns we can get."

Laramie hesitated only briefly, then said, "You're right, we will." He handed the girl his Colt.

Together, they hurried toward the back. They could hear sporadic gunfire as they entered the kitchen. Toddy Hawkins was kneeling at one kitchen window, a rifle poked through a broken windowpane. He fired, then ducked down as a bullet zinged through the window. Laramie scooped Letty up under one arm and fell, taking her weight on top of him, and snaked toward the window.

She began beating against his chest. "Let me go!"

He glanced at her in surprise. Her face was flushed, the gray eyes flashing. "What's the matter?"

"Just let me go!"

He released her, and she rolled away from him. She sat up quickly, straightening her dress, avoiding his gaze.

Laramie got upon his knees beside Toddy and peered over the windowsill. The Apaches were riding hard, single file across the sandy area back of the saloon. From the number Laramie could see, the band had increased considerably in size.

Toddy said, "Why do you suppose they're coming at us from the back instead of from the street?"

"My guess is they're still leery. They've got this strong belief in spirits and they find it odd the the whole town up and left."

"The only spirits I've believed in came in bottles," Toddy said. He shivered. "Now I'm not so sure."

"The thing is," Laramie went on, "They know we're in

here and they're wondering what happened to us, wondering if we're still alive."

Letty said, "You think they'll try and come into town?"

"Oh, they'll come in eventually. When they're sure it's safe to ride right in."

"When they do, what will happen?"

"Now that's the question," Laramie said. "We can't hold them off forever. Let's hope we get some help from somebody. My guess is they'll keep poking at us the rest of the day, stand off tonight. Indians seldom attack at night. But they'll come at us full force and from all directions in the morning."

Laramie saw one Apache veer his pony straight for the saloon, riding with one leg hooked over his mount, using the animal's body as a shield. Laramie leveled his Winchester on the windowsill and sighted down it until the pony loomed large in the sights.

Then, as the Indian poked his rifle around the pony's neck for a random shot, Laramie squeezed the trigger. His bullet struck the Indian's exposed leg, knocking him off the pony.

The Apache sprawled headlong in the dust. He was up and hobbling after his racing pony at once.

Laramie kept the Apache in his sights, but he didn't fire again.

"That's some shooting, hoss," Toddy said admiringly.

Suddenly another shot rang out, the sound loud in the kitchen, and the running Apache pitched headlong to lie still. Laramie glanced around. Marshal Tate was also in the kitchen, kneeling at another window down the room.

"Did you have to do that?"

The marshal met Laramie's glance and grinned lazily. "Like the man said, the only good Indian is a dead Indian."

The man was right, at least under their present circumstances. One less Indian was to their advantage. But something about this man continually rubbed

Laramie the wrong way. He said coldly, "That's a matter of opinion."

"Now what is that supposed to mean?"

"Some people, a train robber, say, might say that the only good marshal is a dead marshal."

His smile disappearing, Marshal Tate's eyes narrowed to mere slits. He spat deliberately, the brown stream barely missing Laramie's boots. "You bucking me, Pinkerton man?"

Laramie held a tight hold on his temper. He knew he had gone too far. The enemy was outside at the moment, not in the saloon. He said tautly, "You'll know when I am."

"Any time, any place." Marshal Tate was drawling again, a faint, derisive grin on his face. "You call the shot."

Although it galled him, Laramie turned back to the window, staring blindly out at the dead Apache.

At his side Letty whispered, "You see? What did I tell you? He's just plain mean!"

Laramie shrugged. "He's right. I had no business saying what I did."

He felt her draw away. "You afraid of him? Like everybody back in Copper Springs? He rules the roost back there. People are afrain to spit unless he gives the word."

Laramie sighed. He said patiently, "Letty, we've got a bunch of renegade Apaches breathing down our necks, and Tate has a prisoner I came for. This is hardly the time to start a personal ruckus with him."

Just then the Apaches came in a bunch, riding hard and yelling, swerving in toward the saloon. Laramie leveled his rifle and began firing rapidly. On one side of him Letty was firing the Colt, on the other Toddy Hawkins was levering his rifle. At the other end of the room, Marshal Tate was also firing.

The Indians swept in very close, a couple so

169

dangerously close Laramie thought they were coming right through the window. Then it was over, the attackers drawing back out of gunshot range. They left behind two dead ponies, and three bodies on the ground, all still.

The cooking smells of the kitchen were now smothered by the stench of gunpowder. It was very hot and close in the small room. Laramie whipped the sweat from his brow and looked around. "Anybody hurt?"

Letty, sagged down with her back against the wall, his Colt cradled in her lap, shook her head. She was very pale and looked worried.

"I'm fine, hoss," Toddy said. He reached up on a shelf for a bottle, tilted it up and drank deeply.

Marshal Tate merely grunted in reply. He was busy reloading his rifle.

Laramie took his Colt from Letty's nerveless hands and quickly reloaded it, dropping it into his holster.

He glanced up at the sound of footsteps and saw the marshal approaching. He was scowling, his demeanor no longer amiable. He planted himself before them on wide-spread boots. Laramie got quickly to his feet, helping Letty up.

"I heard you bad mouthing me, Letty," Marshal Tate said. "I don't take to that kind of talk from a saloon woman!"

"Everything I said was true!" Letty said with a toss of her head.

Marshal Tate raised his hand to strike her, and Laramie stepped in between them. He said evenly, "I wouldn't, Marshal."

The marshal slowly lowered his hand. He slouched, beginning to grin. "You bucking me now, Pinkerton man?"

Laramie let several moments pass, the expelled his breath.

"Not bucking you," he drawled. "I just don't hold with hitting women."

170

"I don't hit ladies, either, but this one's no lady. Oh, I'll admit she's a pretty thing." The marshal's gaze raked Letty slowly, insolently. "Plenty of men back in Copper Springs willing to testify to that, I'd say. And I reckon they'd have reason to know." His grin became malicious. "You'd better be careful, Nelson. She get her hooks in you, you're a gone goose."

He turned away with a careless gesture and strode out of the kitchen.

Laramie glanced at Letty, who was white with rage.

"He's an animal! Can't you see that? That's the way he's been talking to me ever since we left Cooper Springs!"

"You won't be going back there, won't see him again after you reach Yuma. So why let him get under your skin?" He reached out to touch her arm.

She jerked it away. "Leave me alone!" She flounced off.

Toddy was at his shoulder, breath rank with whiskey fumes. "Pesky creatures, females. Always reminds me of a stubborn jenny I once had, only wanted to go where it wanted to go."

Laramie glared at the man with a pulse of anger, then he shrugged and strode off. He was puzzled by Marshal Tate's attitude. The man seemed intent on forcing a showdown; he was literally itching for a chance to draw.

In the other room Letty was at the same table where they'd eaten. Laramie started over, then paused. Marshal Tate stood at the table where the three prisoners were shackled together.

One of them, a squat powerful man of forty, was talking in a complaining voice. "Marshal, pretty soon those redskins are going to come down on this place like a mountain. And we're going to be sitting ducks, all chained together. How about unchaining us and giving us guns?" He grinned wolfishly. "We sure ain't going nowhere with them out there."

Marshal Tate turned to Laramie with his grin. He

worked his mouth and spat, the brown stream sailing past Laramie to splash into a spittoon to his right. Laramie cursed himself for flinching.

The marshal's grin widened. "What do you think, Nelson? Think we can trust them with iron?"

Laramie was silent, thinking. There was something to be said for the prisoner's reasoning. Yet if one of the three was Regan, the man he was after, to arm him would be asking for a bullet the first time his back was turned.

"Oh, that's right, you ain't met these gents yet." The marshal introduced the three men.

Ben Thomas, a lean man of close to forty with the cold, coiled look of a rattler. Hoke Palmer, the squat man who had complained. And Jed Shaw, the biggest man of the three, with the hulking shoulders and ham-like hands of a blacksmith, who glowered at Laramie on being introduced.

Marshal Tate hesitated over each name, as though uncertain of it.

No mention of a Regan.

Laramie caught Marshal Tate's sly glance, looking for a reaction. Laramie gave him none. He kept a poker face as he said, "I think you'd better arm them, Marshal. We'll be needing all the fire power we can muster."

Laramie turned and started toward Letty's table. He met her gaze. She was hostile and bristling. He veered aside and went through the batwing doors.

He paused on the veranda. Monte, rifle cradled in his arms, leaned against the wall.

Laramie deftly rolled a cigarette and lit it, smoking moodily. He wasn't at all happy with the situation circumstances not of his own doing had placed him in. He could smell disaster ahead, like the rain odor of an approaching storm.

They deputy said bleakly, "Looks like we're caught between the devil and the bad place."

Laramie arrowed a look at him and said shortly,

"Yeah. Looks that way."

He stepped down off the veranda and started up the street. He actually had no destination, no purpose, in mind. He simply wanted to escape the tensions of the saloon for a moment. He had little fear of the Apaches attacking again so soon. They would lay out there for awhile and chant war talk, work themselves up to a fever pitch again before coming in.

Again he was struck by the eerie quiet of the town. If it had been a ghost town, the buildings falling down and deserted, empty of everything but cobwebs and broken furniture, it would have been understandable. But these buildings, most of them anyway, were in good repair, some recently painted, all with washed windows sparkling in the afternoon sunlight.

There were recent tracks of men and animals in the dust of the street. It was unnerving. He could understand a little of the Indians' reluctance to ride in and defy whatever spirits lurked about. It would only take a small exercise of imagination to conjure up ghostly shapes lurking behind windows.

He turned into the livery stable.

Wingfoot was dozing in the heat. He raised his head and nickered as Laramie approached his stall.

Laramie stroked his mane. "Yeah, I know how you feel, hoss. I'd like nothing better than to be riding you hell for leather away from here about now."

Wingfoot tossed his head friskily, then rubbed it against Laramie's hand. Laramie searched his pocket and found the glob of sugar he'd filched from the bowl Toddy had placed on the table. He fed it to Wingfoot, then stepped outside again.

Undecided for a moment, he let his glance rake the street both ways. The only living thing in sight was Monte on the saloon steps.

Laramie turned the other way and started going through the building again. He had little hope of finding

173

anything, but it was something to do, a way to pass the time.

This time he didn't look for anything living, but for a clue to the disappearance. He went through the commercial buildings first, then the houses, taking his time and checking every room thoroughly.

Some rooms had beds unmade, as though the occupants had just vacated them. Laramie resisted a strong urge to test the bedclothes for a residue of body warmth. In some of the houses there was partly eaten food on the table. Clothes hung in all the homes, as though the people fleeing hadn't taken time to pack.

The few cats and dogs he encountered were wary of him, skirting around him wild-eyed and scampering away when he tried to coax them near. Back of one house, he found a kettle full of washing, a heap of cold ashes underneath it.

Then, in one small house, he found something of interest. It was a small diary, filled with a child's scribblings. He sat down and leafed through it, reading it with difficulty.

Apparently it belonged to Marcy, a girl of about fifteen; at least there was a mention of a fifteenth birthday party. Most of the diary was filled with gossip about young friends and was of no use to him.

But the last entry, dated just the day before, caught and held his attention. It was only two paragraphs:

Dear Diary; Today the Marshal was shot down on Front Street. Mommy said he was killed by two bad men. He was buried this morning. Then the menfolks all got mad. They put on their guns and rode out after the two bad men. Mommy didn't want Daddy to go. She said the law should handle it. Daddy said, what law. He said, we have to take care of our own or what was the use. Mommy said, pshaw, men. All they can think of is riding and shooting. After Daddy and the men left, only the ladies and the little kids were left.

*An hour ago a cowboy rode in. His horse was almost
dead from whipping. He said he'd seen a band of Indians
on the warpath and coming this way. We've got nobody to
fight them. We're all going up to the old Holmes Mine in
the hills until our Daddys get back. I don't want to go.
Mommy won't even let me take Rex. I've heard Indians
eat little dogs. What will happen to . . ."*

6

The last word in the diary trailed off with a long pencil
stroke, as though the writer had been interrupted in
mid-sentence.

Laramie Nelson stood deep in thought, bouncing the
diary in his hand, debating whether or not to show it to
the others. It could cause a panic. Yet, if he didn't show it,
giving them an explanation for the disappearance of the
townspeople, they would settle down to wait in the hope
the people would return and rescue them from the
Apaches.

At least his surmise about some mysterious plague was
wrong. He supposed that was something to be grateful
for.

Laramie sighed and pocketed the diary. There was
little choice. He had to pass the information on.

He went outside and stood a moment blinking in the
glare of the sun, which would soon be behind the brown
hills to the west. In the wine-clear air the hills stood out
sharply, their silhouette as well-defined as though snipped
out of tin. Dust stirred in the street before a gust of hot
wind, and a tumbleweed rolled lazily past.

Laramie started back toward the Paradise Saloon.
Passing between two buildings, he glimpsed a lone
Apache several hundred yards out, the Indian and his
pony as still, as malevolent, as the dun-colored hills.

Monte was on the saloon veranda, rifle crooked in his
arm, leaning against a veranda post as though dozing.

A shrill scream ripped the quiet while Laramie was still several yards away. It came from inside the saloon.

Letty!

Laramie broke into a run. As he pounded up the steps and past, Monte, the deputy opened one eye and grinned, then winked.

Laramie burst through the doors and skidded to a stop just inside, his glance raking the room. The big man, Jed Shaw, had Letty backed up against the far wall, her shoulders pinned to it with his ham-like hands. The blouse of her dress had been ripped, and Shaw was trying to capture her mouth with his.

Marshal Tate sat at his table, smiling and watching the scene without moving. The other two prisoners, armed now, watched with vast amusement and egged the big man on.

"Go to it, Jed!"

"Give her a big kiss for us, too!"

Toddy Hawkins, weaving drunkenly, ran up behind the struggling pair. He seized a double handful of Shaw's shirt and tugged. "Leave her alone, you big bastard!"

Without even looking around, Shaw whistled an arm through the air like an axe handle. The arm caught Toddy alongside the head and sent him flying across the room. Desperately trying to regain his balance, he careened into a table. Toddy and the table went down in a tangle of splintered wood.

Laramie was already striding across the room. He considered drawing his Colt, but it was too close quarters for that. Letty could easily catch a stray bullet in a gun battle.

He stopped back out of arm's reach of Shaw. He said quietly, "Let her go, Shaw."

Shaw turned a red, sweating face. His small eyes burned with malice, and Laramie had a sickening hunch he had been set up for this.

"What'll you do if I don't, Pinkerton man?" Shaw

176

asked tauntingly. "Shoot me? I don't carry a gun. Don't need one."

He let Letty go and faced around, great arms swinging out from his sides to show that he was unarmed. One thing seemed certain. If it was true he never carried a gun, it would eliminate him as Darr Regan.

Laramie risked a glance at the others. The two prisoners had grown still and watchful. Marshal Tate was leaning back, a huge grin of enjoyment on his face. Toddy had climbed to his feet, leaning against the wall for support. He shot Laramie a shamed look and shambled off toward the bar.

"Toddy!"

Toddy paused. Laramie drew his Colt in one smooth motion and held it out butt-first. "Hold this for me. And if one of those gents so much as moves an eyelash, shoot him!"

Toddy grinned in delight and hobbled over to take the gun. "Yes sir, hoss! Yes indeedy! I'll do just that!" He backed up until his back was against the wall and turned a fierce scowl on Marshal Tate and the other two prisoners.

Laramie stood easy, slouched, his manner deceptively lazy. "Now I don't have a gun, either, Shaw. Does that make us even?"

With a bull roar the big man charged, huge arms already flailing, reaching. Laramie knew he'd be crushed to death if those arms ever enfolded him. It was like facing an enraged bear. He waited until the last possible instant, then stepped nimbly aside and sank his right fist into the big man's gut with all his strength. Shaw's breath left him with a whoosh, and he staggered on for a few steps before pulling up short and facing about again.

This time he approached more slowly, pig eyes wary, breath whistling. Laramie waited, balanced easily on the balls of his feet. He knew he had only one chance. He couldn't trade punches with the man and hope to win. He had to outlast him, using agility and speed to stay away from those sledgehammer fist. .

Shaw charged again and again, roaring and puffing. Each time Laramie danced just out of his reach, pecking at his face with quick lefts and rights. It was like hitting a boulder. Bits of skin ripped from Shaw's beefy face, and blood flecked it, but more damage was done to Laramie's knuckles. They were soon bruised and bloody. And the blows hardly staggered Shaw.

Now and then Shaw connected. Each time he did it was like being struck by a mallet. Twice Laramie was sent stumbling back against the wall, his head reeling, waves of blackness washing over him. Once he sprawled on the floor and was able to roll away just in time as Shaw came stomping at him with his boots.

Laramie began working on the big man's midsection in earnest. He buried his fists repeatedly in the layers of fat. Soon he noticed some effect. Shaw was markedly slower, his swinging punches wilder. His eyes now had the glare of madness, and Laramie knew he'd kill him without compunction if he got the opportunity.

And then, suddenly, it was all over.

Laramie went in low and hammered two quick, hard blows to Shaw's belly. The man staggered past him, lost his balance and fell to his knees. He remained there for a moment, shaking his head.

He blinked up at Laramie.

"I'll kill you," he mumbled through a bleeding mouth.

Laramie stepped in close, locked his hands together, raised them high and brought them down like a meat axe across the back of the man's neck.

Shaw grunted, shook his head woundedly. Then he collapsed slowly, like a tree falling. The building shook as he struck the floor. Laramie stood over him for a moment, fighting to get his breath.

Shaw didn't move.

Laramie raised his head. The other two prisoners were staring at the prone figure of their comrade in stunned disbelief. Marshal Tate's face showed nothing. Now, as he met Laramie's glance, he raised his glass in a mocking tribute.

At the sound of footsteps Laramie turned. Letty, who had remained huddled against the wall all during the fight, was hurrying toward him. She touched her fingers gently to his face. She held the torn front of her dress together with her other hand.

"Your poor face."

A grinning Toddy bustled over, holding out the Colt. "That was some scrape, hoss. That big feller is big enough to take on a whole troop of cavalry. I didn't think you had a chance."

"You know something? I didn't either," Laramie said. He holstered the Colt. "And I lucked out at that."

Letty seized his hand. "Come on, Let's see what we can do with that face."

Laramie allowed her to lead him toward the kitchen. She found a pail of water and a washcloth. As she started to dab at his face, she forgot and let the torn dress gape open. She flushed scarlet and turned around, fumbling in her pocket for a pin. After a moment she faced him again, the dress pinned together clumsily.

She said angrily, "Just because you got that big brute off me, don't think that gives you—rights!"

"Rights? I don't know what you're talking about." His own temper ignited. "Damned if you're not about the thorniest female I ever came across!"

"You'd be thorny too, if you'd—" Tears stood in her eyes. She shook her head violently, as though to dash them away. "Oh, to the devil with it!"

She dipped the washcloth in the basin and began to scrub at the blood on his face. She was rough, hurting. Laramie endured it stoically. Then she probed at a cut on his lip. It hurt, and he winced.

She was instantly contrite. "Oh, I'm sorry, Laramie! I'm a—I should not take it out on you," Her manner softened, and she smiled tremulously. "I'm grateful for what you did for me. You could have been killed. I'm not used to men doing that for me. I guess that's the reason—"

"It was my pleasure," he said with false solemnity. "A good barroom brawl tones up the muscles."

She worked on his face again, gently this time. In a little while she stood back, the basin pink with his blood, and studied him critically. "There! At least you're cleaned up. Of course, it may hurt you to shave for awhile."

He ran his fingers over his face, feeling the various cuts and bruises. He hadn't shaved since the day before, and he could feel the pricking stubble of beard against his fingers.

"Thank you, Letty."

"You're welcome, I'm sure." She stood on tiptoe and brushed his cheek with her lips. Then she turned red again and whirled away.

Toddy came with two steaming mugs of coffee. "I added a little something to yours, hoss. Figured you could use it."

"Much obliged, Toddy."

Cupping the hot mug between his hands, Laramie moved to the window and looked out. Two Apaches stood their horses about two hundred yards away. He felt certain they would be attacking again soon, probing, feeling out the strength they had to face.

Letty moved up alongside him, sipping at the coffee. She gazed out at the Indians.

"Will we ever get out of this? Maybe when the townspeople come back?"

Uncomfortably aware of the diary in his pocket, Laramie said somewhat gruffly, "We'll make it out, one way or another. Depend on it."

She was silent for a moment. Then she went on in a low voice, almost as though talking to herself. "You know those women in Copper Springs—I guess they were right according to their lights. They figured I represented a threat to their security as wives and sweethearts. This country is hard on women."

Her voice took on a note of bitterness. "A few years of marriage, bearing children, hard work, hard times, a woman no longer looks attractive to her man. I was born and raised on a ranch, too, you know. A small one, true. Then my mother died. My father started to drink heavily. He mortgaged the ranch down to the last penny. He finally lost it and proceeded to drink himself to death. There was no money left. I was eighteen. I had to do anything I could in order to eat. I waited tables, worked in a dress shop—What choice is there for a woman out here? You either get married, and I couldn't find a man I'd spit on, much less marry, or you do what I finally did.

"You become a saloon woman. But you don't have to do what some of them do to survive. You have to fight off that part of it, but I guess the women in Copper Springs thought I was like all the rest. I can sing and dance a little." She threw her head back, giving Laramie a burning look of defiance. "That's how I made my way, not by taking drunken cowboys up the back stairs to my room. Not that I'm all that goody-goody.

"I've done some things I'm ashamed of. Had to do them to survive. Sometimes I've thought, what's the use? You've got the name, why not play the game? But I never did!" She had worked herself up into a flashing-eyed temper. "I never did. You hear?"

"I hear. And I believe you," Laramie said soothingly.

"Then you're one of the few who do!" she said hotly. "Those animals in there don't. And that includes the marshal and his fat deputy!"

"Yeah, so you've told me. So settle down. Don't get all het up."

She heaved a weighty sigh. "You're right. We have enough to worry about without me hanging all my troubles out to dry. You know, I've never talked of these things to anyone else. Why now, do you suppose?"

Letty looked up at him, faint color touching her face

again. "I guess I do know. You're that kind of a person. You've got a face that appeals to weeping women—"

"And to cats and dogs and horses?" he said lightly.

She laughed, abruptly in a better mood. "Yes! Those too, I'm sure."

Letty glanced around. Toddy straddled a chair backward, facing out through the window, back to them, a bottle in one hand. Letty stood on tiptoe again and kissed Laramie on the mouth. Her lips were soft and sweet. But she stepped quickly back, face pink as a sunset, gaze averted.

For a saloon woman, Laramie thought sardonically, she does a lot of blushing. He wondered if Marcy, at fifteen. . . .

He touched the diary in his pocket. He didn't want to tell them, but it had to be done. "Let's go into the other room. There's something I have to say." He raised his voice. "You too, Toddy."

7

Obediently they followed Laramie Nelson into the barroom. Marshal Tate was still at his table, working on a bottle. Shaw sat at a table alone, his bloody, battered face brooding. There was a bottle before him, too. It was almost empty, and Shaw was well on his way toward getting drunk.

He glanced up as Laramie came in, and his deep-set eyes blazed with pure hate.

The other two were at the same table, not drunk, just boisterous, talking together in loud voices. They fell silent as Laramie and the others entered.

Laramie stopped at a point midway between the tables, Letty beside him. Toddy went directly to the bar, humming under his breath.

Laramie said, "There's something I think I'd better tell you all. Awhile ago I went through the house again. This time I found something." He took the diary from his pocket.

Marshal Tate sat up alertly. "What is it?"

"A diary. Belongs to a young girl, I gather. She had been keeping it up to date until yesterday." He read them the last page of the diary.

When he was done Marshal Tate grunted, eyes squinting in thought. A curse came from the table where the two prisoners sat.

Letty uttered a small cry. "That means they won't be coming back any time soon. At least, too late to help us any." She clapped a hand over her mouth, eyes stricken.

"I'm afraid it means just that, Letty," Laramie said soberly.

"Marshal." It was one of the prisoners, the one called Hoke Palmer. "What do we do now, Marshal? Set here and lose our scalps to those damned redskins?"

Marshal Tate batted a hand at him to be quiet. "Hey, barfly! What do you know about this marshal killing yesterday?"

Toddy was leaning on the bar, a bottle by his elbow. "Yep, I knew about that. Marshal Coburn was a good old boy. Everbody liked him. Blasted shame about him."

"What happened, Toddy?" Laramie asked.

"Well, I was just getting to that, hoss." Toddy paused to take a drink. "These two hardcases rode in here around noon yesterday. They was a here, drinking up a storm. One hombre got real drunk and mean. He threw Sam—that's the barkeep—through the door and he and the other hardcase started serving themselves.

"Marshal Coburn came to arrest them. He's past sixty, was the marshal. Fast in his day, but he'd slowed up some, and there ain't much call around here these days for gunplay. These hardcases gunned him down. He was dead before he hit the floor."

"But what about all the men riding out after them?"

Toddy shrugged. "Don't know nothing about that. Oh,

there was some talk about a posse. Like I said, he was some popular." He grinned. "This was all before I passed out. I don't know what happened after."

Palmer pounded on the table with his glass. "All this ain't getting us anywhere, Marshal. What are we going to do?"

"I'll have to think on it."

"Think on it! You think long enough we'll all end up dead, with our hair lifted."

Marshal Tate slowly stood up. He turned his head and aimed an accurate brown stream at the nearest spitoon. Although he was still smiling, he was somehow cold and deadly, and Laramie realized again just how dangerous this man could be.

"I gave you men guns against my better judgment, because I thought it might help save your necks. But I'm still the marshal, I still run things, I still give the orders. Don't you forget that for one damned minute, any of you! I can take all of you, one at a time, or all three at once. If you don't think so, try me. Go ahead and try me!"

Palmer didn't move, but he was already backing down, his face paling under the black stubble of beard.

"Hell, Marshal," he whined. "I didn't mean nothing like that. It's just that we're worried about our scalps. I don't see how you can fault us for that."

"Then keep your traps shut or I'll take all that iron away and chain you up again." Marshal Tate spun on Laramie, as though seeking any target for his venom. "And that goes for you, too, Pinkerton man. I'm running things here."

"Concerning your prisoners, sure, Marshal," Laramie drawled. "Speaking for the rest of us, I'd say you're a little out of your jurisdiction."

"I'm speaking as Bart Tate, not Marshal Tate, and my jurisdiction is where I chose to make it. And you're beginning to try my patience. You disagree with anything I've said, spit it out!"

Laramie had had more than enough of Marshal Bart Tate. He let his hand hang close to his Colt. It was a tense moment. A small cry came from Letty, abruptly shut off as though she'd stuffed a hand into her mouth.

All of a sudden the batwing doors swung back, and Monte burse in, yelling, "They're coming again!"

The words were barely out of his mouth before a rattle of gunfire sounded outside.

"All right, Monte," Marshal Tate snapped. "Back out there and keep an eye on the street. If they come at us that way, yell out. Shaw and Palmer upstairs, at the back rooms upstairs. I want to see some dead redsticks when this attack is over. Now get cracking."

Laramie led the way to the kitchen, Letty and Toddy right behind him. As they assumed positions at the window, Laramie resting his Winchester on the window-sill, Letty said breathlessly, "I thought there was going to be a showdown between you and Bart this time."

"It'll come sooner or later," Laramie said tautly. He snapped off a shot and missed. He muttered angrily under his breath, then raised his voice. "I see no way around it. We're bristling at each other like two strange dogs."

"But he seems to be pushing it. Why is that? I know he's mean, I told you that. But why is he spoiling for trouble with you?"

Laramie remembered thinking along the same lines earlier. It did seem the marshal was going out of his way for a showdown. Was it because one of the three prisoners was Darr Regan and the marshal didn't want him taken back and was willing to kill Laramie to prevent it? Then why had he sent the wire in the first place? None of it made much sense.

The Apaches closed in, yelling and firing, and Laramie was too busy for the next few minutes to give much thought to anything else. He fired steadily and methodically. By his side, Letty used his Colt quite effectively. She was level-headed under fire and a very good shot.

It lasted for a quarter hour, and the Apaches crowded in much closer this time. Bullets whined through the room. Once a bunch of arrows, grouped together like a flock of birds, whistled through the window. Laramie threw an arm around Letty's shoulders and bore her to the floor. After a moment he risked a glance over the sill.

The Apaches were pounding away out of range. Laramie snapped off a couple of shots. His rifle barrel was hot to the touch. The Indians had left behind three dead this time.

Laramie glanced down the room. Marshal Tate, his face frozen in that eternal amiable grin, was standing at the other window, carelessly exposed, staring after the fleeing Apaches.

Now he turned to Laramie. "You did good, Pinkerton man. We all did good."

"Yeah, but we're only postponing the inevitable," Laramie said sourly, "and you know it."

The marshal turned his head, spat out the shattered window, then strode back into the other room.

Laramie glanced the other way. Toddy was still kneeling, gingerly fingering his scalp. Blood flowed freely.

"Toddy! You're hit!" Laramie hurried over to him.

The man took his hand away and grinned weakly. "It's only a scratch." He groped along the shelf beside the window for his bottle and tipped his head back, his throat working convulsively as he swallowed greedily.

Letty was there again with a basin of water and a washcloth. She scrubbed the blood away gently and examined the wound. It was only a shallow gouge. The seepage of blood was already slowing.

"It's not too bad," she said in relief.

"I told you, just a scratch," Toddy said with a cackle of laughter.

Laramie gave Letty time to cleanse the wound, then herded them back into the barroom. Marshal Tate was at the same table, the three prisoners lined up at theirs. They were all drinking, the prisoners raucous, crowing over what they considered the rout of the Apaches.

Laramie's thoughts were bleak. At this rate they would all be drunk soon, too drunk to hold a gun, and the Apaches could storm in and take them without firing a shot. He led Letty to a table away from the others.

"I'm going outside for a look around."

She clutched at his arm. "Laramie, don't leave me alone with them!"

"You'll be all right. They're too busy drinking to bother with you. And I'll be within hearing all the time. Here—" He thumped his Winchester down onto the table. "If they get frisky, don't hesitate to shoot."

He went on outside without glancing at the others. Monte was sitting on the top step, rifle across his lap. Laramie's glance swept both ways along the street. It was deserted. The sun was edging toward the distant hills. It would be dark soon.

Laramie stopped at the steps to roll a cigarette. "Anything?"

"Nope," Monte said. "Quiet as a grave. Funny, ain't it, them not coming into town? Always said an Indian ain't the guts of a rabbit."

"Consider yourself lucky or you'd be dead by now," Laramie said grimly.

He lit the cigarette and stepped down into the street. He turned toward the livery stable, intent on checking Wingfoot. He was unhappy about leaving the animal unguarded all this time, but he knew they couldn't spare a man to watch the stable.

At the stable door he toed out his cigarette, then stepped inside, blinking at the abrupt change from bright sunlight to interior dimness.

Almost too late, he heard a swishing sound and a grunt, then a body struck him in the middle of the back, sending him crashing to the ground. His nostrils filled with the rancid grease and woodsmoke odor of Apache, and he cursed his carelessness. He'd been worried about the horses being left unguarded, and he'd stepped right into an ambush, as stupid as any tenderfoot.

He felt a knee in the small of his back, strong fingers tangled in his hair, and he snapped out of the daze just in time to twist his head sharply to one side. A tomahawk whistled past his face with less than an inch to spare and buried itself to the hilt in the ground.

Laramie arched his back and rolled violently to one side. The Apache, overbalanced by his tomahawk's near miss, was thrown off.

Laramie came up on one knee, hand clawing for his Colt.

It wasn't in the holster!

His glance darted to the left. The gun lay in the dust, over ten feet away. Much too far.

He looked back at the Apache in time to see him coming full speed, tomahawk raised high, breech-cloth flapping, stained teeth bared in a snarl of hatred.

Laramie waited until the Apache was close enough so the yellow, hate-filled eyes seemed to fill Laramie's whole world, waited until the tomahawk started its deadly swoop down. Then he launched himself, low, under the slash of the weapon. His shoulder struck the Indian in the belly.

The Apache's breath left him with a whoosh.

Laramie dug his boots into the ground for traction. Then he was driving his attacker back, back until they rammed together into a stable wall.

The impact broke them apart. Laramie fell rolling and was up on his feet instantly, crouching, weaving, his darting glance seeking out the Apache.

He was down on all fours, glaring up. The tomahawk was gone. But just inches from his hand was a pitchfork, prongs buried in a pile of hay. The Indian saw it the same instant as did Laramie. With a cat-like twist the Apache was on his feet. He snatched up the pitchfork and began stalking Laramie Nelson with it.

They were in a stall, and Laramie was cornered. There was no way out of the stall except past the Apache and the pitchfork. A ray of sunlight came through a crack in the rear wall, glinting off the pitchfork prongs like cold fire.

Laramie weaved back and forth, going from one wall to the other in the stall. The Indian was close now, his mouth open in a soundless scream, the pitchfork held high and in both hands.

Laramie plastered himself in the corner, both arms back against the wall, his eyes wide, as though frozen there with sheer panic. The Apache sprang the last few feet, a high yell of triumph keening from him. The three prongs came down, aiming for Laramie's throat.

At the last instant Laramie dropped like a stone.

The pitchfork thumped into the wall where Laramie's neck had been, sinking into the soft wood, vibrating like a tuning fork. The Apache was jarred loose and sent staggering back.

Laramie surged to his feet, reaching up for the pitchfork handle. He wrapped his hands around it and jerked with all his strength. The fork came free.

All in the same motion Laramie spun around, jabbing out blindly with the pitchfork.

The Apache, in the act of charging, impaled himself on the pitchfork, the prongs going in just below his rib cage. A scream of agony was ripped from him. His hands clawed at the sunken pitchfork, trying unsuccessfully to remove it. Blood gushed out around his fingers. He reeled back, bounced off the side of the stall, then collapsed like an empty sack, his eyes already wide and staring.

8

Laramie Nelson, nausea boiling up in his throat like bile, stumbled past the dead Apache and toward the open stable door.

As he passed Wingfoot's stall, the horse whinnied.

"It's all right, hoss," Laramie said weakly. "It's all right now."

He leaned against the open door, his lungs gulping in draughts of air.

It had been a close call. He couldn't remember when he'd been so near death.

He rolled a cigarette with fingers that still trembled slightly. The smoke had a bitter taste on his tongue. He took two deep drags on it, then put it out. He started out of the stable, veered back inside to pluck his Colt out of the dust. Using his bandana, he wiped it free of dust and holstered it.

Outside once more, he trudged up the street. The sun had just gone down behind the low hills to the west. Otherwise, nothing had changed along the street; apparently the fracas had gone unnoticed. Laramie was tired. He couldn't recall ever being so bone-tired. Standing off the Indian attacks, the fight with Shaw, now the fight with the Apache—it had all taken a lot out of him.

His weariness and the deserted town depressed him. For a brief moment he played with the thought of forking Wingfoot and riding out, trying to battle his way through the circling Apaches. The odds were heavy against his making it, especially in daylight, but it would be better than this.

Hell, anything would be better than this!

Then he squared his shoulders, a spare smile curving his mouth, and quickened his pace. He had decided what he was going to do. He didn't look at Monte as he went up the steps into the saloon.

Inside the scene was little changed, except the prisoners were quieter now.

Letty looked up as Laramie entered, a quick smile breaking across her face. Toddy leaned on one elbow on the bar, hugging a bottle.

Laramie crossed to Letty's table. In a low voice he asked, "Is everything all right? Did they bother you?"

"No, nobody made a move," she said softly. "But I'm glad to see you back."

"It may not be for long," he muttered.

Alarm blazed in her gray eyes. "What do you mean?"

He turned away without answering, took a few steps toward Marshal Tate's table. "Marshal, the time's growing short. They're going to get over their fear of spirits. One brave just screwed up enough courage to come in. He jumped me in the livery stable."

The marshal jumped to his feet, face darkening. "And you let him get away to carry the word to the others!"

"No, I did not let him get away. But the point is, others will be filtering in. All it takes is for one to get back to the others and pass the word that there's nothing to fear, no spirits. Then, come morning, they'll pour down that street out there like flood waters."

Marshal Tate dropped back into his chair. "So what do you suggest, Pinkerton man?"

"One of us has to ride for help," Laramie said bluntly. "It'll be dark soon. One man stands a chance. Not very good maybe, but a chance."

"And just who do you nominate for this heroic job?" the marshal asked, head cocked to one side.

Laramie hesitated, then said slowly, "I'm the logical one."

A smothered cry came from Letty. The prisoners stirred restlessly, muttering.

Marshal Tate laughed softly. "Now just how do you figure that one?"

"Well, you can't go, neither you nor your deputy. You have your prisoners to take care of." It was Laramie's private opinion that if either the marshal or his deputy could break free they would keep right on going without a thought of sending back help. "Certainly it can't be either Letty or Toddy. Or one of the prisoners. You know they wouldn't come back."

Marshal Tate turned his head and spat a brown stream without bothering with the spittoon. "And you, Nelson. How do we know you would come back?"

"You have my word on it," Laramie said somewhat stiffly.

"Your word!" Marshal Tate laughed raucously. Hoke Palmer joined in uncertainly. "We'd never see your tail again. Strikes me you're just itching to get away, Nelson."

"I'll be back. Nothing else, I'll be back for one of your prisoners, the one named Regan."

"Regan? Yep, you mentioned him. But none of 'em admitted to being this Regan," Marshal Tate said blandly. "Now did they?"

"You know which one he is."

"And you think I'm going to tell you?"

"You'll tell me," Laramie said grimly.

"We'll see, we'll see," the marshal said comfortably.

Out of the corner of his eye Laramie saw Letty motioning to him. He crossed to her table and sat down.

In an urgent whisper she said, "Laramie, you're not riding off and leave me with them?"

He sighed heavily. "Letty, somebody has to do something. We can't just sit here and wait to be butchered. And I'm the logical one to go, Can't you see that? They won't dare do anything to you, not when they know they'll have to account for it later."

"That's all you know. You're like all the rest," she said with a burst of the earlier bitterness. "To you, I'm nothing but a saloon woman, fit for nothing else."

"Letty, I never said that, and I don't think that."

He tried to take her hand, but she jerked it away.

"Leave me alone!"

"Hey, Pinkerton man!" Marshal Tate said in a jeering voice. "What are you two whispering about? You going to take her with you? Use her out there for bait? They wouldn't have her. They're too particular."

Laramie looked at him without answering. His glance moved to the window. While he'd been inside, the desert night had fallen fast. It was pitch black outside. Toddy Hawkins was going around the saloon lighting lamps.

Laramie reached back for his Winchester leaning against the wall and got to his feet. "Toddy?"

Toddy looked around. "Yes, hoss?"

"Go to the door and call that deputy in here. Tell him he's needed at once." Laramie swung the rifle to cover the men at the other tables. "The first one of you to make a wrong move gets an arm shot off."

Marshal Tate's right hand jerked toward the edge of the table.

Laramie brought the rifle to bear directly on him. "Touch your gun, Marshal, and I'll kill you."

The marshal's lips drew back over yellowed teeth in a wolfish grin, but his hand stopped moving. Carefully he inched it forward until it was wrapped around his glass once more. "So you're turning tail on us, huh?"

"Call it what you want," Laramie said unemotionally. "Toddy?"

"Yes, hoss, I'm going."

Laramie didn't take his gaze from the four men as he listened to Toddy's uneven footsteps toward the door.

Letty said tightly, "You're going, then?"

"I'm going, Letty. I have no choice. But you'll be all right. I'll be back. That's a promise."

He heard Toddy call to the man outside. He risked a glance at the door as Monte appeared, halting abruptly.

Laramie motioned with the Winchester. "Over there with your boss, Monte. And don't try anything foolish. Leave your rifle by the door."

The man placed his rifle against the wall and drifted down the room to the marshal's table, his gaze never leaving Laramie.

Laramie said, "Toddy, go down to the livery stable and saddle my horse. He's in the second stall on the left going

193

in. Bring him back and tie him to the rail outside."

"Sure, hoss, right away." Toddy hurried out again.

"I hope those redsticks catch you and lift your scalp," the marshal said with sudden viciousness. "But not before they tie you to an anthill for a couple hours first."

"You'd better hope that doesn't happen," Laramie drawled. "They'll stay out there tonight. But come sunup, they'll be moving in. You won't stand a chance in hell unless I'm back with some help by then."

"Oh, sure, you'll be back! We'll never see you again, Pinkerton man. You're yellow. You're running to save your own hide."

"If that's true, then you're better off without me." Laramie darted a glance at Letty. "You'll be all right, Letty. I'll tell Toddy to keep an eye on you."

"Toddy! He'll be about as much help as a housecat." She half rose to her feet as Laramie began edging toward the door. "Laramie, don't—" Then she subsided with a shrug. Her full mouth curved in a crooked smile, and she said softly, "I'm sorry. I'm thinking of nobody but myself. Good luck, Laramie. And be careful out there, you hear?"

Laramie acknowledged her concern with a nod, his glance jumping back to the other men. They all waited in tense silence until Laramie heard the thud of hooves in the street.

Laramie said, "You all stay put until I'm long gone. I'm giving Toddy my Winchester and instructions to shoot anyone who pokes his nose through that door. Toddy may be a barfly, but he can shoot real good. You know that, Marshal, you saw him."

The marshal gestured, turned his head and spat contemptuously. "Go on, Nelson. Hightail it! Good riddance to you!"

Laramie backed through the batwing doors and turned to Toddy, who stood on the top step. It was so dark he could barely make out Wingfoot saddled and waiting at the hitching rail.

194

He held out the Winchester. In a voice loud enough to be heard inside, he said, "Shoot the first man who sticks his head through that door, Toddy. Hold 'em in there until I'm away and gone."

Toddy drew back. "But hoss, I ain't no gunnie."

"You can shoot. I watched you!" Laramie deliberately made his voice rough, abrasive. "Now's your chance to be a man. Show that marshal in there that you're more than a barfly." He lowered his voice. "Toddy, do you believe I'll come back?"

"Well, sure, if you can. You ain't the kind of a man who'd—"

"Well then?" He jabbed the rifle, butt first, into Toddy's midsection.

This time Toddy took it, his face blooming in a slow grin. He seemed to stand taller. "By God, I will! Yes indeedy!"

"And watch out for Letty, will you? If they get nasty with her, whistle a bullet alongside their head!"

He started down the steps.

"Mr. Nelson" Toddy's voice was soft. "Good luck, hoss. You're sure by God going to need it out there!"

Laramie waved a hand without looking back. He spoke gently to Wingfoot and gathered up the reins without mounting up. He led the horse down the street a distance, then turned in between two buildings.

At the end of the alleyway he paused. It was cooler now, and the desert looked like an unbroken field of snow stretching away toward the end of the world. The night was clear, moonless, the heavens vaulting overhead, distant stars glittering like an inverted field of diamonds.

Laramie stood perfectly still for a long time, letting his vision adjust to the darkness. Nothing moved out there. The only sound was the far-off howl of a coyote, lonely and quivering in the still air like a lost soul's plea for help. Laramie strained his eyes until his head began to ache but he could see a little.

The Apaches were out there. It was a feeling, a sort of sixth sense. But he knew they were there, and they would be alert for anyone trying to slip through them. Laramie figured he had one slight advantage. They were spread pretty thin. If he had exceptional luck, he could drift through the cordon without being noticed.

He also knew it wasn't likely to be all that easy. The Apaches also had a sixth sense, the instincts of a hunted animal, unusually good hearing, and a strong sense of smell.

A misplaced pebble, just a whiff of the scent of the hated white man, and they'd be on him, raging, ablaze with a killing lust.

Laramie longed for a cigarette, but he couldn't risk it. He didn't know how much time he had before those in the Paradise Saloon might work up enough courage to push past Toddy and come looking for him.

Yet there was one thing he had to do. It should have been done in the stable, with the aid of a light, but he couldn't have trusted the job to Toddy.

He fumbled behind the saddle and unknotted the saddle blanket. With his knife, working as quietly as possible, he ripped it into four roughly equal pieces, then sliced off four long narrow strips.

He spoke soothingly to Wingfoot, then knelt by the animal's front leg and raised it off the ground. He wrapped a piece of the blanket around the hoof and used a narrow strip to tie it as securely as possible.

Working in the dark, working by feel, he had no way of knowing how efficient the job was. Finally it was done, all four of the animal's hooves muffled. He stood and roughed Wingfoot's ear.

"Now you're going to have to be quiet, hoss. Or we'll both end up as fodder for the buzzards come morning."

Laramie knew the Apaches would be concentrated the heaviest on the road coming in and leading out of Indigo Flats, so he led Wingfoot due east, at a right angle from the road. Earlier, he'd spotted a deep gully in that direction, probably a dry wash. He had to stay off high ground. Even on a night as dark as this one, a man and a horse could still be seen lined against the skyline.

He went very slowly, stopping every few yards to listen intently. The mouth of the gully was about a half mile away. Soon he was in it, the night looming darker on both sides.

The floor of the gully was strewn with small boulders. Laramie stumbled a couple of times, but Wingfoot picked his way daintily around the rocks. The thud of his hooves barely audible.

But Laramie knew that an Apache with his ear to the ground could detect the faint tremors set up. He moved deeper into the gully, more cautious with each step. They were in the most dangerous territory now, roughly at the edge of the circle of Apaches.

Then it happened.

"Ai-ee!"

9

The shrill yell sounded off to the right and up on the ridge above the gully. Gunfire bloomed orange in the night, and a bullet pinged off a rock a few yards to Laramie Nelson's right.

He vaulted into the saddle in one supple twist and sank his spurs cruelly into Wingfoot's flanks. Wingfoot snorted at the unexpected jab and bolted.

Laramie sent him pounding down the wash. Gunfire poured down at him from both sides, bullets pelting around him like a deadly rainfall.

Laramie didn't bother drawing his Colt to return fire. He knew it would be a waste of bullets, and would only serve to make him a better target.

Then one bullet found him, slamming into his left shoulder. The impact was severe. Only by grabbing at the saddle horn at the last possible moment was he able to remain in the saddle.

The pain came in a little while, came in waves of agony. He held on grimly, clinging to the saddle horn with both hands. He let Wingfoot have his head, made no attempt to guide him.

The gully opened up, the ground leveling out, and Wingfoot ran flat out. The gunfire fell behind, reduced to flashes of fire like pinpricks in the dark, then fell behind entirely. Laramie let Wingfoot run on for a couple of miles.

Finally he reined him in, then slid out of the saddle. Pain pounded at him as his boots hit the ground, and he had to hold on to the saddle as waves of dizziness assaulted him. It passed after a little while, leaving a dull throb in his shoulder.

Wingfoot was sweating heavily, his sides working like giant bellows. Laramie listened intently for sounds of pursuit. He could hear nothing. Evidently the Apaches had given up and gone back to the ones they had pinned down instead of chasing a great horse and one white-eye through the night.

Laramie began walking Wingfoot slowly. If the horse cooled off standing still, he'd get stiff, might even go lame. As he walked the animal, Laramie began working his way back west. Eventually he would hit the road going out of Indigo Flats to the west, toward the range of brown hills. There was a good-sized town about a four-hour ride in that direction.

The pressing question was, could he make it that far in time?

His shoulder wound throbbed. He probed at it gingerly, could feel no fresh blood, but the waves of pain nearly drove him to the ground. From the saddle bags he took an extra shirt, tore two strips from it and wadded it around the wound, then used the rest of the shirt to make a crude sling.

198

He pulled Wingfoot in and knelt in the dust. Most of the blanket strips had been torn off during the hard run. Laramie removed what remained, then felt along the horse's legs and flanks. Wingfoot was dry now, his breathing no longer labored.

"It's going to be a long night, hoss," Laramie muttered, "and it's going to be up to you from here on."

With difficulty he mounted up and set Wingfoot at a faster pace, letting him pick his way in the dark. It was mostly flat country now, with only a few shrubs along the ground, and Wingfoot never faltered once. An hour later they hit the trail Laramie had been seeking. He turned Wingfoot west and clucked at him. The horse flowed easily into a ground-eating lope. The animal had an easy stride. Even so, every time his front hooves struck the ground, the pain in Laramie's shoulder was excruciating.

He hung on grimly. Now that the Apaches knew someone had broken clear of their ring and was likely on the way for help, they would be certain to attack the saloon at first daylight. Laramie figured he had about eight hours, and most of that would be taken up with the ride to the next town and the ride back.

If he could find anybody willing to ride back with him.

Time seemed to stretch out before him like a road into eternity. He suffered through long periods of near-unconsciousness, searing flashes of pain keeping him from going under. He did pass out at times, but only for a few minutes at a time.

And then, without any warning or transition, Laramie found himself lying on the ground, his face in the dirt, something cold and wet nudging his neck.

He had fallen out of the saddle, and the something cold was Wingfoot's nose. Laramie climbed slowly and painfully to his feet, using first the stirrup, the saddle girth, then the saddle itself to pull himself erect. He had absolutely no way of knowing how long he'd been on the ground unconscious. It was still dark, of course, but that could mean anything from a few minutes to half the night.

His face was dry, hot, his lips cracked, and his thirst was something terrible. He was burning up with fever. And in his haste to get away, he'd committed the unforgivable error. He'd ridden out into a desert country without a canteen of water. The wound felt spongy and wet; he knew it had started bleeding again.

It took him a long to climb into the saddle again. Wingfoot stood patiently, without moving, once or twice turning his head and nudging Laramie's leg with his nose, as though trying to boost him up.

Laramie finally made it aboard. He removed his belt and looped it tightly around one thigh and then around the saddle horn. If he went under again, at least he wouldn't tumble out of the saddle.

He clucked to Wingfoot, his voice fuzzy. "Move along, hoss. Move along."

Wingfoot started at a walk and no amount of urging would make him move faster. Finally Laramie prodded him with the spurs. A second time in one night. Wingfoot loosed a snort of indignation and broke into a gallop.

More time passed, for Laramie a time of agony, of even briefer periods of consciousness, the rest pain-filled blackness.

Abruptly he became aware that Wingfoot was standing still. The horse had his neck arched around, nudging Laramie's leg. With an effort Laramie opened his eyes and forced himself erect. They were in a town, and Wingfoot was standing at a hitching rail before a saloon. A few wall bracket lamps along the street were lit, but the street was deserted. There was a faint light coming from inside the saloon, but no sounds of human activity.

For a moment Laramie thought that Wingfoot had somehow turned around and taken him back to Indigo Flats and the Paradise Saloon. Then his blurred gaze made out the sign over the door: *Last Chance Saloon.*

Laramie called weakly, called again. He received no

response. It had to be very late; probably everyone was asleep. With care he unbuckled the belt from around the saddle horn and eased to the ground, clinging to Wingfoot for support.

He drew his Colt and fired it into the air, waited a moment and fired it again. He saw lights go on in some of the buildings, heard the murmur of voices.

Laramie fired a third time, lost his grip on the saddle and slid slowly to the ground.

Dimly he heard footsteps pounding toward him. Dimly he heard snatches of conversation:

"—drunk, most likely—"

"A shame, being woke up in the middle of the—"

"No! He's hurt! Look! Hurt bad!"

Gentle hands picked him up and started carrying him.

"Get the doc, somebody!"

Laramie fought to stay conscious, but he lost the battle, and a wave of blackness moved over him. He sank down and down, drowning in it.

He awoke to pain like a red hot poker rammed into his shoulder. A plump, kindly face swam before his eyes, and a voice said soothingly, "It's all right, cowboy. I've found the slug. It'll be out in a minute."

"I've come for help—" The words came from Laramie in a straining whisper.

"You're getting help." The doctor, if that was who he was, winked companionably. "What do you think I'm doing, using your shoulder for a checkerboard?"

"No—don't understand. Have to talk to your marshal—"

"Plenty of time for that in the morning. Whoever did this to you won't have time to get far—"

Laramie seized the doctor by the arm, fingers digging in with all his strength. "No, no—"

Then the pain slammed into him again, and he passed out.

A girl was chasing a small dog that always kept the

same distance in front of her. "Rex, Rex... Don't run away! Come back, come back!"

Laramie struggled along behind the girl trying to catch up. "Marcy, Marcy! Wait, wait! don't leave There's no plague, nothing is going to hurt you."

Behind him a mocking voice roared, "That's what *you* think, Pinkerton man!"

With an enormous effort Laramie twisted his head around. Right behind him came Marshal Tate. The marshal laughed uproariously, worked his mouth and spat. A brown stream came at Laramie like a bullet. He twisted and dodged and squirmed, but there was no avoiding it. It slammed into his shoulder.

Laramie cried out and came fully awake. He was stretched out full-length on the bar in a small saloon, several men gathered around him. The man whose face he'd seen earlier was nearby, just closing a small black bag.

He saw Laramie looking at him. He winked as he had before. "You'll be fine, son. A week or so of staying flat on your back and you'll be fine."

Laramie remembered. Everything came flooding back. He struggled to sit up, clutching at the doctor's arm.

"Easy now, easy." The doctor tried to stretch him out again.

Laramie resisted. "You don't understand! Is there a marshal here?"

A lean man with a full black beard stepped into Laramie's vision. "I'm the town constable, Ned Watson. Only law we've got around her."

"I came for help. Seven people... Pinned down by Apaches in Indigo Flats—"

The constable laughed with a flash of strong white teeth. "Apaches! You must be joshing us or out of your head with the fever. Ain't had an Apache on the warpath around these parts in four, five years now."

"Renegades. At least I think that's what they are."

Laramie swallowed, waited for his voice to steady. "You know Marshal Tate?"

Watson nodded. "Sure. Bart Tate's marshal of Copper Springs."

"Well, he was taking a wagon load of prisoners to Yuma. They were waylaid just outside of Indigo Flats. They're held down there now. And they'll be massacred come morning, if they don't get some help."

Watson's yellowish eyes quickened, but he still remained skeptical. "How about the men folk of Indigo Flats? Can't be all that many redskins, if you're telling us the gospel, that they can't staind them off."

"The town was empty of people when we rode in. Everybody had left, men and women."

"Ah now! Everybody just up and rode off, leaving their town to taken over by a band of Apach?"

"No, that isn't the reason." Laramie tried to reach into his trouser pocket. The doctor restrained him. "Constable, I'm not just some saddle tramp yarning you. I'm with the Pinkerton Agency. I have papers in my back pocket to prove it."

Watson and the doctor exchanged looks.

"What do you think, Doc?"

"Least we can do is check."

The doctor probed in Laramie's back pocket. Laramie lay back, exhausted, as the two men read the papers.

Watson scrubbed at his chin. "Seems you're on the up and up. Doc. Is he out of his head?"

The doctor shook his head. "No, he's weak from loss of blood, but I'd say he's clearheaded enough."

"All right then!" Watson became crisp, commanding. "Jake, roust out every able-bodied man who can ride and shoot. Have them in front of the saloon here in thirty minutes. Get a move on!"

The man called Jake left the saloon in a dead run. Laramie, through a combination of will and painful physical effort, managed to sit up and swing his feet off the bar.

The doctor glanced around in time to see him.

"Here now!" he said in alarm. "You can't be sitting up. You have to spend at least a week in bed."

Laramie said stubbornly, "I'm riding with them, Doc. I have to. I promised somebody. Besides, I have a job to do back there."

"You ride, it's against my advice."

"Against your advice or not, I'm riding." He grinned weakly. "I'm a stubborn cuss, Doc. But don't you worry none. I'll take the responsibility. The constable here will bear witness. Nobody will blame you for what happens to me."

10

The doctor shrugged philosophically after Laramie's declaration and did what he could to make Laramie Nelson comfortable. He bound the injured shoulder tightly, made a sling for it, and Laramie nipped at a bottle of whiskey until the men were all collected in the street outside, ready to ride.

It was close to two o'clock, and daybreak came shortly after five. They would have to ride hard and steadily to make it.

There were some thirty men, of various ages, all armed to the teeth and itching to go.

As one leathery oldtimer put it, "We ain't had a good Injun squabble around these parts in ages. Forgotten what it's like." He threw back his head and howled like a wolf.

A ripple of agreement went through the assembled men.

Laramie's shoulder was stiff, sore, the pain reduced to a dull ache, and he was weak, but he found he could ride when helped aboard Wingfoot. Wingfoot, seeming to sense his rider's condition, adopted a rolling gait that wasn't too bad.

Even so, after an hour in the saddle, the pain was back again, and Laramie had to hold on tightly to keep from tumbling from the saddle. At least there was no problem of getting lost, of Wingfoot having to find his own way. Laramie kept him back in the center of posse as it pounded down the trail.

They stopped three times on a signal from Watson to let the horses rest for ten minutes or so. Laramie remained in the saddle the first two times, rolling and smoking a cigarette.

The third and last time Watson came down the line on foot. He stopped by Wingfoot. Light glinted off a bottle in his hand. "I brought this along for medicinal purposes. Doc told me you might be needing it just about now."

"I sure could," Laramie said gratefully.

With Watson's help he slid from the saddle, took the flat bottle and slugged it back. The liquor flowed through his veins like a reviving drug.

He returned the bottle. "Much obliged."

"My pleasure." Watson belted the bottle, then jammed it into his pocket. "You said something about a job to do back in Indigo Flats. Mind telling me what it is?"

Laramie hesitated for a moment, then blurted it all out.

At the end of the story Watson said slowly, "Bart Tate's a strange one. At one time Bart was the best lawman in this end of the country. He's still one of the best men with a gun I know, but something's happened to him in recent years. He's gone sour.

"I recollect the last time I talked to Bart. He was complaining about putting his life on the line all these years for thirty dollars a month and what did he have to show for it? Well, all I could say was what did any of us have to show for it? Except a job well done. That didn't seem to sit too well with Bart.

"I haven't seen him since—" Watson turned away with an abrupt gesture, as though he'd said more than he intended. He raised his voice. "Mount up, mount up! Let's ride!"

Laramie got back on Wingfoot with difficulty and had to use the spurs on him again to catch up to the others.

"I know, hoss, I know," he muttered. "When this is over, I'll throw my spurs away. All right?"

After some more hard riding dawn turned the eastern sky pink. Ahead lay the low humped hills. Just beyond those hills was Indigo Flats.

They were all alerted by the sudden crackle of gunfire. Watson, riding a big roan in the lead, rose in the stirrups and swung a long arm forward. The riders began spurring and yelling at their horses.

Laramie, who had been in a half doze of pain and weariness, snapped fully awake. He leaned forward and spoke into Wingfoot's ear. The big horse responded powerfully, passing one horse after another. As they topped the brown hills, Wingfoot was neck and neck with the leaders.

Laramie was clear-headed now. Although his shoulder was stiff and still ached dully, it didn't bother him too much. It was full light, though yet short of sunup, as they swept down the hills and thundered across level ground toward Indigo Flats.

There were no Apaches waiting outside of town for them. Apparently the Indians had decided to storm in, make a clean sweep of the town and ride out before the rescue party, if any, arrived. As the road made a looping bend and straightened out, Laramie could see the length of the main street. Dust roiled up in a yellow cloud as the Apaches raced up and down the street, pouring a heavy volley of firepower into the Paradise Saloon.

Laramie had his Colt out and bucking in his hand as he rode into town past the first buildings. Others beside him were firing as well. Laramie steadied his Colt on one

Apache and fired. His bullet knocked the Indian off his pony.

That was the first inkling the Apaches had of the rear attack. But before they could rally to it, the rescue party was in among them, firing at close range. The Indians rallied then, fighting back viciously.

Within minutes it turned into hand-to-hand combat, Laramie and the others using their handguns and rifles as clubs, the Apaches fighting back with rifles, spears, tomahawks, whatever they had.

Horses screamed and went down. Indians and whites locked together in the street in deadly infighting. Dust rose from the street to mingle with gunsmoke, and it all hung like a pall over the scene.

Laramie kneed Wingfoot off to one side and reloaded his Colt. It was awkward with the wounded shoulder. He finally managed it and charged back into the melee.

Wingfoot turned and twisted like a cutting horse, Laramie clinging to the saddle horn with one hand and firing his pistol with the other. Then the gun was empty again. Before Laramie could reload a second time an Apache, hideous in war paint, mouth open in a scream that went unheard in the din, charged at Wingfoot.

The Apache left his pony in a leap like a cougar springing at his prey from a wind-whipped tree limb. Copper arms wrapped around Laramie, and he was propelled from the saddle. Pain licked at his wounded shoulder like a tongue of fire.

They rolled over and over in the street. The Apache was unarmed, and Laramie's Colt had been knocked out of his grasp by the impact. The Apache clawed like a wild animal, his long nails gathering Laramie's skin like mush. His breath was fetid and hot.

Then Laramie was on the bottom, the Apache's hands locked around his throat. Laramie thrashed and bucked to no avail. The hands remained knotted around his throat like steel talons. Laramie fought for breath. Dimly he realized he had only a few seconds of consciousness left.

He managed to work his hands up between the Apache's arms. Then he went limp, as though losing consciousness. For just an instant the Indian relaxed his grip slightly. Laramie drove both hands outward with all his strength, striking the Apache on the forearms with the edges of his hands. It broke the Apache's hold.

Laramie swarmed all over him. He struck him twice in the face, dazing him, then pinned him to the earth with one knee and locked the fingers of his unwounded arm around the copper throat.

He squeezed with all the strength he could muster, squeezed until black dots danced before his eyes. The Apache's struggles grew weaker and weaker, finally ceased altogether. He was dead.

Laramie crawled off him. He crouched for a moment on his knees, head hanging. His shoulder was a solid mass of pain. But his head was still clear; the fever seemed to have burned itself out.

He raised his head and glanced around. It was all over, or almost so. The Apaches were routed, fleeing in all directions, leaving several dead on the ground. The rescue party was also scattering, giving pursuit to the edge of town, then stopping to watch the Apaches ride off.

Wingfoot stood a few feet away, head down. Laramie got to his feet and made his way over. He ran a hand over the horse, murmuring gently under his breath.

The animal was exhausted, but otherwise seemed all right.

Laramie turned away. He was directly in front of the Paradise Saloon. As he crossed unsteadily toward the steps, the batwing doors swung out. Marshal Tate, Monte, and one prisoner, Hoke Palmer, stepped through. Palmer had a pistol in his hand.

"Well, Nelson," the marshal drawled. "It appears I had you figured wrong. It seems you came through for us after all."

He spat a brown stream into the dust and turned to his right, all in one motion. He chopped at Palmer's wrist with the edge of his hand. The Colt flew out of Palmer's hand and bounced down the steps, coming to rest a few inches from Laramie's boots.

"Why'd you do that, Marshal?" Palmer whined.

"Because you're my prisoner and I don't allow my prisoners to carry iron around," Marshal Tate snarled. He fastened his hand around Palmer's wrist.

"Come along."

He started down the steps, pulling Palmer after him. Monte fell in a few steps behind. Marshal Tate turned his head. "You stay here, Monte."

"But Bart, I've got a right to—"

"Damn it, I said stay here! Now do as I tell you!"

Laramie hadn't paid a great deal of attention to the byplay. He had been watching the door for either Letty or Toddy to appear. It seemed they weren't going to. He turned his head to watch the marshal lead Palmer up the street, wondering idly where they were going.

Then he forgot them in his anxiety about Letty. He mounted the steps, paused beside Monte who was scowling after the marshal. His plump face had the look of a petulant child.

"Where's Letty? Is she all right?" Laramie demanded.

Monte jerked a thumb inside without glancing around.

Laramie went past him, hurrying now. He pushed open the door and went in, apprehension driving him past caution. Squinting against the dimness, he swept the saloon with a single glance. Shaw, his head bloody and one arm hanging stiffly, fingers dripping blood, stood at the bar, drinking out of a bottle. The third prisoner, Ben Thomas, was sprawled on the floor by the front window. Laramie didn't need to go over to tell he was dead.

209

Neither Toddy nor Letty were to be seen.

"Letty? Toddy? Where are you?" Laramie called.

He heard a faint answering cry from the kitchen.

The kitchen was a shambles, everything turned over and smashed. Toddy was on the floor, Letty kneeling beside him, working on him. Laramie couldn't see the man's face until he stood over him.

It was a mess, nose smashed and bloody, lips cut and swollen, several teeth missing, the skin peeled off in a dozen places. His eyes were swollen shut. It looked as though he'd been beaten about the head with a club.

Laramie dropped to one knee beside them. "What happened?"

Letty turned a weeping face to him. "He tried, Laramie. Don't blame him. He tried!"

Toddy stirred. He tried to open his eyes and couldn't make it. He said weakly, "That you, hoss? You make it back all right?"

"It's me, Toddy. I made it back all right and with some help. The Apaches are on the run. But what happened to you?"

Letty gave a choked cry, leaped to her feet and ran out of the room.

Toddy's ruined mouth worked in what could have been an attempt at a smile. "It was my fault, Mr. Nelson. Everything was all right most of the night. I had about decided they weren't going to bother Miss Letty. I guess I put away too much red-eye again. I went to sleep on the bar some time afore morning, just a nap. When I woke up, Miss Letty wasn't around. The marshal and that sod Palmer wasn't to be seen, neither.

"I heard a scream out here in the kitchen. I ran out here and found them at her. I piled in and did what I could. They turned on me. The marshal took my Winchester away and used it on me like a club. I should've shot them both first instead of trying to jump them, but I wasn't thinking straight. They'd just about beat me through the

210

floor and had turned back to Miss Letty again when the redskins hit us. I reckon that saved her. Certainly wasn't me."

Laramie groped for the man's hand. He pressed it gently. "You did fine, Toddy. You did the best you could. That's all anyone can ask. The thing is, how bad hurt are you?"

Toddy did smile this time. "I'll be all right, Mr. Nelson. I'm some bunged up, but I've been knocked around before. One thing—they broke my bottle. Could I have one from the bar? I reckon now the redskins are gone, folks will be coming back, and that'll mean the end of free red-eye!"

As Laramie stood up, Letty came back. The tears had stopped, but he noted details he'd missed before. One eye was almost swollen shut, there were several scratches on her face, and her dress was practically in ribbons.

A cold, killing rage filled him. "Did they—"

She shook her head, trying to smile. "No, Laramie. Honest, nothing really happened."

"It's not because they didn't try!"

"That's not the whole of it. I've been thinking. I invited it. I invited it because I was more or less expecting it. I represented a challenge to them. If I hadn't been so afraid, they probably would never have bothered me."

Laramie thought differently. He had a strong hunch that the attempted attack on Letty had been aimed at him. He had taken her under his protection, and Marshal Tate resented that. "I have a score to settle with our marshal!"

Alarm showed on her face. "Don't, Laramie. Don't put yourself in the way of getting killed on my account."

"It's more than just on your account. It's you, Toddy, and my own business with him, the reason I'm here in the first place."

He wheeled back into the barroom. Letty started after him, calling his name, but he strode on. He went behind the bar for a bottle. Shaw hadn't moved from his position

211

at the bar, and he gave no indication he was even aware of Laramie's presence.

Laramie took the bottle back into the kitchen. He squatted by the man on the floor. "Toddy?"

This time Toddy managed to open one eye. A beatific smile spread across his face at the sight of the full bottle. He took it in both hands and cradled it reverently against his chest. He whispered, "I thank you, hoss."

Letty gave a small cry as Laramie stood up. "Your arm! Why's it in a sling?"

"It's fine, nothing to worry about. Letty. You stay here with Toddy. I have a job to do." He started off.

"Laramie—"

"Yes?" he said impatiently.

"Take care of yourself."

He looked at her then, and smiled slowly. "What else?"

11

The plump deputy hadn't moved from where Laramie Nelson left him. He was still staring resentfully up the street in the direction Marshal Tate and his prisoner had taken.

Laramie drew his Colt, stepped quietly up behind the deputy and jammed it against the back of the man's neck. Monte stiffened, his breath escaping him gustily.

"Monte, You know what this is." Laramie cocked the Colt, the sound loud, ominous. "I'm going to ask you a couple of questions. It's been a long, hard night, and my patience is at an end. If you don't give me the answers I want, I'm going to blow your head off. You hear me, Monte?"

"I—" Monte cleared his throat softly. "Yes, I hear you, Mr. Nelson."

"Now—Is one of your three prisoners the man I'm after, Darr Regan?"

"Uh—Yeah."

"Which one?"

Monte hesitated, swallowing.

Laramie jabbed the gun brutally, the snout burying itself into the soft folds of the deputy's fat neck.

Monte said hastily, "Palmer. Hoke Palmer."

Laramie sighed, some of the tension draining out of him. "I had a hunch he was the one. Why is it Tate didn't want me to know?"

"He—The marshal knew about him, knew Regan had near to twenty thousand dollars from his last train holdup hid away. The marshal wants that money. He sent the telegram to you, then told Regan about it. He offered to make a bargain. If Regan would lead him to the money, he'd let him go. Otherwise, he was going to turn him over to you. Regan finally agreed. That's why we left Copper Springs before you got there."

"And the money's here, in Indigo Flats. Right?"

Monte hesitated once more, and Laramie increased the pressure, screwing the Colt muzzle into the thick neck.

"Yes, it's here! We were heading here when the Apaches jumped us. If we got the money, the marshal was going to let Regan escape between here and Yuma."

Watson was coming up the steps toward them. The rest of the rescue party was collected up the street. Watson's gaze was curious. "What's going on, Nelson?"

Laramie motioned him quiet. To Monte he said, "Is that where they're gone now? To get the money?"

"Yes, Marshal Tate finally made Regan tell him this morning. Regan said it's cached up the street in the rooming house where he was staying just before we picked him up."

Laramie glanced up the street. The marshal wasn't in sight.

Watson asked again, "What's going on?"

Laramie told him, quickly, succinctly, easing the pressure of the Colt slightly but keeping it against Monte's neck.

Watson swore harsely when he'd heard the story. "Looks like Bart's gone over the edge, turning outlaw."

"I'm going after them, Watson. Keep on eye on Monte, will you? I don't want a bullet in the back."

"I have no authority here, Nelson."

"Neither does Tate, but that doesn't seem to have bothered him," Laramie said harshly. "I'm only interested in two things, that stolen money and Darr Regan. After that, you people can do what you want with this one and his boss. Turn 'em loose, for all of me."

With one swift motion Laramie holstered his Colt and started down the steps without looking back. He was still several yards from the rooming house when Marshal Tate stepped through the front door, saddlebags draped over his left shoulder. He came down the three steps, Palmer—Regan now—right behind him.

Laramie said, "I see you found it, Marshal."

Marshal Tate halted. "Found what, Nelson?"

"The holdup money. Monte told me the whole story."

"That yellowbelly!" Marshal Tate said venomously. "I'll hang him up by the heels and let the buzzards pick his eyes out!"

"So I'm taking my money and *my* prisoner."

"Are you now?" The marshal relaxed, visibly his smile coming back. "It ain't going to be all that easy. Like the man said, over my dead body."

"If that's the way you want it," Laramie said steadily.

Out of the corner of his eye, Laramie saw Regan step quickly back and to one side. He was still unarmed, so he represented no danger. Laramie held his gaze intent on the marshal.

Marshal Tate let his left shoulder droop, allowing the saddlebags to fall to the ground. Then he took two steps to one side and planted his feet wide apart in the dust. His right hand hung inches from his holstered gun. He flexed his fingers and drawled, "Any time you're ready, Pinkerton man."

Laramie didn't move, didn't speak. He kept his eyes on the marshal's smiling face.

A full minute passed. Neither man moved nor spoke. Laramie could have sworn the marshal didn't even blink once.

Then, without moving his head, Marshal Tate spat a brown stream at Laramie's feet. Laramie's gaze didn't waver even fractionally. He had been expecting exactly that. He suspected it was a ruse that had cost many men their lives in a gun battle with Marshal Tate.

While the stream of tobacco was still in the air, the marshal went for his gun. He was very fast, his hand a blur of speed. He was faster than Laramie by a fraction of a second and got off the first shot. But it was hurried and the bullet whistled past Laramie with the sound of an angry hornet.

Laramie's bullet slammed into the marshal's chest just over the heart. It sent him staggering back, his second shot also wild, the bullet sailing harmlessly over Laramie's head. The marshal crashed down into the dust on his back, twitched once and then was still.

Laramie, crouching slightly, swung his gun around to bear on Regan, who was inching away. "Hold it right there, Regan! I can gun you down before you even get started!"

Regan froze in his tracks, his hands going up. "All right, all right. Don't shoot, for God's sake!"

Laramie stepped over to the marshal's prone figure. His eyes were open, staring sightlessly, the always-present smile now frozen in a grotesque death's-head grimace.

His Colt still centered on Regan, Laramie dropped to one knee and rummaged in the saddlebags. They were stuffed with greenbacks, the holdup money. Brock Peters would be pleased. Both the money and Darr Regan. He might even go so far as to hand out one of his rare compliments.

Laramie stood up with the saddlebags and motioned

215

Regan to precede him up the street. As they neared the Paradise Saloon, Letty came running down the steps to meet him. She hurried to his side.

"Laramie. Are you all right?"

"I'm fine, just fine." He smiled down at her anxious face. "It's all over now."

Watson and Monte hadn't moved from the top step. Watson said, "I expect Bart's dead?"

"He's dead. I could say I'm sorry, but I'm not sure I'd be telling the truth."

Watson studied him for a sober moment. Then he nodded at Regan. "That the man you came after?"

"That's the man. I've also got the holdup money."

"Then it's seems you've got what you came after," Watson said, somewhat sourly. "Which means you'll be leaving us. I can't rightly say I'm sorry."

He turned away into the saloon, nudging Monte in ahead of him.

Laramie stared after them for a moment. He could understand Watson being upset. Marshal Tate had been a friend of his. Still, a town marshal had no more right than anyone else to step outside the law.

Letty said, "If we're leaving, Laramie—My clothes are in rags. I'm ashamed to be seen. Do you suppose I could find something around here?"

"Why not?" Laramie said lightly. "Toddy got his fill of free red-eye. I can't see why you aren't entitled to a free dress. I saw a ladies shop up the street. I'm sure you can find something in there to fit you."

An hour later Laramie was riding Wingfoot west out of town at a leisurely pace alongside the jail wagon. Letty, in a pink and white dress that was a perfect fit, rode in the front seat. She had insisted on leaving money to pay for the dress. The driver was a man Watson had sent along to drive the wagon to Yuma. Locked in the wagon were Shaw and Darr Regan.

Laramie had agreed to deliver Shaw to Yuma Prison,

then he would ride north with Regan and the money.

"Laramie," Letty called over to him.

He kneed Wingfoot in close.

"You're going to just leave me in Yuma?"

"I have to, Letty. My job isn't finished yet. My boss is going to be foaming at the mouth as it is, wondering why I'm taking so long for a simple job."

The gray eyes were shadowed with melancholy. "Then I'll never see you again?"

"Oh, I wouldn't say that." He smiled easily. "In my job, I get around quite a bit. Don't be at all surprised to see me riding back this way at any time."

They were climbing up into the brown hills now. Laramie reined Wingfoot in. Shading his eyes against the sun, he looked back and down at Indigo Flats.

A plume of dust on the road leading out of town to the east caught his attention. After a moment he made out wagons, buckboards and horses strung out on the way to town. The women and the children and the old men somehow knew of the departure of the Apaches and now considered it safe to return to their homes.

"I hope you find Rex, Marcy, and he's all right," Laramie muttered.

Startled at the sound of his own voice, he glanced around in embarrassment. But he hadn't been overheard.

The jail wagon had continued on without pause and was just disappearing over the crest of the distant hill.

Laramie Nelson clucked to Wingfoot and sent him pounding after it.

ZANE GREY

LAST OF THE DUANES

Buck Duane's father was a gunfighter who died by the gun, and, in accepting a drunken bully's challenge, Duane finds himself forced into the life of an outlaw. He roams the dark trails of southwestern Texas, living in outlaw camps, until he meets the one woman who can help him overcome his past—a girl named Jennie Lee.

___4430-7 $4.99 US/$5.99 CAN

Dorchester Publishing Co., Inc.
P.O. Box 6640
Wayne, PA 19087-8640

Please add $1.75 for shipping and handling for the first book and $.50 for each book thereafter. NY, NYC, and PA residents, please add appropriate sales tax. No cash, stamps, or C.O.D.s. All orders shipped within 6 weeks via postal service book rate. Canadian orders require $2.00 extra postage and must be paid in U.S. dollars through a U.S. banking facility.

Name_____
Address_____
City_____ State_____ Zip_____
I have enclosed $_____ in payment for the checked book(s).
Payment <u>must</u> accompany all orders. ❏ Please send a free catalog.
        CHECK OUT OUR WEBSITE! www.dorchesterpub.com

TIMBAL GULCH TRAIL

MAX BRAND

"Brand is a topnotcher!"
—New York Times

Les Burchard owns the local gambling palace, half the town, and most of the surrounding territory, and Walt Devon's thousand-acre ranch will make him king of the land. The trouble is, Devon doesn't want to sell. In a ruthless bid to claim the spread, Burchard tries everything from poker to murder. But Walt Devon is a betting man by nature, even when the stakes are his life. The way Devon figures, the odds are stacked against him, so he can either die alone or take his enemy to the grave with him.

__3828-5 $4.50 US/$5.50 CAN

THE
KAINTUCKS

The Natchez Trace is the trail of choice for frontiersmen heading north from New Orleans. But for Dan'l Boone and his small band of boatmen, the trail leads straight into danger. Lying in wait for the legendary guide is a band of French land pirates out for the payroll he is protecting. And with the cutthroats is a vicious war party of Chickasaw braves out for much more—Dan'l Boone's blood!

4466-8 $3.99 US/$4.99 CAN

Dorchester Publishing Co., Inc.
P.O. Box 6640
Wayne, PA 19087-8640

Please add $1.75 for shipping and handling for the first book and $.50 for each book thereafter. NY, NYC, and PA residents, please add appropriate sales tax. No cash, stamps, or C.O.D.s. All orders shipped within 6 weeks via postal service book rate. Canadian orders require $2.00 extra postage and must be paid in U.S. dollars through a U.S. banking facility.

Name_____

Address_____

City_____State_____Zip_____

I have enclosed $_____ in payment for the checked book(s).

Payment <u>must</u> accompany all orders. ❑ Please send a free catalog.

KIT CARSON

KEELBOAT CARNAGE
DOUG HAWKINS

The untamed frontier is filled with dangers of all kinds—
both natural and man-made—dangers that only the bravest
can survive. And so far Kit Carson has survived them all.
But when he sets out north along the Missouri River he has
no idea what lies ahead. He can't know that the Blackfeet are
out to turn the river red with blood. And when he hitches a
ride on a riverboat, he can't know that keelboat pirates are
waiting just around the bend!

___4411-0 $3.99 US/$4.99 CAN

DAVY CROCKETT

BLOOD HUNT

David Thompson

With only his oldest friend and his trusty long rifle for company, Davy Crockett explores the wild frontier looking for adventure, and has the strength and cunning to face any enemy. But even he may have met his match when he gets caught between two warring tribes on one side and a dangerous band of white men on the other—all of them willing to die—and kill—for a group of stolen women. It is up to Crockett to save the women, his friend and his own hide if he wants to live to explore another day.

__4229-0 $3.99 US/$4.99 CAN

Dorchester Publishing Co., Inc.
P.O. Box 6640
Wayne, PA 19087-8640